A KISS
— BEFORE —
DYING

H. D. THOMSON

Lynn,
I hope this book
keeps you up at night!

H. D. Thomson

A KISS BEFORE DYING By H. D. Thomson

Published by Bella Media Management.

To Tim, my constant companion on this amazing journey.

AUTHOR NOTE

Myths and legends are usually inspired by fact or history. While doing research for Gabriel Martinez's backstory, I wondered what he might have endured while leaving his home country of Spain. I also found myself fascinated with the history of mercury.

Each civilization had its own legends regarding the silvery-white metal. Its use ranged from medicine to various talismans. Mercury could protect a person from death by murder or poison, guard them against treason, and if placed beneath the head during sleep, it could produce prophetic dreams.

Gabriel's story is pure fiction. I took the great liberty of changing time periods, adding conflicts where there were none, and creating my own unique world.

Some characters in Gabriel's history did, in fact, exist while others were pure fabrications on my part. When reading about Aztec lore, like any other writer, I thought of *what if.*

I hope you enjoy Gabriel's and Amanda's story.

PROLOGUE

Almost there," Mark muttered through gritted teeth. Both his shoulders brushed rock as he crawled on his hands and knees and squeezed deeper into the tunnel, surrounded by limestone. Moist air clung to his face. The sudden hint of a breeze, a sign of a possible live cave, urged him forward. To actually find a cave no one had discovered.... *Calm down.* After all, he and his cousin had been searching for two years now and found nothing but empty mine shafts, dead caves, and sinkholes. The light attached to his helmet illuminated a few feet in front of him as he edged forward. Anything farther was a black wall of the unknown facing him.

"I think you said that half an hour ago," Jason grumbled from behind him.

"Yeah, yeah." Mark paused on all fours and tried to see his cousin over his shoulder, but his helmet butted up against rock. As he faced forward, he continued, "I know, but you don't have to—"

Lurching forward, he lost his balance and tumbled headlong into black space.

Grunting, he landed on his back, the wind knocked from his lungs. He shifted his legs. Thank God. Ending up paralyzed wasn't something he planned in this life.

The helmet with the flashlight remained attached to his skull. Well, that was something.

Shuffling echoed into the chamber, and a moment later Jason appeared standing to his left, his helmet's light glaring from above. "You sure make things difficult for yourself, don't you?"

The pain in his hip made him snap back, "Like you haven't had a couple of close calls. If I hadn't gone first, you would have been the one landing on his back instead of getting forewarned long enough to rappel down to here."

"Too true." Jason offered his hand.

Mark took it and scrambled to his feet. He stepped forward gingerly to gauge his injury and sank a foot into a puddle. Forget aches or pains! He'd landed in water which meant—

Something dropped on Mark's forearm. He glanced up. More water.

Hot damn. It looked like they'd found a live cave.

Jason unhooked another flashlight attached to his belt and shined the beam upward a good twenty feet and toward the entrance where they'd entered the cave.

Mark gasped in unison with his cousin. Excitement rushed through his body, and he thought for a brief moment his chest might explode from the sheer power of it.

"Holy crap," Jason whispered, turning slowly, the scrape of his boots hollow against the rock floor. The beam from the light on his helmet arced along the wall. Tube-like formations gleamed. "This has gotta be virgin territory. I think I need to sit down before I pass out with happiness."

Mark glanced up at the cave's ceiling. "Damn! Do you see all those soda straws? I've never seen anything like it."

The distinct drip of water hitting water merged with the sound of their breathing.

Jason edged forward. "A pond. The humidity in here is amazing."

Cold, musty air rushed into Mark's lungs. "I can't believe we found a freaking live cave. All these years of vague rumors but no one knowing exactly where the hell it was." He aimed the beam at his cousin.

Jason flashed him a toothy grin. "Just think of the money."

"You know it's not the money."

"Still... It'll be an added bonus along with the recognition." Jason's flashlight caught on some type of odd-shaped formation on the ground several feet in length. "Hey, what's that?"

Mark unhooked his light from his belt and raised its beam to meld with his cousin's. Stepping carefully to avoid ruining any formations, he moved toward it. "Not sure..."

Something brushed his ear. Shivering, he swiped at his neck and glanced around. He could have sworn he'd heard wings.

Bats?

He peered up at the ceiling. The light only penetrated so far. He hadn't seen any signs of bats—no tell-tale squeaking, droppings or smell. Unease prickled the back of his neck.

As they drew closer to the mound, unmistakable disquiet entered Jason's voice. "What the hell is it? I swear it looks like a—" The other man sucked in a harsh breath. "Jesus."

Their flashlights illuminated what appeared to be a man's decomposing body. Sections of skin and flesh had dissolved. Time must have eaten the skin and tissue of his lips. The teeth and upper and lower jaw gleamed white, while the man's eyes had caved into the skull's sockets. By the side of the body, a helmet rested, its light extinguished. For how long, he couldn't even guess.

Mark grimaced. "The poor bastard."

"What do you think happened? Do you suppose he got trapped in here and just wasn't able to get out? He couldn't have been stupid enough to go spelunking alone."

They both pivoted around and angled their lights around them in a complete circle. Stalagmites protruded from the cave floor, and the ground to their right sloped downward to the motionless pool. A thick black, impenetrable wall cut off deeper parts of the cave and the area above where they'd entered the chamber.

"I don't see another body," Jason murmured. "I'm not an expert on dead people, but I'm guessing that he's been dead several months."

"You think?" Mark avoided glancing at the body. It just creeped him out too much. But that lasted all of two seconds. Morbid curiosity won out over repugnance, and reluctantly he gazed back at the corpse.

"Hell if I know." Jason grunted. "I can't imagine dying in this place alone and being unable to see a damn thing. I'd have gone insane before I finally bit the bullet."

"He might have been alive for a good while. He could have easily broken a leg or something and couldn't get out, and then possibly starved to death." The corpse's chest looked odd; he stopped scanning with his light. "Then again, maybe not…"

That same morbid curiosity urged him down on his haunches to get a better view. This close to the body, both his flashlights revealed a chest torn apart. "Shit. This guy didn't die from anything broken. It looks like a wild animal got to him."

"That's crazy," Jason argued, his voice thick with unease. "This place is locked up tight. Nothing that big could survive down here."

"Tell that to the dead guy." There was a round, somewhat oval object between the size of a golf and tennis ball. "Hey, what's that between his arm and body? A rock?"

His cousin aimed his light at it. "I don't know about that. Too porous…"

"Jesus!" Mark jumped up and back, almost falling on his ass in his haste to get away from the body. "I think it's his heart."

"No!" Jason bent over and peered down. "Uh, is part of it missing?"

"Missing? It looks worse than that. It looks like someone ripped his heart out of his body. That's what it looks like!" Mark backed farther away. "Let's get the hell out of here." Gooseflesh rose along his spine and across his neck. He peered into the blackness around him again, unable to shake the sudden fear digging into his muscles and kicking up his heart rate. Any second now he expected a wild bear or rabid wolf to attack.

"Wait. Not yet. There's something else…" Jason hunched even lower and pulled at something in the corpse's hand.

"Just forget it. It's not important."

"No. This guy found it important. He was clutching it like a lifeline." Jason tugged harder.

At the sound of bone snapping and giving away, Mark winced. Bile rose from his stomach to catch against the back of his throat.

Jason lifted some type of silver rope into the air.

They both angled their lights at the object. It wasn't a silver rope but a thick chain with a large fist-sized medallion on one end.

The pendant swung back and forth before Jason steadied it. Then he raised his palm. The silver winked beneath the flashlight's beam.

Mark was wrong again. The object wasn't really a medallion or a pendant, but a necklace. And attached was a blood-encrusted cross.

CHAPTER 1

"And here I thought the town of Spirit Lake didn't have much crime," Amanda Douglas murmured, her gaze fixated on the corpse.

Standing beside his partner of two weeks, Gabriel Martinez rubbed his neck, but that didn't ease the tension, which cut a swath across his neck and into every part of his body. Holy Mother, he was getting tired of this. He had been working for the police department for five years now. Like Amanda, he had escaped to Spirit Lake, a small town of around five thousand in northern Iowa, in hopes of never coming across sights like the one in front of him, which just proved he would never escape.

Amanda, face blanched of much of its color, stepped cautiously away from the body. "Two years in Chicago as a cop, I'd seen my share of murders, but after moving here almost a month ago, I get this, this... What type of crazy is running around in your town?"

They stood in the middle of Jack Blunt's living room. Along with the fan's overhead light, every other lamp in the room illuminated the area in bright, glaring detail. With the drapes open wide, the night, a silent witness to the crime, clung to the front window, while winter air intruded through the open front door.

"It appears someone crazy with rage." Gabriel

looked at the corpse sprawled on one side of the sofa as if Blunt had been tossed there as an afterthought.

Fully clothed in jeans and sweatshirt, the male victim didn't appear to have struggled against his murderer. No contusions on his arms or hands, no broken fingernails. But above his torso… Holy Mother. That was a different story. It looked like someone had used a serrated knife and shredded his neck until they'd gotten past tendon, muscle and bone.

As for the head...

There was none.

At least they hadn't come across one. They'd checked beyond the living room with no luck. Blood immediately around the victim had seeped into the leather, and there were some large puddles two yards away from the couch and the victim—as if someone had been standing there watching the man while dripping blood.

The metallic scent permeated the air. Gabriel wrinkled his nose and backed up, but the odor still clung to his senses.

According to dispatch, the call had come in from the mother of one of three kids selling cookies door to door. The girls had seen the victim from the front window and had run screaming to the mother hovering on the sidewalk. They would have nightmares for weeks.

Hell, at that age, Gabriel would have too. The whole tableau was nauseating.

Amanda whispered, "Those poor little kids. Nicole could have been one of those girls. She could have easily walked up those stairs and looked into the window and found this… this..." She waved a trembling hand at the body.

"But she didn't, and she was not anywhere around this place." Gabriel tried to reassure the new patrol officer. "You checked on her on our way here, and she is home watching her favorite television series with your babysitter. Did you not tell me that yourself?"

"Yes, but still..." She took a deep breath. "I don't get it. What type of person would do something like this?"

"I don't know." Gabriel rubbed the bridge of his nose. "Maybe he had a pet that attacked him."

"Seriously? A pet?" She turned her startled gaze toward him, disbelief in her large brown eyes. "A pet that runs off with a human head?"

Gabriel shrugged. "Probably not any type of pet I have ever had."

"Well, the only type of pet I can think of would be some exotic animal no one's seen or heard of." She rubbed her arms and backed up another step. "It looks worse than an animal. Almost like someone took a small chainsaw to him."

"I'm sure he didn't have a tiger running loose, and as for the chainsaw, I haven't a clue." Gabriel noticed the fine sheen of sweat on her brow. "Are you going to be okay?"

He cupped her elbow, his hand gentle against the fragile bone and muscle, then brushed a finger along her inner arm. What would her skin feel like beneath her long-sleeved shirt? No doubt better than he could imagine.

Supple, silky.

Holy Mother. Sudden awareness of her being a woman and not just a coworker rushed through him. He should not have touched her. She stiffened under his hand, and he let go, but the warmth and texture of her flesh against his palm still lingered. Suddenly awkward, he dropped his hand to his side.

"Yeah, sure. I'm fine." She jerked her head a couple of times. "I've seen some dead bodies. I'll get over this one too. Maybe not as quickly."

He suspected she would probably have herself a nightmare, too, after their shift was over. "Do you want to wait in the patrol car until someone from the Medical Examiner's Office arrives? You don't have your jacket, and you can crank up the heater."

Alarm flashed in her eyes. "No. I'd never live it down if the rest of the department got wind I couldn't stomach a scene like this."

"They wouldn't hear anything from me, and you are not in Chicago." Gabriel tried to give her an out. "Your reaction is understandable. No one is going to give you flak for being human."

"Well, I'm feeling a little green, probably look it too. You, on the other hand, seem unfazed. I'm sure you've got some years on me and faced your share of grisly crime scenes."

"A few." *If only she knew.* Gabriel decided to keep his mouth shut on the details. "It's always harder when you know the person, though. I played poker with Jack and some of the locals on a number of Friday nights."

She shook her head, clearly dismayed. "I'm sorry. I didn't know. But then, this being such a small town, you must know everyone."

Some more than he wanted to. "Yes, pretty much." Gabriel searched the room. Other than a couple of magazines littering the coffee table and a few gold-framed pictures sitting on the end table, nothing else revealed the owner's personality. Like the living room, the rest of the house was clean but sparsely furnished. "We're going to have to call his family. His sister lives in Omaha, and I know his parents retired to Florida. I think, Miami."

"I can do that if you like."

"They know me. I think it's best coming from me."

"Sure."

"Are you positive you're okay?" Gabriel was a little worried she might pass out on him. "You can sit down outside until the medical examiner gets here. The cold air might do you some good."

She stiffened. "Like I said before, I'm fine." Jaw taut, she looked at the corpse. "Obviously the person was enraged when they killed him. Possibly jealous? There has to be a motive."

"Why does there need to be a motive?"

"Well, because"—she frowned and trailed a hand down the chestnut-colored ponytail draped over her shoulder—"if there isn't, then we're dealing with a psychopath who gets their kicks out of ripping apart people's chests." She twirled the tip of her ponytail between her long, elegant fingers again and again.

So far, Gabriel had only seen her with hair swept back from her face. The severe hairstyle emphasized the regal curve of her cheekbones, the arch of her nose, the strong, graceful sweep of her jaw and the long, smooth column of her neck. Too many times, he had imagined that same hair loose around her shoulders, her naked beneath him, arching into his body in complete surrender.

Longing and hunger, intense and jaw-grinding, raged through his body. How the hell a woman could look sexy in a navy-blue police uniform and padded bullet-proof vest was beyond him, but somehow Amanda managed it. He had been salivating over her from the moment she joined the local police force. He had it bad. But no one would find that out from him.

"Gabriel?"

He returned to reality with a sickening thump. Amanda was staring at him with a question in her eyes, and he had no clue what she had asked him. "I'm sorry?"

"I was just wondering if you knew of anyone he'd pissed off recently."

"He had a nasty divorce years ago. Then there were a couple of complaints over the last few years about him getting too loud and obnoxious at the bar when he was drinking too much. But I can't think of one person enraged enough to cut off his head like that."

The headlights of a car arced into the room then disappeared. The medical examiner's vehicle pulled into the driveway.

Jennifer Barnes and a crime scene tech stepped into the house. One look at the victim and Jennifer's jaw slackened. "What the hell?" She walked over and joined them.

Amanda looked at her. "You probably haven't seen a death like this one."

"That I haven't." After her initial shock, Jennifer's voice thickened with obvious excitement. "Where's the head?"

"Not sure." Gabriel rocked back on his heels. "We didn't find it in the house."

"It'll be interesting to see if the perp is trying to mask the cause of death. Actually, I don't think I've gotten something this fascinating in years."

Amanda pressed her mouth into a tight line. "Yes, well, fascinating as it may be, I'm afraid I've been looking at it a little too much."

"On that note"—Gabriel headed for the door—"we will let you and your tech get to work on the crime scene."

After getting behind the wheel of his patrol car, Gabriel looked over at Amanda. Lights from the house illuminated a face devoid of feeling, but it was probably only a fragile mask, and she was shell-shocked. "I think we need a break before we get through a mountain of paperwork. I'm sure you're not up to eating, but how about some coffee?"

Shoulders sagging, she cranked up the heat and sank into the passenger seat. "How about some decaf? I think I've got enough adrenaline to keep me going for a while."

"Decaf, it is."

Five minutes later, he pulled into Wombats, the only twenty-four-hour restaurant in town. The place was owned by an Australian couple who visited Iowa a decade ago and liked it so much they'd never moved back. After Blunt's murder, they might think differently.

The moment they stepped into the diner, the night manager, his body shaped like a bowling pin, rounded the cashier's counter. Scott frowned at them. "What happened to Jack?"

Gabriel wanted to groan aloud. "How did you find out so quickly?"

"Susan told me. Her kid was selling cookies and is traumatized. A rumor's going around that it was a wild animal."

He should have known it wouldn't take long for the word to get out to the general public, but even for Spirit Lake, this was close to a record. "You know I can't tell you anything, Scott."

The dreadlocked man rolled his eyes at Amanda. "He's one of the most close mouthed cops we have. Care to let me in on the details?"

Amanda shook her head. "Sorry. Can't do that. I might be green, but I'm not stupid."

At Scott's rabid gaze, Gabriel laughed. "Cut it out. No one is going to tell you a thing."

"Fine. Be that way." Scott wrinkled his nose. Then a sardonic smile tipped one corner of his mouth. "So what are you wanting to eat? Steak? How about something a little extra rare and bloody?"

Gabriel narrowed his eyes. "Funny. I wouldn't be making any jokes. You could end up a suspect. Everyone knows you and Jack never got along. Especially after that last poker game the two of you were in."

The other man's smile congealed.

Gabriel arched a brow. "We both would like a cup of decaf coffee. And not some of that stuff you've had sitting on the burner for the last couple of hours."

When they reached their booth and were out of earshot, Gabriel sat down on a well-worn bench. "I bet you're not used to town gossip or Scott's lack of empathy."

Amanda twisted her lips as she dropped into the opposite bench. "Hmmm, no. But you're efficient when it comes to shutting it down."

"I try my best." He sank back and smiled, relieved to see color bloom into her cheeks. "Scott is one of our top gossips. Actually, there are four or five who can beat him hands down, but I would say he thrives on it the most. I wouldn't be surprised if he gets back at me for not spilling my guts about tonight. He might retaliate by serving a poisoned donut one day soon."

"That sounds scary. Someone vindictive enough to poison my prized breakfast food." She teased him with a smile that revealed the dimple in her left cheek, while her eyes warmed to chestnut.

Gabriel inhaled sharply and broke eye contact before he gave himself away. Where was Scott with their coffee? Amanda had no clue the power she held over him with just a look or gesture. Yes, she knew he found her attractive, but it went beyond any physical release, and she needed to remain clueless about his feelings. But the hunger, the driving need to taste and touch her... He clenched his hand on the seat and forced his mouth into a semblance of a smile.

He knew she felt something for him. At times the sexual tension between them locked him in place, froze his thoughts. He had caught her staring at him several times with her lips parted, cheeks flushed. It wouldn't take much to have her succumb, to—

"You don't look like the donut type." Those incredible eyes held his gaze. They were light brown, almost caramel in color. A lioness. Fierce. Protective. Loyal to her young. She was all of those things and more.

"Donuts   are   not   my   favorite   food"—he smirked—"only because I refuse to be the stereotypical cop. Give me another five years, though, and that might change. I could gain a couple of spare tires around my middle."

Maybe if he cleared the air, talked about this attraction between them, it would go away and lose its power. Or maybe they should act on it, get it out of their systems and move on. Something had to give. He couldn't take much more of this.

"I find that hard to believe." She laughed, a deep throaty sound filled with sensual pleasure that caressed his senses.

"Here." Scott plopped two cups of coffee and creamer on the table with such force that it sounded like he'd used a hammer to pound them onto the table. He disappeared without another comment.

Amanda blinked, thankful for the timely interruption. She'd been eyeing Gabriel's physical attributes far too closely. The man was muscle, sinew, and sexy as hell. There wouldn't be a spare tire around Gabriel's middle. If his biceps were any indication, a person probably could bounce a quarter off his abs or any other body part.

Enough. The last thing she needed was to start an affair with a coworker. She'd just started work two weeks ago. A new town, a new job. No need to ruin everything with a fling. At least not this quickly.

"See what I mean?" Gabriel rested an arm on the back of the bench, accenting the wide breadth of his chest and shoulders. "Scott now has it in for me. It will take a week before he warms up."

"Remind me to keep on his good side."

Gabriel slid the creamer across to the table toward

her and shifted, his knee brushing against hers. The action underscored their close proximity and how important it was to keep her distance so she didn't get completely distracted by his maleness.

In a hurry to take the container from him without touching his hand, she spilled cream over her own. Heat rushed into her face, and she bit back a four-letter word. Even with three yards and a table between them, she still got flustered. Any shorter distance and her brain would combust, short-circuit, or cease to do anything for the foreseeable future. Only two more days of training and getting familiar with the department, and then she would have her own patrol car. Those two days seemed a hell of a long time. She couldn't exactly sit in the back behind the cage while he chauffeured her around town, now could she?

The silence between them thickened. Awkward— with a capital A. At least *she* found it awkward. Gabriel might be completely oblivious to how she thought of him and that three letter word that screamed at her every time he stepped within her radar.

SEX.

Amanda shifted, and air whooshed out of the leather bench. Well, awkward might be putting it mildly.

Gabriel rubbed a thumb over the rim of his coffee cup again and again.

She desperately tried not to think of those large hands on her body.

"Taking tonight out of the equation, how are you liking Spirit Lake?" Gabriel finally broke the silence.

Maybe he didn't find anything awkward, and all this sexual awareness between them was just her wild imagination.

"Love it." She managed a decent reply. Cool and composed, at least, she hoped so.

"You don't find it too boring? There is really not much nightlife in the area."

"I like boring." She eyed his bland expression. What was going on inside his head? "But after tonight, I'm not sure I'm going to get boring."

Leaning forward, he set both elbows on the table and slowly searched her face. "I am not sure what to tell you. Before this, Spirit Lake's violent crime has been non-existent. We get busy in the summer. The Great Lakes area here is a popular tourist destination, especially for families and college students. The most crime we get is during the summer—disorderly conduct and boating while intoxicated, while our main emergency calls are due to people passing out from dehydration."

"The lack of crime is why I moved here with my daughter. I was hoping to raise her in a safe place with a sense of community."

"Before this evening, I would have told you this place is perfect for the both of you. Everyone watches out for each other's back. Many of the locals still don't lock their car or house doors." He leaned back against his bench. "There is only one downfall…"

"And what's that?"

His eyes crinkled into a smile. "Trying to avoid someone, especially during the winter here, is near impossible."

She laughed, relaxing at the warmth in his gaze. The interest in his eyes did something to her insides she hadn't felt in a long while. It was hard to consider it a good thing, though. She didn't need any complication right now, not on a personal level.

His expression turned serious, and the light in his eyes darkened suddenly to rich chocolate. "Hopefully, you'll have an opportunity to meet new people and to laugh more here. Freer mentioned something happened to your daughter. I don't know all the details."

"I-I-"

"Oh, I am sorry." His hand cupped hers on top of the table. "I didn't mean to make you feel uncomfortable."

She quickly withdrew her hand, but the brief heat of his palm still lingered on her skin. So much for confiding in Bill Freer, the Chief of Police, and expecting him to keep it private. She struggled to keep her voice even. "I just didn't realize he'd been talking."

"He didn't go into any details. I walked off before he could. He tends to stick his nose where it does not belong and gossip more than most, and I have never been one to listen to hearsay."

She stared at the remaining coffee in her cup as if it were suddenly fascinating. Her uniform and bullet-proof vest turned constrictive. She didn't want to talk about Nicole. It would only make her feel terribly inadequate at her parenting skills.

"Hey."

She looked up.

"I didn't intend to upset you. Tonight has been upsetting as it is. The last thing you need is for me to make you feel even worse."

The sincerity in his eyes made her smile.

"You know…you have a beautiful smile." He flushed. "Forget I said that."

How could she? "Consider it forgotten."

Sudden tension filled the booth. Gabriel drummed his fingers on the tabletop, while she cleared her throat before taking a sip of cooling coffee.

He rubbed a palm against the back of his neck. "The two of us getting involved is not a smart move. Not when we have to work together."

Amanda sucked in a breath. Now that was a surprise she hadn't planned on, him addressing the sexual tension between them. So much for hoping he'd ignore it or pretend it didn't exist, like she'd been failing to do for days now. "Absolutely." She nodded. "I should be able to keep my hands to myself." At her asinine attempt at a joke, a blush rapidly heated her neck and face. But could she control herself? Yes, she had Nicole to think of. Nicole, traumatized and emotionally fragile, needed a strong, capable, and protective parent. Still, no matter how much she wanted to deny it to herself or anyone else, a part of her was lonely, craving something more than being a parent, traffic cop, and fully functioning and responsible adult.

A secret part of her wanted to be wildly irresponsible…

"That is good to know." He stared at her with eyes gone dark with some indefinable emotion. "I hope to do the same."

"Well then, it seems we're on the same page." Amanda's pulse quickened and her body stirred with undeniable longing. Having sex with Gabriel would be stupid, irresponsible, and completely selfish on her part. She needed to think of Nicole. The move, on top of everything else the past year, had been a traumatizing change for her daughter.

When the staticky voice of the dispatcher came over the radio attached to Gabriel's shoulder, Amanda thanked the heavens for the interruption, that is, until Becky's next sentence.

"We have a possible 240 at Christopher's Crossing. Someone heard screaming."

Amanda tensed while Gabriel swore under his breath. He clicked on his radio and replied, "10-4. We will go check it out."

For the briefest of moments, they stared across the table at each other. Then Amanda said what they were both thinking. "I hope to hell we don't have another victim on our hands."

CHAPTER 2

Back in the squad car, Amanda rubbed her brow with a thumb and index finger. "Where's Christopher Crossing? I haven't heard of it."

"After a while, you'll hear about it plenty enough. It's inside the city limits." Gabriel guided the vehicle from the restaurant's parking lot and drove a good mile before pulling onto the highway.

Brief glimpses of snow-dusted farmland appeared on both sides of the road as the vehicle devoured asphalt and the yellow median line sped by. "And?"

"It's a teenage hangout. We are always getting calls about loud music and fighting—teenagers blowing off steam. During the summer, a lot of kids go fishing there and drink more than they should. We make appearances to keep them in line, but the fear of landing in jail does not always work. We usually get fewer calls during the winter, though. I guess the natives have gotten bored and are in need of some excitement."

"Dispatch said a 240. Assault, I can understand with a bunch of drunk teenagers. Screaming's a whole different matter."

"Hmmm. Well, let us hope it's nothing more. I don't think either one of us wants to deal with another dead body."

"I'll take rowdy teenagers any day of the week."

"Is that so?" Gabriel was obviously amused. "Does that mean you can relate, and you were rowdy yourself as a teenager?"

Amanda's lips twisted into a wry grimace. "Just a typical one. I'm sure you have far wilder stories under your belt than I do. I think the craziest thing was a bunch of us going skinny-dipping."

"Skinny-dipping, eh?" He chuckled, his next words growing deep and smoky. "I would have liked to have been there to see that." He slowed the car and turned it onto a dirt road.

The headlights bounced off patches of snow, dirt, and several pines. A deer leaped across the road and disappeared into the brush.

"I'm sure you would have," she quipped, turning and catching the flash of a smile in the car's interior. His eyes glowed a metallic golden brown and his large shadow suddenly took up too much of the front seat.

Oh, no. She sucked in a breath as her chest tightened with desire. She hated how her brain ceased to function just because of a little smile. After all, she'd been fighting this attraction since the moment she walked into the police department and saw Gabriel seated at his desk that first day.

As they rounded a bend, a fire flickered in the distance, while smoke billowed into the night sky. Flames revealed a good half-dozen people. Couples sat on the tailgates of two trucks backed up to the fire.

The group must have seen them. Two people started kicking dirt and snow into the fire. Others jumped into their cars.

"See what I mean?" Gabriel guided the vehicle

down the dirt road layered with potholes and patches of ice, both of which impeded their speed.

"I'm sure we're putting the fear of God into them."

"It's possible, but not probable. And as for the screaming from the looks of the group, they were just getting rowdy and loud."

Headlights flashed. Engines rumbled. Dirt and snow kicked up into the air as vehicles fishtailed from the area. Taillights disappeared.

"It has become a bit of a game," Gabriel explained. "We have never arrested anyone yet. Maybe if they get out of hand and do more than regular teenager stuff, that might change."

By the time Gabriel pulled the car to the side of the dirt road and angled the headlights, only embers glowed in the fire pit.

"Not even a beer can left behind." Amanda peered around the cleaned-up area. No signs of fighting or foul play. She relaxed. Just a bunch of teenagers letting off steam. "I'm pretty impressed. You can't even fine them for littering."

"They clean up the area after themselves, and we pretty well let them go on their way."

"What about drunk driving?"

"Doesn't happen often. But we should check the place out and make sure we've got a dead fire."

"Well, shoot. We didn't even get to see the whites of their eyes."

Gabriel laughed. "There's always next time. There always is."

Amanda unbuckled her belt and tried to open the door, once, twice.

"Is that thing sticking again?" He shook his head. "You would think they'd learned that a bit of WD-40 doesn't always do the trick."

Amanda checked to make sure it wasn't locked, and this time shoved at the door. It didn't budge. "I guess I don't have enough muscle to unjam it."

"Damn budget cuts. Nothing seems to be working. God forbid if anything breaks down. If it does, you are going to have to wait until you retire to get it fixed." He muttered a four-letter word under his breath. "Here, let me." He reached over to grab the door with his right hand.

"No, that's fine." She squished up against the backrest to avoid his touch. It didn't work. Even through the bulletproof vest, bra, and shirt, his arm burned through to her breasts as he caught at the handle and twisted.

The scent of his aftershave drifted toward her. Oh, crap. The smell was divine. Musky, male, woodsy, clean, and something else Amanda couldn't decipher. A wild, hungry scent was the only way she could describe it, but the smell was distinct and pure Gabriel. She'd gotten too close to him a couple of times and hadn't been able to avoid inhaling.

Double crap. Her body started to respond. Desire roiled through her limbs to pool in the pit of her stomach.

"The thing is worse than before," he muttered.

In her panic to get away, she grabbed the door handle herself, entwining her fingers with his as she yanked at the metal.

He twisted around and used his other hand instead,

which made everything worse. Now his chest angled toward her. His cheek brushed against her lips. His upper torso pushed into her breasts.

"Just leave it alone!" Her voice was too loud, too emotional in the close confines of the car.

With one hand resting on the side of the backrest by her shoulder and the other clasping the handle, he froze. His cinnamon-scented breath whispered into the car's interior.

Her pulse thundered. *Please don't turn. Just, please don't turn.* Gabriel made her feel too needy, too lonely for a man. She was afraid—one touch from him and she'd cave.

He turned.

Inches separated their lips.

They both jerked back at the same time.

But then he pushed up against her again, sending her heart ricocheting inside her chest.

"Move!" She twisted against his chest and tried to edge closer to her door, using her feet to get a better grip on the vehicle floor. Her heels skidded, and she lost her footing, sliding across the leather bench to land on her back.

He reached for the dashboard for balance, missed, and landed on top of her, his legs entwining with hers. "Damn it. I can't."

"Bullshit."

Her breath came out in quick, shallow pants.

Gabriel was now plastered over her body.

She grabbed his arms. Beneath the fabric of his uniform, his muscles bunched beneath her fingers.

"I am stuck somehow," he said by her ear.

His breath sent a delicious shiver down her spine. She wanted to kiss him. No, she wanted to do more than kiss him. This wasn't good. Not good at all.

"What do you mean?" She managed to get the question out as she touched her cheek to his and looked between their bodies.

Somehow they'd twisted this way and that, to the point that he was almost on top of her. She couldn't take this; she was going to do something stupid.

Like kiss him.

"My badge is caught on yours."

"That's impossible." She squirmed harder. Her hips twisted and meshed with his, and, and—

"Damn it," he demanded. "Just stop. Stop it right now."

Beneath him, she stilled and looked up into his face.

The moon had risen over the trees to stream into the vehicle from the window, illuminating the hard angles of his face, the gold flecks in his eyes.

His erection burned against her pelvis.

My God, he wanted her just as bad as she wanted him. If she moved just so and arched up— *Whoa. Stop right there.* But by God, she couldn't remember one moment, one instant where she was drowning in desire like this.

"To hell with the badge." He caught her lips in a kiss, thrusting his tongue into her mouth, tasting, touching as if he wanted to devour her.

She kissed him back with equal fervor, brushing her fingers along his nape to caress the fringe of his hair, then slipping them through the silken strands until she tugged at his scalp, urging him on.

He shoved a hand beneath her body until he cupped her ass and pressed her deeper against his groin.

She squirmed until her thighs cradled his hips.

He pushed into her again.

Perfect, so perfect. Except for the clothes keeping them apart. She wanted to rip them off. Feel naked skin against naked skin. She wanted—needed more.

Hunger eclipsed all thought.

Clawing at his shirt, she pulled the hem from his pants until her fingers encountered flesh. She caressed the small of his back with shaking hands, rimmed the inside of his belt loop, then edged higher, but his bullet-proof vest impeded her from caressing his back or anything above his waist.

With one hand beneath her head and the other on her hip, pressing her deeper against his erection, he kissed her jaw, temple, earlobe. The wet heat of his lips trailed along the arch of her neck.

My God. She cried out at the pain of unfulfilled desire. The ache between her legs was unbearable. Near frantic, she inched back into the padded seat of the cruiser and tried to get her hands between them to disentangle their shields and get to the buttons of his shirt and beyond.

The badges disengaged. Freedom! Quickly she twisted at his buttons, opening each with frantic fingers. She needed to get at his skin, touch it, taste it...

The sound of a horn ripped into the car's interior.

For a moment Amanda didn't understand. Oh, hell! Her foot had connected to the steering wheel and was digging into the padded horn.

"What the—" Gabriel jerked away from her. He

grabbed onto the dashboard and the back of her seat to keep from crushing her.

She came to with a resounding crash. Fog clung to the windows, shielding her view from beyond the vehicle. They'd misted the glass in a thick film like a couple of randy teenagers.

My God. She'd been about to have sex with her partner. Even worse, while she was on duty. What the hell was wrong with her?

"Jesus." Gabriel pulled away from her.

Shadows masked his expression, but she sensed his need. Felt the desperation and tremor in his hand as he stroked wayward strands of hair from her face.

He kissed her brow, his breath quick and unsteady against her temple before he drew away. "This is what I was talking about." Raw hunger laced his voice. "This attraction, this need between us. It's much worse than I thought. Especially now that I have had a chance to taste you."

"It's only because it's been a while for me." She pulled herself into a sitting position and tried to keep her voice from cracking.

"Come on, Amanda. I am a cop. I can read bullshit with the best of them."

She pressed her lips tightly together. "Fine. It doesn't mean we have to give in."

"Can you honestly say this is not going to happen again when we're alone?" With a hand curled around the top of the steering wheel, he stared at her across the barely two-foot distance between them.

"I…" Her body ached. "No. But I'd like to think the two of us are more than animals and can handle keeping our hands to ourselves for the next two days. After that, I'll have my own car and the only time we'll be in each other's company is at the office."

Her cell buzzed. In relief, she slumped against the cushioned backrest. Topic closed for the moment. She pulled the phone from the case at her hip. "It's my daughter. I've got to get it." Time to switch gears. "Hey, honey. What's up?" She made a point of not looking at Gabriel. It was hard enough focusing on her daughter with him only feet away.

"I can't sleep." Fear peppered Nicole's voice.

"Nightmares?" Amanda groaned silently.

"Yeah."

"I'm so sorry, sweetie. I thought they might have disappeared. You haven't had one since we moved here."

"Katie didn't hide all the knives after dinner. She said she would, but they were all in that big wooden box thingy. And the other ones were still in the drawer."

Amanda's shoulders dipped. "I'll talk to her again and make sure she understands how important that is." Though she wasn't yet ready to get into any great detail about Nicole's past with the babysitter.

"Oh, Autumn asked if I could spend the night tomorrow." A hint of excitement overshadowed Nicole's sadness.

"And?" Hope bubbled up in Amanda's chest.

"I want to."

"That's great." She broke into a smile. Finally, just when she thought an overnight stay would never happen. Maybe moving to Spirit Lake *was* the best thing she'd done in a long while. She tried not to think of the savage attack on Jack Blunt. "I'll be home in a little over an hour, and we can talk about it more, but just remember that I'll have to pick you up from Autumn's the next morning for volleyball practice."

When she hung up, Gabriel looked at her, his brow creased. "Is everything okay?"

"Yeah, Nicole's spending the night at a friend's house tomorrow night." She smiled with genuine pleasure. "It's a first. She's never done that before. She's finding her wings when I thought she never would."

"Well, it could be she has wanted to stay close to home all this time because she has such a special mother."

The mood had changed, thank God, and she was going to make sure it stayed that way by keeping to a safe topic. No detours back to where they were. "I'm trying. Motherhood is something pretty new to me. Nicole might be eleven, but I've only had her a year."

"I am sure she realizes how lucky she is."

Amanda adjusted her clothing and slipped on her seatbelt. "The adoption was final just last month."

Gabriel started the car and rubbed the condensation off the window in front of the steering wheel. "So, she is going to be over at a friend's house tomorrow night."

"Yes…"

"We both have that night off." His voice turned husky.

"Uh-huh."

"So, you are going to be alone."

Amanda couldn't find the willpower to lie. Her heart rate kicked up a notch. "Yep." It was hard to keep her voice steady.

"Did you want me to come over?"

"I-I don't know…" The idea sent a new wave of desire roiling through her. Did she have the power to say no if he showed up at her door? Actually, she didn't think she wanted to say no.

Gabriel left it at that as he turned the car around on the dirt road and drove them back to town.

CHAPTER 3

Shoulders slumped with weariness, Amanda slipped through the side entrance of her house and into the kitchen, softly closing the door behind her. What a crazy, exhausting work night. Lows and highs, and then more lows. Talk about being twisted into a mental pretzel. She was just glad she was home with her body and part of her mind intact.

Above the counter, the babysitter had left on a nightlight, which illuminated the brown-flecked countertops, ceramic floor, and maple kitchen table and chairs. The warm, cozy feel of the place took the edge off the tension digging into her shoulders, back and neck. A hot shower would remove the rest. Sleep would have to wait a little longer.

She pulled her gun out of its case and set it on top of the refrigerator. As she started tugging open the top button of her uniform, the whisper of footsteps announced Nicole's approach. Her daughter appeared from the hallway leading toward the bedrooms. Tousled blonde shoulder-length hair framed a round, freckled face with an upturned nose. The smile was what caught Amanda's attention. Natural and genuine. It lit up Nicole's large blue eyes. Thankfully, Amanda was seeing more and more of those smiles the past couple of months. Even more since they'd moved to Spirit Lake.

Back in Chicago, she'd tried to keep Nicole insulated from all the news on the television and Internet. Shootings, robberies, carjackings, or kidnappings, were all terrifying to a normal eleven-year-old, but even more so for Nicole. They hadn't been able to get away from the violence. How ironic that Amanda's job involved all of it. She couldn't give up Nicole, though, and she believed without her, Nicole would never have survived the system intact. She was too fragile, too sensitive.

Hence, the small town of Spirit Lake and its historically low per capita crime rate.

At least, until now...

"Hey, Sweet Pea." She hugged Nicole for a brief moment and inhaled the clean scent of soap and lavender shampoo. "Couldn't get back to sleep?"

After grabbing the gun from the top of the fridge, Amanda led the way to her bedroom. Mindful of Katie asleep in one of the bedrooms, Amanda shut the door as her daughter launched herself onto the queen-size bed.

"I tried to snuggle with Katie, but she takes up too much of the bed and moves around a lot."

"Sorry to hear that." She put her gun in the safe and locked it.

Nicole grimaced "*And* she snores."

"I guess I should have asked those questions when I was interviewing for a babysitter." Amanda shrugged out of her uniform and tossed her top into the laundry basket in the bathroom. Then she worked at the velcro to get out of her vest. "Things working out with her still?"

"Oh, yeah." Nicole flung herself backward and into the pillows. "She can be really funny and makes really good peanut butter cookies."

"She does, does she?" In the closet, she hung up the vest while smothering envy's green-eyed monster. There was no need to compete with Katie. "Give me fifteen minutes. I need to take a shower, and then I'll make you some chocolate-chip pancakes. But you need to take your own shower and start getting ready for school. Also, you've got to put your overnight things for your sleepover into your princess bag."

"Shower, smower." Nicole scrambled from the bed. "But heck, I'd do anything for chocolate-chip pancakes. I can't remember the last time you made them."

Amanda wasn't going to feel guilty. There were a ton of mothers out there who didn't cook so well. A great chef didn't make for a great parent, she told herself as she scrubbed off the night's worth of grime in the shower, slipped into a pair of sweats, and started the pancakes—all in less than fifteen minutes.

Nicole popped into the kitchen soon after and smelled even better than before.

When Katie stumbled into the room, sleepy-eyed and rumpled looking, Amanda asked, "I take it, you didn't get much sleep?"

"I had enough." The older girl plopped onto the kitchen chair by Nicole. "We had a couple of bad dreams last night."

"I couldn't sleep." Nicole's lips twitched, and she flicked her gaze to the ceiling. "Katie snores like crazy."

"Nicole!"

A pink flush raced into Katie's cheeks.

"Apologize to Katie." Amanda grabbed a bowl from the cabinet and sent Nicole a fierce look.

Her brow wrinkled. "Why? It's the truth."

"Even so, you don't broadcast that to everyone. It's rude."

"Amanda, she doesn't have to apologize." Katie shook her head.

"Yes, she does."

"Sorry," Nicole grunted.

Amanda raised a brow at her daughter.

"I'm really sorry, Katie." Nicole's voice turned sincere. "I didn't mean to hurt your feelings."

"Don't worry about it." Katie smiled, her gaze softening. The girl exuded a gentle aura, which had first drawn Amanda in their initial interview.

Amanda opened the kitchen drawer and found two trays of silverware inside. One held forks, spoons, and blunt utensils, while the second contained butter and steak knives and other wicked-looking cutlery that gleamed beneath the room's light. "Nicole, turn around."

"Why?" There was a brief pause, then understanding flashed in Nicole's eyes. She latched onto the chair's arms with tight fists before she swiveled her chair to look at the wall.

With Nicole's back turned, Amanda took the tray from the drawer. She retrieved a butter knife before stuffing the tray in another cabinet behind some plastic containers and mixing bowls while Katie watched. Yeah, it looked odd, but if it made Nicole feel happy and safe, she'd do that and so much more.

"Good to go." Amanda sensed the tension leave Nicole in one long rush.

"So, how many pancakes do I get?" Nicole's eyes twinkled, and she nudged Katie's thigh with a slippered foot. "We get chocolate-chip pancakes this morning. You're going to stick around, aren't you?"

"Stay for breakfast," Amanda urged as she gathered ingredients, suspecting Katie didn't put much in her mouth without thinking of her figure. Ah, teenage self-confidence. Thank goodness, she'd gotten through that phase in one piece. It helped having a mom who praised and encouraged her in areas other than her looks, unlike society's almost fanatic focus on a person's physical appearance. "Having breakfast once in a while won't hurt you."

Pancakes appeared to be a hit. Both girls didn't talk much because they were too busy feeding themselves. Breakfast tasted pretty darn good, Amanda had to admit, as she finished her own stack and sank back against her chair.

Nicole pushed her plate away. "Can I be excused?"

"Of course. Don't forget to brush your teeth."

She wrinkled her nose. "I know. You don't have to tell me."

As Nicole trotted from the kitchen, Amanda stacked dirty plates and silverware. She carried them over to the counter and tried not to act surprised when Katie followed her.

Katie ran a thumb back and forth along the edge of the counter, then glanced at the door leading to the hall and back to Amanda. She lowered her voice. "I saw you hide the knives. Sorry, I forgot to do that last night."

Amanda sighed. This was not her favorite topic. "Yes, well...can you remember to do it next time you use them?" She leaned a hip against the counter and met Katie's gaze. "It's important."

"Yeah, sure." Katie stared at Amanda's hand as she continued to slide her thumb up and down the counter's edge.

"Is something wrong?" Amanda finally asked. It wasn't like Katie to be vague or shy away from a topic.

"No, but I was just wondering…"

"What?"

"Why is she so scared of knives?"

"Right now, that's not something I'm willing to tell you."

∞

In total darkness, Gabriel paced the confines of the living room.

Friday night.

Amanda's daughter was probably now safely over at her friend's house. He had a good idea Amanda was home alone. From the first moment she had moved into town, he found himself fascinated with her to the point he had a good idea of her routine and who she associated with. From what he could tell, she had not started dating or hanging out with friends on the weekend.

Holy Mother. He had turned into some sick stalker. All because of a woman. Common sense told him to keep away from her, to ignore the hunger that flooded his senses any time thoughts of her whispered into his conscious mind. She embodied everything he loved in a woman—soft, womanly, independent, protective of the people she loved. Having a sexy body didn't hurt. And that quirky smile of hers. The way her mouth would curve into a grin just on one side, and how laughter would lighten her brown eyes to caramel. He was half in love with her.

He glanced at the clock. Eight o'clock. Night clung to the windows. Within ten minutes he could be at her front door.

Damn it. He should leave Amanda alone.

But when had he ever listened to shoulds?

Gabriel needed to keep his hands to himself.

But Mayor wasn't around anymore...

He peered outside. Streetlights illuminated the snow-covered ground and added a sheen to the asphalt. There was no flash of headlights or pedestrians taking an evening stroll. After the slaughter of Jack Blunt, pretty much everyone hid in their homes, thinking they were safe inside. But being inside a house could be a trap in itself, escape impossible behind a locked door.

He hoped the killer had moved on to another city, another state.

It wasn't Mayor. Mayor had a signature when it came to leaving a corpse. But someone else was marking their territory.

Damn.

He had liked Jack. The man had not deserved to have his life end that way. No one did.

Gabriel grabbed the remote and turned on the television. After a couple of minutes, the drone of voices and canned laugh track that followed every comedic punch line grew old. He hit the off button and stared at the blank screen for a couple of minutes. Maybe he should go to the gym, sweat off some tension, and then add a cold shower to the mix.

Holy Mother, who was he kidding? The gym was not going to do a thing, never mind a cold shower.

He could not stop thinking of Amanda. The idea of her mouth on him…

Damn it.

To hell with it. He grabbed his coat and keys from the counter and drove across town. He pulled into Amanda's driveway and parked beside her economy car. For a moment, as he stared at her house, he clutched the shift lever and debated whether or not to back out and drive off. But memories of her beneath him, her hips flush with his, the scent of her hair—with that touch of coconut and tangerine—bombarded his senses and decimated any lingering willpower. Sighing, he shut off the engine and slipped out of the SUV.

Amanda's place might not have a white picket fence, but it came pretty close. A porch light illuminated an older, red brick home with a wraparound veranda. She had bought the place herself. In a town of a little fewer than five thousand inhabitants, word got out as to who did what and where pretty quickly.

He climbed the stairs and snow crunched against the soles of his shoes. A swing hung at one end of the porch, while a light inside seeped through the cracks of the blinds and the sides of the drapes—a pretty good sign that she was home for the night.

Briefly, he stilled on the top step. What was he doing? For all of one second, he again argued with himself to turn back and retrace his steps. Visiting her was an all-around bad idea.

Again, he was not good at shoulds. So he climbed the last step and hit the doorbell with his thumb. He didn't have to wait long for the door to open.

She stood there, brown eyes dark with emotion, pink lips parted.

Suddenly unsure, he dragged in a calming breath and took in her scent. Coconut and tangerine—reminders of warm sunshine, relaxing summer days, and a time he had almost forgotten existed. The light bathed her in a romantic glow, caressing her brown hair in such a way that she looked better than any angel he'd ever envisioned—he just hoped to God he never caused her to fall from grace.

"You came." Her words were soft, husky, and so damn sexy.

"I couldn't keep away." He stood rooted to the porch. The excitement, mixed with trepidation and desire in her voice, stoked the hunger roiling through his body. "Is Nicole gone for the night?"

"Yes."

He placed both hands on either side of the doorway but didn't step across the threshold and inside. "Well?" he whispered. "Are you going to invite me in? But I want to warn you. Once I step inside, there's no going back."

Her smile faltered, and a beautiful pink blush rose up her neck into her face.

Gabriel inhaled sharply. She was gorgeous and so vibrant.

Her breasts rose and fell in rapid succession as she took in quick, shallow breaths. She was obviously just as hungry, just as excited as he was. "Come in."

The moment the words left her mouth, he strode

across the threshold, ripped off his jacket to toss on the coat rack, slammed the door shut with his heel, and hauled her in his arms. His mouth caught her gasp of surprise. He didn't bother with preliminaries. His kiss was all about hunger and desire. He wanted to drink in her essence, lose himself in her arms; for the briefest moment, he wanted to feel like a human again.

She slid her hands up his arms to his shoulders, squeezing, caressing, as if trying to memorize the feel of him.

He cupped her face with both palms, savored the silken touch of her skin and rubbed his hips against hers.

She returned his kiss with a hunger that rivaled his, but then she shivered in his arms and drew back enough to mutter, "This is all wrong."

"Is it?" He unbuttoned her blouse and pulled the long-sleeved garment from the smooth slope of her shoulders. The material parted and revealed her breasts in a black lace bra that accented her flawless marble-like skin. He spread his palms around her waist and caressed her ribs. Cupping both breasts, he ran his thumbs across their tips through the lace cups.

"We work together." She shrugged out of her shirt as he unhooked her bra. "This is the last thing we should be doing."

After he eased the silky material from her skin, the feel of her plump breasts—taut nipples against his palms—dragged a groan from his mouth. "But it feels great."

A soft, little moan whispered past her lips. "Doesn't it, though?"

Their mouths fused again as he cupped her bottom and pressed her harder against his erection. "Damn straight," he murmured between a deep, slow kiss.

She broke away, breathing heavily, then slid a path across his jaw with her lips. "You'll have to leave"—she kissed his temple—"before seven." She nibbled on his earlobe. "Nicole has volleyball practice in the morning."

"Sure," he murmured, pulling away long enough to yank his shirt off his back. "Where's your bedroom?"

"Down the hall. Second door to the right."

That was all he needed to hear. He swept her into his arms and moved swiftly down the hall to her room.

Amanda gasped at Gabriel's sheer strength. She wasn't light, but he made it seem like she weighed little more than air. Then there was his scent—moonlight and evergreen and something just a little wild.

He hit the light switch with his elbow. A lamp on a table in the corner threw the room into muted shades of mauve and white. Two steps and he gently draped her over the comforter. Then he unhooked his belt.

Leaning back, resting on her elbows, Amanda sucked in air and savored the moment and how the soft light caressed the curves, indentations, and slope of his shoulders, the hard wall of his chest, and the lines and shadows of his ribs. The scar on his chest did nothing to detract from his rugged good looks.

Her gaze dropped lower, past his flat belly to his jean-encased hips where his erection pressed against the blue fabric. Her heart rate stumbled, then quickened. She wanted him, the feel of his body on her own, the taste of his skin on her lips.

Quickly, he discarded the rest of his clothes and deftly removed her jeans from around her hips and legs.

Clad in only a black lace thong, Amanda found it hard to catch her breath when she met the fierce hunger in his gaze. "You're beautiful." The words came unbidden from her lips.

He smiled, but there was nothing gentle in the harsh lines of his face. "Now, you are being kind. I am nothing compared to you. Everything about you takes my breath away." He sank down over her.

She arched into him, loving the cool, subtle texture of his naked flesh against hers as she helped him remove her underwear. Then he kissed her again, his hands gentle, sure, experienced on her breasts, stomach, and hips, and she stopped thinking and fell into sensation. Lifting her head off the comforter, she met his lips with a demanding kiss.

She caressed the long line of his spine, the dip at the small of his back and cupped his ass with both hands, urging him even closer than he already was. Delicious, how he quivered under her touch, the quick intake of his breath when she slipped a hand between their bodies and glided her fingers over the silk length of him.

Groaning, he grabbed both her hands and shackled them above her head. He rubbed up and down along the juncture of her thigh with the thick length of his erection, mimicking what was to come.

He urged her legs wider with a knee. With feather-light fingers, he teased, fondled, and stroked her until she was squirming beneath him as anticipation, intense, even painful, curled into her stomach. Then finally he pressed the tip of his cock at her entrance and slowly glided into her body, filling her with his length, his width.

His mouth muffled her cry of pleasure as he started moving.

She wrapped her legs around his hips, urging him faster, harder with her hands and hips, loving how his muscles flexed beneath her palms.

Then with one deft move, he flipped them until he was on his back and she was astride, his hands on her hips, urging her with slow, sure movements.

She looked down and met the fierce glow of his gaze. Nothing about him was soft or gentle. He was protector and predator.

Sighing, she bent over his body, caught his hands and fisted them with hers just above his shoulders. She moved above him, her breasts brushing his chest as pleasure danced through her body. She nipped at his lip, then licked the spot where she'd used her teeth.

Growling, Gabriel flipped her once again on her back. The beat of her heart pounded against his chest as he stroked in and out of her. He caught her ass with both hands and pulled her tighter to him. Her gorgeous, long legs twined with his. She twisted her head to one side, exposing her neck, as she arched into him again and again, her chestnut-colored hair flowing over the white comforter...

The light from the lamp glowed across the smooth expanse of her throat and neck before she shifted and met his gaze. He was the first to close his eyes, afraid she could see beyond his carefully manufactured façade, afraid she would find him lacking. But he couldn't hide from himself. He had tried. Holy hell, he had tried to keep away, tried to tell himself he was not falling.

The scent of her sex, the way she moved intoxicated him, pushed him further to the edge. He wanted to drown in her essence.

Amanda cried out, growing rigid beneath him as she orgasmed. Her body writhing beneath him, her quick, ragged breaths, her pure excitement, pulled Gabriel under, and he came into her.

For the briefest of moments, he forgot everything. The taste and touch of this one woman choked back thoughts of despair and loss. In Amanda's arms, he forgot, and for just a moment, there was a whisper, a possibility of hope.

Her soft sigh washed across his temple. He kissed the corner of her lips, her brow. Her eyes fluttered closed, and she curled into his body as they shifted onto their sides. He lay there for a moment, his mouth against the soft down at her nape, his arm around her slender middle, and he cherished the feel of her body flush against his.

Fifteen minutes later, he pulled back the comforter and urged her beneath the sheets as he slipped from the bed. She rolled onto her back. Lamplight illuminated the rise and fall of her breasts, the shadow of her lashes against her cheeks as she slept.

Opening and closing his hands, he stood frozen, unable to turn away, unable to stop staring. He'd lost control and taken. This thing between them was not some fling that would disappear in the morning.

He forced himself to turn away, dress, and leave the house, quietly shutting the door behind him. As he stepped out into the frigid night, a strange, inexplicable lightness unfurled from his chest and latched onto his breath.

Hope.

How strange. Gabriel had almost forgotten the feeling.

He trotted down the stairs. As he drove home, he could not keep from grinning like a crazed idiot. He wanted to get to know Amanda. It was a bad idea, they were wrong for each other, and it wouldn't last. How could it? She would never understand his past, but that didn't erase the crazy rush of excitement at the idea of getting to know Amanda more. She was a fierce little thing, and not just in bed. She gave as much as she got, and from what he had witnessed so far, she was a great employee, mother, and friend. He had the feeling she would protect the people she loved until her dying breath.

After pulling into his garage, he stepped through the entrance into the kitchen and paused with his hand on the front doorknob. The rank smell of rotting flesh slapped him, the scent so strong he gagged. Shock rammed into his chest. He moved into the kitchen, his gaze assessing the room quickly.

Moonlight streamed through the slats of the blinds across the kitchen window. Shadows clung to the doorway leading into the living room. Silence coated the house. No ticking clock, hum of the fridge, or sound of the old house settling.

To the left, he eased the kitchen drawer open on silent hinges. He locked a hand around the handle of his Glock. Blood pounding in his ears, he inched across the kitchen tile. Tension cut across his shoulders and his back.

As he edged farther into the house, he checked behind the large sectional sofa in the living room, the desk and loveseat in the office, and inside the closet and bathroom.

Nothing.

Yet.

He climbed the stairs, mindful of the places on the wood steps that creaked. As he searched the master bedroom and bathroom and the other two bedrooms, no signs of an intruder materialized, and the scent of death dissipated.

He didn't relax. A person could not replicate the smell of a corpse. It was too distinct an odor.

He retraced his steps to the first floor, his hand firmly on his Glock. When he reached the living room, the stench increased. Frowning, he followed the scent into the kitchen and flipped on the light switch. He eyed the refrigerator to his right. Dread crawled up his spine. He grabbed the handle with his free hand and opened the door, expecting the worst.

A gallon of milk. A pint of orange juice. Ketchup and a plastic container with leftover pizza.

Nothing. This was like some sick horror movie.

Still, he didn't relax. The odor leached the breath from his lungs. He blinked back the sting of tears. He could not take it anymore. He pivoted away from the fridge and strode toward the window above the sink to get some air into the room.

"Son of a bitch!"

A severed head rested in the sink. The mouth gaped open as if in a silent scream. The half-closed, blind eyes stared at nothing. Hair matted from dried blood clung to the skull, while marbleized flesh gleamed beneath the fluorescent light. The frigid temperatures had slowed the decomposition enough to help Gabriel identify the victim.

Jack Blunt.

CHAPTER 4

Amanda's cell phone started vibrating on the nightstand. Lying on her stomach, she pulled her head from beneath the pillow, brushed her hair from her face impatiently, and glanced at the digital clock in bright green neon. Five o'clock. She'd wanted another blessed hour of sleep. Just one hour. Was that too much to ask for?

She grabbed the phone, and Bill Freer's name flashed across its face. Work. Great. Just what she needed.

The pillow beside her was empty; the sheets were cool on the other side of the bed. Gabriel had left a long time ago.

Groaning, she flipped over on her back to stare at the ceiling. "Amanda Douglas."

"You need to get your ass into the station."

Her body snapped into a sitting position. She didn't like the sound of Bill's voice. Something was definitely up. Related to Jack Blunt? "What's wrong? Do we have another murder?"

"Hell, no. It's worse than that. I want you here in ten minutes." Before she had a chance to respond, he disconnected the call.

My God, had Gabriel confessed to Bill that they'd

slept together? Bill hated fraternization of any kind. She'd heard from one of their dispatchers that Bill considered dating within the police department taboo and wouldn't tolerate it. Something about a lawsuit, divorce, and a brawl inside the department several years ago, but the gossip was sketchy on details. Sure, there wasn't anything in the policies or procedures manual on it. Sexual harassment policies had long since replaced something like that, but that didn't stop supervisors like Bill from reaming out their subordinates about fraternizing.

No, she argued. The idea of Bill finding out so soon was crazy. Word didn't get out that fast, no matter how small the town. Granted, Gabriel had left his car in front of the house a good part of the night. It was just the previous night, for goodness' sake. No, it had to do with the murder. Maybe the autopsy had revealed a clue to the killer's identity.

After quickly showering, she didn't bother with makeup. She tugged on a pair of jeans and a T-shirt and rushed from the walk-in closet. Unable to find her usual hairbrush, she crouched to grab a spare from under one of the bathroom cabinets. In her hurry, she rose and pivoted into the open medicine cabinet. The corner rammed into her neck.

"Damn it!" She slapped a hand against the side of her throat and gasped from the sudden pain. She blinked a couple of times. As the pain receded, she pulled her palm away and looked in the mirror. A red welt had formed, but at least she hadn't broken the skin.

Okay, time to calm down, slow down. She didn't need another accident, particularly not a car wreck on her way to work.

She called Katie, just in case she couldn't get out of work in time to pick Nicole up from her friend's house. Who knew how long she was going to be at work. Bill's barking sure wasn't a good sign.

Her stomach churned during the drive to the station. Again, how could word of her and Gabriel have gotten out to Bill? But what else was she supposed to think? Bill had sounded angry at her, not at something or someone else. She considered calling Gabriel. No, that was a stupid idea. Better to keep her mouth shut and deny everything if Bill brought up the subject.

After parking and stepping out of her car, she rolled her shoulders to relieve the tension snapping at the muscles in her back and neck and strode into the main entrance of the police department. According to her cell in its case on her belt, she'd managed to make it in twenty minutes. Not bad, but not good for this particular situation. Tardiness was another of Bill's pet peeves. He expected punctuality, and probably a person's firstborn.

After crossing the lobby and security, she walked into the main offices and paused at the entrance. A couple of officers sat at their desks, but no sign of Bill. Yet.

"He's pissed." Warner, a rookie who'd started less than six months before her, nodded toward Freer's closed door. "He's in a meeting, but I don't think he's going to calm down by the time it's over."

"Thanks for the heads-up," Amanda muttered before heading to her own desk to go over the autopsy reports from the Medical Examiner's Office. After pulling up her work email, she opened the attachment. She skimmed the toxicology section. No surprise, nothing of importance. After scanning the first several paragraphs, she got to the meat of the report and gaped at the screen.

She pulled up an image of Blunt's headless body, dragged in a sharp, ragged breath, then whispered, "My God."

She wrinkled her nose; the scent of his dead body was just as vivid in her mind. She hadn't seen anything like it, and she never wanted to again. But the images would be branded into her brain for some time. She stared, then frowned at his chest. How strange.

After reading for a couple more minutes, she grabbed her phone to talk to Jennifer. The woman worked most weekends. She knew that only because she'd met Jennifer under different circumstances, over cookies and punch during a school holiday party, since the woman's daughter was in the same class as Nicole. They'd even gone out for a drink to reminisce about old boyfriends and the big city; Jennifer and her husband had escaped the crowd and crime for small-town life. But it looked like no one could fully escape from the darker side of society, no matter how badly they wanted to.

"I knew you were going to call," was Jennifer's first comment.

"Of course I was. Who wouldn't? It's not like I've seen this before." Amanda grabbed a pen from her desk.

"Right there with you. Everything about Blunt's death is macabre."

"But you don't know what type of weapon it was?" Amanda rocked the pen between her two fingers, then tapped one end against the desk.

"Some type of sharp instrument with a serrated edge, but right now, we haven't been able to figure it out. It's not steel or any type of metal we know of. I'm hoping more tests pull something up."

Amanda frowned and tapped even faster against the desk. She couldn't calm the rapid beating of her heart. "There's also that mark on his chest. I hadn't seen it at the time."

"Blood was masking much of it." Jennifer grunted. "Fuck. That's also strange. They took the time to carve a design into his chest. It's a simple marking, but hell if I know what it is."

"I've seen something similar."

"Where?" Jennifer's avid interest came through the phone.

"In Chicago, on some gang members. They have inked tattoos, not carved designs like Blunt's. And they're far more intricate than this one."

"Gangs? Oh, hell. That's just what we need."

"It's not something that makes me feel all warm and fuzzy. You can't get much worse than the Mexican Mafia."

"Shit." Jennifer grunted again. "What the hell are they doing in this area? There's nothing here for them. Drugs? You can't hide drug or gun running through Spirit Lake."

"Maybe the Mexican Mafia thought differently. Or maybe they don't care."

"Unless it was a revenge thing. Why carve that into someone's body? Maybe they were telling him and his type to get the hell out of town?"

"Blunt? He's a middle-aged white guy."

"Nix that, then. That's a crazy thought. Or is it? Maybe he was dealing drugs or guns all this time and had us all completely fooled."

"You knew him far more than me. I just got into town."

"Welcome aboard."

"Thanks." Amanda matched Jennifer's sarcasm.

After discussing a couple more items on the report, she hung up. It was almost like she knew less than when she'd first called. She swiveled around in her chair and grabbed both arms to stop herself from jerking backward in surprise.

Bill loomed over her, all six feet seven inches, using his height, no doubt, to intimidate as he scowled down at her and demanded, "What the hell did you do to Gabriel? Can you tell me that? Martinez quit. No explanation, no nothing."

"What?" Amanda's jaw nearly unhinged.

"Don't look so shocked."

She straightened but didn't roll her chair away from his angry bulk. She wasn't going to show him any weakness or reveal just how shocked she really was at the news. He'd just bully her that much more. "But I am. I never once got the impression he was unhappy with his job."

"He wasn't!" Bill growled at her. "Not once has he complained about the department. For five bloody years he's been working here with not one grievance from anyone. You hear? Five years, and you're here less than two weeks and he decides to chuck his career. You haven't even gotten a freaking paycheck yet, and look what you've done!"

"Come off it!" She jumped up from her chair. She wasn't going to be someone's scapegoat. "That's crazy. I have nothing to do with Gabriel's decision to leave. You're giving me far more power than I can possibly have."

"Then why the hell did he up and leave! Can you tell me that?" His hot coffee breath fanned her face.

"There could be a number of reasons. A gruesome murder could be a probable cause." She tugged on the tip of her ponytail. "Maybe you should talk to him."

"He won't tell me."

Amanda raised her brows.

"Don't give me that look. It's got to be you. Something's been going on between the two of you. Anyone with a pair of eyes can see it, and everyone in this office has a set. It's not a damn secret. Ever since you've started, the two of you have been making goo-goo eyes at each other. I'm surprised no one's caught the two of you in the bathroom or storage room." He waved a hand at her, the look of disgust evident in the curl of his lip and narrowed gaze. "Just look at your neck. You've got yourself a damn hickey. What the hell are we? Teenagers? Jeez, I thought you had a hell of a lot more class, Douglas."

The heat of mortification crept up her neck and into her face. She hated the silence that stretched the length of the room. No phones, no talking. Nothing. Because everyone in the place was listening to their conversation with avid interest. And who wouldn't? It was too tantalizing for anyone with an ounce of curiosity to ignore.

There had to be a reason for Freer to lay into her like this.

"I don't have a hickey." She stopped herself from

lifting a hand and touching her neck. Explaining about hitting the medicine cabinet wasn't going to do anything to change his mind. For some reason, he didn't like her. She'd heard she looked a lot like his ex-wife, but that didn't give him cause to act like an ass.

"Oh, next, you'll be telling me you burned yourself with a curling iron. Yeah, I've heard that excuse too many times from my daughter."

"I wasn't going to say that at—"

"Save it. I'd fire your ass if I thought it would get him back here." He pulled up his pants by his belt loops. "But I've got a better idea. I want you to get your ass over to his place and beg him to change his mind. I don't know what type of fight you got into last night after the two of you hooked up and I don't care. I just care about getting him back at his job. He's going to screw up his career. You don't just leave like that without notice. That's unheard of. And there's no way in hell I'm going to replace him with a new hire, especially when I've got some newbie like you already screwing things up."

Amanda stiffened. "That's uncalled for, and you know it. I'm damn good at what I do. I may not have the experience that most of you do, but the recommendations from my superiors are—"

"Blah, blah, blah. That's all well and good, but it doesn't get Martinez back. No one's been able to reach him by phone.

"If you value your job, I suggest you get your little ass over to his place and make nice. I expect you at work tonight at your scheduled time and Martinez in tow. Clear?"

"As crystal!" Amanda snapped her teeth shut with

a click. She opened and closed her hands. The temptation to say something really nasty or deck him with a fist was overwhelming. Instead of doing either, she pivoted, rounded her chair and desk, and marched across the room, avoiding the gazes of onlookers. Tears of impotent rage misted her eyes, and she blinked several times to clear her vision. She needed her job. She didn't have the luxury of doing what she wanted. Nicole also needed as much stability in her life as possible.

The door slammed behind her with a loud bang. Good. Too bad the glass panel didn't break and Bill had to clean up after her. The guy was a prick. Had been since she'd started. She'd thought chauvinists had died a good decade ago, but there seemed to be one wobbling around like a Weeble in Spirit Lake, Iowa.

Never, ever, had she been so humiliated. Freer could have at least had the decency to call her into his office to talk instead of broadcasting about her 'hickey' to everyone within hearing distance.

When she slipped into her car, she flipped down the window visor and snapped open the vanity mirror. Craning her neck to one side and then the other, she bit her lip. Damn it. Bob was right. An unmistakable, large welt marked the side of her neck. She touched the area with tentative fingers. She'd forgotten about the reddened skin and never thought to cover it with foundation on the off chance someone might consider it a hickey. Hell. After being reamed out like that, she wished it had been. Gabriel sucking on her neck would have been preferable to being injured by the corner of a medicine cabinet.

Well, there was nothing she could do about it now.

Sighing, she snapped the mirror shut and readjusted the window visor. She'd been up less than two hours, and she was exhausted. The past twenty-four hours had been mentally draining. She wanted peace, quiet, some form of calm, but she wasn't going to get it, not by going over to Gabriel's place. It took all of five minutes to drive to his house. She'd never been inside but had seen him pull out of his driveway a couple of times while she'd been en route to work.

Partially hidden from view from the street by a couple of large oak trees and shrubs, his house rested at the back of his property. The brick home had a high-pitched roof and was one of the older houses in town.

She pulled up into the driveway. His SUV was parked in front of the garage. God, she didn't want to be at his place. He couldn't have quit because of her.

It was impossible.

Or was it?

Yes, it was ludicrous to think he'd left a good-paying job because of her. She didn't have an extra body part, and she hadn't acted psychotic to the point where he'd wanted to escape from her bed. If she thought too hard about the whole situation, she'd start getting an inferiority complex and think sex with her was so bad it made normal, rational men flee town.

But the sex hadn't been bad. It had been great. At least she'd thought so…

A sudden flush of anger burned her cheeks. He must have known he was leaving the previous night when he'd shown up at her door. He'd decided to keep it to himself before he got into her pants. Pretty nervy on his part.

She was getting good and angry. To hell with any embarrassment or awkwardness.

After stepping out of her car, she eyed the two-story house with ambivalence as she walked by his black-and-chrome SUV on the way to the front door.

After a fortifying breath, she hit the doorbell. And waited. No sound from the other side.

She thumbed the doorbell again. When Gabriel still didn't appear, she rapped her knuckles on the storm door. Although she hated the idea of talking to Gabriel, she hated showing up at the department alone and facing Bill even more.

She glanced to either side of Gabriel's property. Houses in this neighborhood were on good-sized lots. His was more secluded than most, with trees and a fence line. Private. Like Gabriel. After working with him for two weeks, she still didn't know much about him. She hadn't a clue if he had brothers or sisters, where he'd lived before Spirit Lake. Or if he might have a wife tucked away somewhere.

Nope. She wasn't going there...

"I know you're in there!" she called out. "It's Amanda. I need to talk to you!"

Still no answer. She glared at the door. Obviously, Gabriel didn't want to talk to her. Fine!

Frowning, she backed away from the door. Talk about the strangest one-night stand... Jeez. Nothing made sense. She'd never thought of Gabriel as someone who avoided conflict. It wasn't like she was going to make a scene if he thought he'd made a mistake sleeping with her. She'd just appreciate the truth instead of avoidance.

As she retraced her steps, she paused by his SUV

and peeked into the driver's side window. No empty coffee cups, loose change, or food wrappers inside the black interior. The inside was far more immaculate and neater than her car. There was a large medallion hanging from the rearview mirror by a thick chain. It looked old, worn, and silver. Actually, she wouldn't be surprised if it was an antique.

For some reason she never thought of Gabriel as highly religious, but how else could she explain a cross?

CHAPTER 5

Amanda drove the squad car down Hill Avenue. Alone. All the retail shops had since closed for the night, and a line of cars was parked in front of the Sportsman's Bar. Even frigid temps couldn't keep people away if they wanted a cold one and company. No calls of disorderly conduct so far. That might quickly change when the bars hit near closing.

The beams from the streetlights slipping and in and out of the vehicle's interior were strangely relaxing as she guided her car down the town's main street and turned onto 71. So far nothing unusual had hit, but the way the day had gone, who knew…

She'd called Gabriel's place twice more that afternoon with no answer. Not bothering with leaving a message, she'd then given up trying to get a hold of Gabriel and shown up at the department for work, expecting the worst. She'd been given a reprieve. Bill had left for home. Something about a 'family' emergency. Goodness knew, she'd eventually have to face him. At least she finally had her own patrol car, and it looked like she was without a partner from here on out.

The dispatcher's voice came over the radio. "We have a 10-54 over at the Jeffersons' property."

At the mention of a dead body, Amanda's adrenaline kicked in. So much for nothing unusual. She'd quickly learned very few serious crimes happened in Spirit Lake, unlike the other night with Jack Blunt. Public records showed only two murders in the town or surrounding area in the past thirty years. That was one of the reasons why she'd taken the position. She'd expected, even hoped for, the job to be boring. Traffic tickets, disorderly conduct. That's what she wanted—the perfect place to raise a troubled child. But now trouble with a mammoth capital T was hitting the town. Something Amanda never could have guessed.

She hit the radio's communications button. "Thanks, Becky. I'll take a look."

"It's probably nothing. You might not have been here long, but you've already gotten a taste of how Helga acts when she starts drinking. Two years ago, she swore a couple of aliens landed on her front yard."

Amanda laughed. "Maybe she should keep it down to a pint of beer instead of a pint of vodka."

"You can tell her that when you see her."

"Yeah, right." She'd already met the woman the Saturday before. No one told the sixty-five-year-old how to run her life.

"Well, she saw the body over by that large meadow north of the Jeffersons' house."

"Got it. I'll let you know if we've got ourselves an alien or dead animal."

Fifteen minutes later, she pulled up on the side of the road in front of the Jeffersons' two-story ranch house, which rested in the middle of a good five acres. Helga's place was on the south side, while the state forest lay to the north of the property. The windows from the Jeffersons' home stared back like dark, emotionless eyes. No sign of life beckoned from within. Like a good number of residents in Spirit Lake and the surrounding lakes, the Jeffersons vacationed in the area for the summer with fishing and boating in mind. Come winter, though, many retreated back to places like Miami or Phoenix.

She stepped out of the cruiser and grabbed her flashlight from her belt. Icy air scraped across her face and exposed hands. A breeze moaned around her. Having lived with the noise of a large city much of her life, she hadn't yet gotten used to the sound of the wind through the pine needles. That night the wind reminded her of death, of that one last breath before a person passed to the other side.

Shivering, and not necessarily from the cold, she flexed her fingers against the frigid temperature. No joking around with Gabriel. If she told herself enough times she didn't miss his company, maybe she'd start believing it.

A light flickered from Helga's home through an outcropping of pines. It looked like she was home after all. Right now, the woman was probably peering through her kitchen or living room window with a whiskey in one hand. Alone, afraid, and getting slowly drunk with her cats.

Stars glittered from the sky above while a crescent moon cut a swath of silver across the snow-covered clearing. Immediately, she saw what Helga must have been talking about. A dark object lay just on the outskirts of the pines. Probably a fallen log. No doubt the snow had melted earlier in the week and exposed the dead tree trunk.

After she climbed over an old waist-high wood

fence lining the property, she trudged through the snow that crackled in protest beneath her weight. Her flashlight picked up some type of track as if something had been dragged over the snow. But she didn't see any footprints. She crisscrossed the beam. Flecks of red stained the snow.

Blood.

Amanda's grip on the flashlight tightened, and her heart rate leaped into a gallop. The wind continued to groan through the pines as if to warn her to retreat, to get back in that damn cruiser. Moments like this made her wonder why the hell she'd ever thought of becoming a cop.

To help people. To make a difference. To be a better person—a woman like her mother.

But right then, helping only herself sounded far safer and saner.

Instead of retreating, she pulled the collar of her jacket higher against her neck, and while avoiding the markings in the snow, she moved forward, across the clearing and toward the line of dense pines. She glanced over to her right and the Jeffersons' place. Maybe the house wasn't so lifeless after all. Perhaps someone was peering from one of those windows right at that moment.

As she drew closer, her nostrils flared. The wind carried the scent of death and cut into her lungs. Damn! The object protruding from the snow wasn't some old, forgotten log or dead animal.

Her flashlight illuminated a body on its back, arms and legs splayed. A man with his jacket and shirt ripped open.

And the blood...

Holy shit. There was blood spatter everywhere.

Five more steps and…

The odor of death hit her harder. The unexpected strength of it made her gasp. Nausea roiled and rose from her stomach. Clutching her throat, she struggled to keep the bile down.

Steam rose from the body. Jesus. He hadn't been dead long. The smell of urine lingered in the air. She came to a stop two feet away and forced herself to get down on her haunches and run the light over the body. Unlike Jack Blunt, this victim still had his head. She paused the beam below the neck and gasped. The chest cavity had been plundered, and it looked like the heart was missing. Two ribs had been broken off, while pieces of skin, tendon, and muscle littered the area around him.

It also looked like some animal had ravaged the body and run off without finishing its meal, but if that was the case, it didn't explain the lack of paw prints in the snow around the victim or leaving the scene. But the man had been dragged across the snow to this spot and ravaged.

The smell. Jesus…

Gagging, she pivoted away from the body and took two stumbling steps before she heaved her stomach's contents onto the ground. The smell of bile mingled with the scent of blood and the victim's entrails.

Death.

She'd never witnessed anything so grotesque. Not even in her nightmares had she come across such a sight.

Amanda struggled to her feet. That's when she realized she wasn't alone.

CHAPTER 6

Gabriel threw a suitcase into the back of his SUV. He could not stay another night in Spirit Lake. He needed to get out of town and as far away from Amanda as possible. Once he figured out where he was going, he would get a company to pack and move the rest of his stuff.

Damn it.

He scrubbed at his jaw and chin with a palm. He should have kept away from Amanda from the very beginning. What was wrong with him? What had happened to his self-control? Obviously flushed down the toilet. He had been a fool to think he had gotten used to being alone.

For a crazy moment, he had felt hope, a possibility of happiness. But then the decapitated head in the sink brought him savagely back to reality.

He slammed the hatchback shut and hurried back into the house. The sound of the dispatcher broke into the living room as he moved into the kitchen to pull out the perishables from the fridge. He had turned on the radio the moment Amanda had started her shift, wanting to make sure she was doing okay without him.

He grunted. Hell, Amanda was far better without him. No doubt Amanda thought the same after he had walked away from her, his job, and soon, Spirit Lake, without a goodbye or any explanation. Staying there wasn't an option. He would just bring death to the people he cared for.

The dispatcher's voice came over the radio. "We have a 10-54 over at the Jeffersons' property."

Amanda answered, "Thanks, Becky. I'll take a look."

"It's probably nothing. You might not have been here long, but you've already gotten a taste of how Helga acts when she starts drinking. Two years ago she swore a couple of aliens landed on her front yard."

A prickle of unease crawled across Gabriel's neck. Not another dead body. It was way too soon. He didn't like the idea of Amanda looking into it, or for that matter, anyone. They didn't know what in God's name they could be walking into. Blunt's murder was beyond the norm. His killing was not from a jealous lover, a person out for money or some vendetta. It had been savage, filled with rage. The killer had not been sane. Could not be sane.

He crossed the living room and stopped at the front window to glance at the neighboring houses. No one stirred behind their closed doors or over the snow-covered yards. Silence hung in the night air. It looked like a typical evening in Spirit Lake—quiet, tame, and quaint in appearance. It was all a façade. Everyone was panicking about Blunt's savage murder. Not that he could blame anyone. He was close to panicking himself.

Fear for Amanda's safety swelled to the point where he tasted it, smelled it.

How could he walk away when her safety could be in danger?

No way.

He grabbed his keys from a hook on the wall by the fridge and slammed out of the house.

If the body was another murder victim, it wouldn't be the last, and Spirit Lake was headed toward a bloodbath.

Laughter drifted in the wind from behind Amanda. She jerked around and stumbled in her hurry to see. Her heel caught on a patch of ice, propelling her backward into the snow. Her butt hit the ground hard, and she dropped her flashlight, its beam going wildly up in the air before it landed on the ground and shined a short path across the snow. Icy air cut into her lungs as she gasped and scrambled wildly to her feet, unsnapped the leather casing, and clutched at her gun's handle.

Gaze narrowing, she yanked the gun from its holder and aimed at…nothing.

"Son-of-a…" Her words drifted into the silence. She searched the clearing, the road, and then her cruiser, a good hundred yards away. The Jeffersons' house remained dark, empty, and lifeless to her left. Helga must have turned off her light. Moonlight illuminated nothing but an empty snow-covered meadow. Absolutely no human being in sight.

A sudden spark of light flashed between the pines. Possibly metal or something else.

Shit. Not wanting to take a chance, she lunged backward, almost tripped over the dead body in her hurry to take cover. Snow kicked into the air as she pivoted and rushed toward the tree line. Breathing heavily, she whirled around a large trunk, snapping off small branches in her hurry to hide, and smashed her back against the bark. Twigs caught in her hair and scraped at her face. She impatiently brushed them aside as clouds of icy air billowed from her mouth.

She grappled to rein in the fear crawling across her skin and shivered. It dug through her flesh and sent her heart ricocheting inside her chest. She shifted. The snow cracking and snapping under the soles of her boots sounded like a boom in the night's stillness.

Calm down. Panic didn't solve anything. She hit her com at her shoulder to call dispatch. "I'm in the field north of the Jefferson property. I've got a dead body and the killer possibly in the vicinity."

She only half listened to Becky's response about a backup. Mindful of the snow beneath her feet, Amanda edged to one side, her hip scraping along the trunk as she peered around its side and eyed the pines where she thought she'd seen the flash. Anyone with a gun or weapon aimed her way could be lurking in the deep shadows, and she wouldn't be able to tell.

The moan of the wind blowing sounded far too creepy through the pine needles and grated on her already frazzled nerves. She waited for another sound or sign she wasn't alone. The silence lengthened. The laughter had been deep, throaty, and indistinguishable as to whether it had come from a man or woman.

Unless she hadn't heard laughter.... Maybe it had been the wind? Her wild imagination? Crap, she'd come across a bloody and mutilated body. Yeah, she was a cop, and saw plenty of ugly things, but nothing like at the

Jeffersons' property or when she'd come across Blunt's body. Who wouldn't overreact?

A shout exploded into the night air.

Tension snapped through Amanda.

A man in a navy jacket and jeans came around the corner of the Jeffersons' house and ran across the clearing. His brown hair gleamed beneath the moonlight.

Gabriel.

Thank God, she had some backup. But what the hell was he doing running out in the open like that? Was he nuts?

"Over here!" She waved a hand but didn't venture into the clearing.

"Are you okay?" Gabriel asked when he reached her side. Plumes of fog wafted from his mouth and into the frigid night air. Even in the shadows, obvious concern etched lines across his face as he stared down at her. "I heard the call on the police scanner at my house…"

"I'm fine, but we've got a dead body, and it's not pretty. The sick freak ripped open the victim's chest. What type of person does that?" She asked him in disgust and horror but didn't expect or wait for an answer. She dipped her chin toward the tree line. "There was some movement over in the trees. It could have been caused by the killer, who, might I add, could have taken you down with a clear shot to the head the way you raced out in the open like that. If I'd had an itchy trigger finger, I could have shot you too, if I hadn't recognized you quickly enough."

He shook his head. "I wasn't worried. I parked down the road a good ways, did a quick search, and didn't see anyone. Were you able to get some type of visual on them?"

"No. Nothing. Just a flash of light." When she said it aloud, she realized how much she might have over-reacted. A flash. Laughter. Both of which could have easily been her imagination. But then there was a dead body involved, so no, she needed to stop second-guessing herself.

Gabriel peered around the area. "I am sure they are long gone by now."

Then, as if in perfect timing, a light flashed in the same area. Tension cut a swift path across Amanda's shoulders and back again. "Did you see that?"

"Yes…"

"You don't sound or act worried."

"You're probably seeing Esposito. He does a lot of welding and sells much of his artwork out of state. He's probably replenishing his stock after the holiday season."

"Yes, but…" She wanted to argue as to why Esposito was doing welding outside at night and in winter, but then she thought of Helga and realized Esposito might also have his own peculiar way of coping with life. She decided to let it go and hit her com. "That's a 10-22 instead, Becky. I just need a crime scene unit out here."

Frowning, she eyed Gabriel's shadowed frame. He was far too tall and far too close. His hair looked mussed as if he'd run his fingers through the strands again and again, and then some more for good measure, while the jacket looked like he'd tossed it on as an after-thought. "Why are you here? I can take care of myself. Believe it or not, I've been involved in some high-risk and dangerous situations in Chicago. I'm not a rookie."

"I was concerned." He edged closer to her.

She didn't have room to back up, with the tree on one side and branches on the other, unless she wanted to climb the trunk or get even more scratched up with twigs. Nope, she wasn't going to give Gabriel the satisfaction of showing how much she found his nearness agitating.

"Concerned? Really? You've got a novel way of showing it. I didn't think you gave a crap." She snapped her mouth shut before she started a verbal tirade, then nodded in the direction of the clearing. "The body's over there. You can't miss it. I left my flashlight with it." She didn't tell him she'd dropped it in a full-blown panic. The less he knew, the better.

He left the safety of the trees and trudged through the snow, purpose in his every movement. Amanda cursed softly, eyeing the tree line. Not seeing any sign of someone lurking between the branches and trunks, she cursed some more and hurried after him. If he got them killed, she swore she'd kill him again.

Stopping a little over two yards away from the body, Gabriel sank down on his haunches.

Amanda slipped her gun back in its holster and retrieved her flashlight. Well, if she hadn't been a target before, she was now. But then, if anyone out there wanted them dead, they would have done something by now. Amanda forced herself not to turn her head away as she moved the flashlight's beam quickly over the victim's chest and rested it across his face.

Gabriel rubbed the bridge of his nose and shook his head, his voice thickening with emotion. "His name is Clark Swanson."

"I'm sorry. Did you know him as well as Jack Blunt?"

"Kind of. In a different way, though. He's a neighbor." He rose quickly to his feet. "He didn't deserve this."

"No one deserves *this*." She waved her free hand at the body, then looked along the tree line again just on the off chance someone decided to show themself. The killer was beyond sick. The person had to be filled with mind-numbing rage. "This new murder is going to get the town into a full-blown panic if it hasn't already. It's only a matter of time before this gets out to the general public beyond Spirit Lake. I can see it hitting the national networks with a vengeance. It doesn't take a genius to figure that one out."

"Then we will probably have a media circus in town." He continued to stare at Swanson.

The tension emanating from him came at her in thick waves. Something in Gabriel's voice made her frown with puzzlement. It took her several minutes to recognize the emotion.

Fear.

Since she'd been with him—granted, it hadn't been for very long—she'd always seen him unflappable— even when they'd come across Jack Blunt's mutilated body. "What is it?"

"Nothing."

"This is far from nothing. We have a wacko walking around this town, and I have an idea it's not going to be simple to catch this killer. Everything about both killings is out of a horror movie. This last one looks like they took the victim's heart."

He turned to stare down at her, and light from the outer sphere of the flashlight revealed the intensity of his gaze. There was something in his eyes that was more than fear.

Amanda grunted and moved back a step. "I'm not surprised." Bitterness crept into her voice. "You're not going to tell me anything. That seems to be your M.O."

"What are you getting at?"

She was pissed. Pissed at Gabriel and doubly pissed at herself for being so emotionally involved with him. "I thought you left town."

"Not yet."

"I appreciate the notice. So nice of you. You could have at least texted about leaving town and your job. Freer was furious. He blamed me for ruining your career." She jammed her free hand on her hip and glared up at him. "Why? I don't get it. Quitting without notice? That's unheard of."

"I did call him."

"Wow, how nice. Well, Freer wants me to convince you to come back to work." Her anger increased with each of her words. "For some reason, he thinks I'm the reason you quit. And I'd like to know how he got such a stupid idea." She opened her mouth to yell at him but realized it wasn't the time and then snapped it shut.

She wanted to get out of the area and away from the intolerable situation. One minute was too much right now. Hell. She just wanted to write up traffic tickets, not deal with crazy, sick people or savage murderers. Or for that matter, deal with Gabriel. She'd never been very good at the relationship game. Two failed attempts had made her leery of diving into another relationship, especially with a cop. And she had Nicole to think of. The girl didn't need her world disrupted by Amanda's lack of relationship know-how.

Forcing down her own fear, impatience, and desire to flee the scene, she edged back to the body and flashed her beam across the victim. The steam from the insides of his chest had since dissipated. He must have died not long before Amanda had arrived on the scene. What would have happened if she'd been quicker? Would she have seen the actual attack? And what the hell had the killer used to butcher a seemingly strong, capable man? A hatchet? Axe? At the thought of different weapon scenarios and the actual attack, Amanda's stomach started to roil with nausea.

"Helga called it in," she murmured, needing to focus on something other than the ruined body in front of her. "I wonder if she saw more and didn't say anything."

"It's possible. The detective assigned the case will find out. That'll probably be Reznick, unless he's pulled and bigger fish are assigned. Resnick is pretty good at what he does."

"Really?" Amanda arched a brow. "And just how much experience does he have? Other than Blunt and this latest, I didn't think there'd been any murders in Spirit Lake for years."

"Funny." His teeth flashed, but he didn't look amused. "He's originally from Seattle. There was a serial killer case he was assigned to several years back. I think it did a number on him and it's probably why he moved here."

Amanda grimaced. She could relate. She moved the beam from Swanson's face to the wreckage of his chest and over other areas of his body. Much of his shirt had been ripped from his body. She inwardly cringed at the brutal carnage, and her stomach did a dangerous flip. She paused, allowing the light to illuminate several odd markings on his stomach she'd missed earlier. "Hey. Look at this. How odd." She sank down on her heels and let the technical aspect of her mind take over. "There's something on his stomach."

As she edged the flashlight's beam a little lower and along the victim's pants line, she realized someone—most likely the killer—had etched a pattern onto his skin with some type of sharp object.

Gabriel lowered himself beside her and rested a hand on his knee. "It looks like some type of symbol."

Frowning, Amanda inched a little closer, but because of forensics, she didn't want to disrupt any more of the scene than she already had. The arcs and lines formed a primitive design. It was some form of a bloody tattoo. "I've seen something like this just recently."

"You have?" His expression was curious but guarded.

"Yeah, Blunt had something similar on his body. We both missed it at the scene—probably because of all the blood. Jennifer at the Medical Examiner's Office sent me the report. You would have known that too if you hadn't decided to—"

He jerked to his feet.

"What?"

"Nothing."

Her gaze narrowed as she looked up at his face. Tension again radiated from him in waves. Something was definitely wrong.

"This isn't the first time I've seen similar designs,"

Amanda murmured, gauging his reaction as she, too, rose to her feet.

"And when was that?" His face turned neutral, his control fully back in place.

"A couple years back in Chicago."

"Chicago? That's a long way from Spirit Lake."

"Not really, when it comes to logistics. But what was carved on Swanson's body and Blunt's is pretty close to the tattoos of murder victims I've come across in police reports in Chicago. I didn't actually see the victims myself, but they were all murdered within a four-year time frame while I was at the department. After some research, it was discovered the tattoos of the vics all had some type of correlation to Aztec symbols."

"Aztec symbols?"

She met his gaze but still couldn't read anything beyond his bland expression. She suspected very little cracked his composure. Probably from too many years as a cop who saw more than anyone had a right to.

"They're used a lot with the Mexican Mafia. I saw a lot of it on the streets in Chicago. Many of the tattoos consist of a circular calendar with a number of Aztec gods on the outer rim; the sun god with a protruding tongue is in the center. The tattoos are usually on their chests and arms. Most are elaborate. But they can be pretty simple if done in prison." She shook her head. "But none of it makes sense. What would the Mexican Mafia be doing in Spirit Lake?"

One crazed killer was bad enough, but murders from a criminal organization like the Mexican Mafia sent dread crawling across her skin. Shivering against the cold and her own fear, Amanda stepped back from the body. Her heel caught on a slick patch of snow, and she stumbled.

"Steady," Gabriel murmured, moving quickly to her side to catch her elbow.

The warmth of his breath fanned her brow. Cinnamon. He always chewed cinnamon gum. She loved the scent on his breath.

Upset with herself, she pulled her arm from his grasp and backed away. She shouldn't love anything about him. Having him touch her brought all the anger rushing back. How dare he leave town without at least letting her know. Better that sentiment than the fear. She strode back to her department cruiser. When he followed her to her vehicle, she muttered, "You can leave. I've got the area secure. I don't need you around."

"I would feel more comfortable if I stayed until someone from the Medical Examiner's Office arrives."

"Well, it doesn't make me comfortable," Amanda argued. "Far from it. I'd prefer to be alone. And anyway, you quit, remember?"

A tense silence followed. Then Gabriel said in a low voice, "I am sorry."

"Sorry? That's it? Jeez!" For a wild moment, she wanted to use the flashlight on his noggin. "I thought you'd already left town." She forced the words through gritted teeth. She deserved some explanation. "Can you at least tell me why?"

"Why?"

"Yes, you-you—"

"Because it was best for everyone, including you."

"That's a stupid answer, and no answer at all. Freer seems to think you were leaving because of me."

He looked down at her with a strange metallic glow in his brown eyes. "He's right."

Her mouth gaped, but she couldn't find words.

"You have me doing things I know I shouldn't. I can't stay away from you. And because of that, I decided I needed to put as much distance between us as possible."

Deliberately, she looked at a point over his shoulder. She sure as heck didn't want to see in his face the longing she heard in his voice. It would just make her that much more susceptible to him. "But to leave town? Freer threatened to fire me if you don't change your mind."

"Damn it. He can't do that!"

"Well, he seems to think so, and I don't want to test him out to see what he'll do. Is there any way you'll change your mind? I need this job. I left Chicago for a more stable environment for Nicole. It's a new start for both of us. Granted, with these killings, things are far from stable, but at the same time, if I move her again so soon and she has to deal with another change, I really don't know if she can come out of it fully intact— mentally and emotionally."

Headlights flashed, indicating the arrival of the crime unit.

"After tonight, I can't leave even if I wanted to." His voice was hollow and defeated.

Before she had a chance to demand an explanation, Jennifer stepped out of her car and strode toward them, while an unmarked car, no doubt the detective on duty, rolled up behind the medical examiner's vehicle.

CHAPTER 7

Gabriel pulled up in front of Amanda's house as the late afternoon sun dipped in the west. Tapping a thumb against the steering wheel, he sat with the engine running. The past two days had been quiet. Freer had greeted him the next day with a firm nod and little else. No acknowledgment of Gabriel having walked out without notice, which was fine by him.

No new murders since the last discovery. Which was also fine. But word of some of the gruesome details about the latest attack had leaked out to the public. Which was not so fine.

People were getting skittish and leery, even about the locals they had known for years.

During his patrol, along with the obvious questions on what was getting done, he witnessed subtle unease and anxious whispers from Spirit Lake's residents.

Patches of dead grass and mud leaked through the melting snow of Amanda's yard. That was soon to change. Another cold snap was expected to hit in a couple of days, and with it, a pile of snow. Amanda and Nicole stood outside in front of the porch steps and were focused on a light-blue mountain bike. It gave him a moment to take in the scene.

Nicole's voice carried over the yard, but his closed window muffled the words.

Amanda shook her head. A moment later, Amanda smiled and slid a finger across the girl's temple as if to move a blonde strand from her face.

Nicole broke into an answering smile, a look of adoration flashing across her face as Amanda wrapped an arm around the girl's shoulders and drew her against her side for a quick, hard embrace. Then Nicole's laughter floated in the air toward him, youthful, and filled with undeniable joy. The glossy sheen of her hair flashed platinum beneath the sun's rays, so unlike Amanda's darker locks. They might not be biological mother and daughter, but there was no mistaking the bond between them.

Gabriel's hand tightened on the steering wheel. Suddenly he was thrust back to another time and another girl. As a child, his sister had been filled with such enthusiasm for life. She would cajole and pester him and his brother in all manner of ways. She had been precocious and the darling of the family. But that was another life. A life before all the horror.

Amanda glanced his way, and the moment she recognized his vehicle, the pleasure leached from her face; her brow dipped and her lips thinned.

He hated the idea he did that to her. God, he missed her. But how could he keep her safe and maintain his distance? It was a difficult, if not impossible, task. Amanda was not going to let him slip back into her life. And he could not try mending their relationship. Events were now in motion. He could not stop them. He had been stupid to think his life had possibilities, that hope *was not* a four-letter word.

She stepped away from Nicole and walked toward his SUV.

He loved how Amanda moved, a low rolling gait filled with feminine confidence. She had dragged her hair into her standard ponytail. It suited her, but that didn't mean he did not want to pull the tie off and let her hair tumble around her shoulders, so he could dive his fingers into the silken strands and lose himself in their scent. As she drew nearer, he dragged in a breath.

The crease between her winged brows didn't let up. She would have looked happier if she had downed a gallon of prune juice.

After turning off the engine, he slipped outside and shut the door behind him. He stopped himself from wiping his palms across his jean-clad thighs. Holy Mother, it had been a long time since a woman had the power to get him rattled. He joined Amanda at the end of the walkway where it reached the street and glanced over her shoulder at Nicole, who looked preoccupied with her bike as she started pushing down on the seat as if testing its suspension.

"Why are you here?" Amanda stopped in front of him and searched his face with a guarded expression. She stuffed her hands inside the pockets of her down jacket, which she'd left unzipped to reveal a red sweater with a V-neck that dipped low enough to expose the shadow between her breasts.

His lips firmed. Sex was on his brain and Amanda had not said more than one sentence. Whenever she stepped within a five-foot radius of him, he turned useless, and at the moment he was feeling awkward. Yes, he had a good excuse for coming by, but it was not the real reason why he had shown up. "I think I left my badge at your place."

She frowned. "I haven't seen it—"

"I think in my hurry, it came off my clip." Mindful of Nicole not far off, he lowered his voice. "It might be under your bed. If you remember, we were—"

"Yes—yes. Let me check." A flush crept from her chest, up her neck, and into her cheeks as she avoided his gaze. "Stay here."

He hadn't meant to embarrass her. All he wanted… Was what? Have her see him in a different light? Make her realize he was not a jerk? Not likely. He had been a jerk. Right then, the only thing he could do was keep her safe.

She turned her back on him and trotted up the stairs. The shapeless jacket covered her butt, but her jeans hugged an incredible pair of legs. A pair that had wrapped around him—fully naked and amazing to touch. The door banged shut behind her. Sighing, he turned away and walked over to Nicole. He had seen her from a distance but never officially met her. Again, her blonde hair reminded her of his sister…

He frowned. He didn't like thinking that.

By the bicycle, Nicole sank down on her haunches.

He lowered himself to her level and grimaced at the deflated tire. "Looks like you have a bit of a problem."

She turned. Piercing blue eyes, rimmed with silver, regarded him. For a moment he was disconcerted. He wasn't sure why. Maybe how wise her eyes looked? As if they'd witnessed too much horror, too much despair?

Her stepfather. That had to be the reason she appeared old beyond her years. Who wouldn't, after having to deal with a monster like him? Freer had mentioned a bit about Nicole's past, but Gabriel had walked away before learning any more of the details. He didn't think it was right for him to listen to something so private unless Amanda wanted him to know.

Nicole stared at him for the longest time, then finally said, "Yeah. I usually ride back and forth from school."

He rose, lifted the bike, and hooked a finger around one of the spokes, then let go. The wheel rotated a full circle with a whisper. "I can get you a tube," he found himself saying, "and you'll be as good as new for tomorrow."

"Are you sure? Mom isn't good at this stuff. She messed up the garbage disposal last week."

He nodded before he changed his mind. His throat tightened. The girl reminded him too much of his sister as a child. "Sure. Tell your mom I'll be right back."

When he returned with the tube, Nicole had disappeared, but she'd left an air compressor on the ground by the bike. For a brief moment, he stared at their home. They were probably inside at the moment chatting about the day's events. Smiling. Laughing. Living. Lips firming, he focused on the bike. A life like that was not, and never would be, one he would live.

With quick, angry movements, he repaired the bike within five minutes. After tossing the old tube in the garbage on the side of the house, he dusted off his hands and walked back across the driveway just as a pizza delivery car pulled up in front.

A kid with a partially shaved head and outdated skinny jeans trotted up the sidewalk.

"Here, I'll take that."

He traded cash for the pizza and climbed the stairs

with purpose. He still needed to check if Amanda had his badge. Nicole answered the door and glanced past him to her bike. A huge grin split across her face. "You did it! Now I can ride to school tomorrow."

The girl opened the screen door. "You can put the pizzas on the kitchen table."

He stepped into the kitchen as Amanda appeared around the doorway from the hall.

"That's not a good idea." Amanda took the two boxes from him and set them on a round kitchen table. "I told you I didn't want you riding your bike to school anymore."

"But—"

"It's not going to happen." She met his gaze from behind Nicole's shoulder. "I'll drive you, and if I can't do it, I'll get one of the other parents to do it."

Despite her neutral expression, Amanda had to be frightened. Everyone in town with any sense of self-preservation was.

Nicole opened her mouth, shut it, and then shook her head. Her rueful smile turned into a cheeky grin as she glanced over her shoulder at Amanda.

"Sure, but only if Mr. Gabriel stays for dinner."

Was he missing something? The last thing he needed was a matchmaking eleven-year-old.

"I don't think—"

"But he just fixed my bike…" A look of reproach and disbelief flashed in Nicole's eyes as she turned to face Amanda. "We should feed him. You always said—"

"Yes—yes, you're right, but I'm sure he already has dinner plans." Amanda's brow creased, while a look of uncertainty flashed in her eyes. She didn't outright say no.

Of course, that didn't mean he was off her enemy list, only that she had a hard time saying no to Nicole. Maybe given time…

Damn it. He was asking a lot.

"I don't have anything planned, but I don't want to intrude." He didn't like the idea of going home. He had been alone a very long time, but this was the first time in years he felt bone-weary lonely. At the same time, he did like the idea of being under the same roof and being able to keep an eye on both of them, even if it was only for a while.

"Why not?" Amanda relented and walked over to the cabinets beside the stove. She pulled out three plates from inside and placed them on the kitchen island, then paused and regarded him with a cool smile. "What do I owe you? I need to at least pay you for the pizza."

"Don't worry about it. I owe you." Hard to believe they had been under the same roof and unable to keep their hands off each other days before. After he retraced his steps and shrugged out of his navy jacket to hook over the coat rack, he moved deeper into the kitchen to rest both hands on the edge of the kitchen island that separated them. From across the counter, he glanced at her sweater's low neckline—he could not help it, given his vivid memories of cupping and caressing those beautiful breasts—before he looked up and locked his gaze onto hers. He wanted his hands on far more. He wanted them on every curve and indentation of her body. That had not changed. Far from it. The need had gotten worse.

"You're staying! Great. Mom's always talking about you, but now I get a chance to hear some stories."

"I hope it's all good." He arched his brows.

Amanda didn't take his bait, just stared back with that frosty expression she had used on him on more than one occasion while working together.

Gabriel inwardly sighed. Only feet separated them, but it might as well have been a foot of impenetrable ice.

"Oh, yeah." Nicole surprised him with her answer, as she rummaged in a drawer and pulled out three forks before grabbing napkins and placing everything on the table. "She always has great things to say about you."

"Really?"

"Yes, really." Amanda pulled a pitcher of water from the fridge, while Nicole set down glasses and the plates from the kitchen island by the silverware and napkins. "Your co-workers have always had the utmost respect for you, and I could see why, with—"

"You never gave that impress—"

"It doesn't matter. Not after the stunt you just pulled a couple of days ago where—"

"Yes, well, let's not travel down that route right now." He glanced at Nicole, who looked far too interested in their conversation.

"Not now, but after dinner, we need to. At least I do. And don't tell me you're working tonight and don't have time. I'm on nights, but we both have five minutes." Amanda set the pitcher on the table with a loud bang.

From the hard line of her jaw, *chat* wasn't what she was getting at, more like interrogation. She wanted answers to why he had acted like a complete shit and decided to walk away from her and his job. So now he knew why she agreed to have him stay. It was not because of some softening toward him or relenting to please Nicole.

Amanda did deserve an explanation, and he would give her one. She didn't need to know it was a lie, and he would have to quickly decide what that lie would be.

He sat down at the table. He took the pitcher of water a smiling Nicole offered—she was a sweet kid—and filled his glass. Her worldly eyes gleamed with kindness and warmth and even a strange innocence—a complete contradiction. He stilled as he held his glass of chilled water while Nicole talked about her day with Amanda. Everything about the scene screamed of family intimacy, of love, of caring. He cleared his throat, then looked down at his untouched pizza. The cheese had hardened into a shell.

"Aren't you going to eat?" Nicole asked.

"Ah, sure…"

"I'm not hungry anymore myself." Nicole picked the layer of cheese from the top of her second piece of pizza and set it to the side. "When can I start riding my bike again? I haven't gotten a chance all week."

"I don't know…" Amanda blew out a breath.

He met Amanda's gaze across the table. They both knew the reason why Nicole wasn't allowed to ride her bike to and from school.

"They're going to catch him," Nicole suddenly announced.

"Who?" they both asked.

"The killer."

Amanda, as if in slow motion, put down the glass

she was drinking from. "Of course we are. I didn't know word had gotten out to your school."

"The teachers are talking about it. They think we're stupid and can't hear all their loud whispering."

"They mean well," Gabriel assured, "and think they're protecting you."

"Was the person stabbed?" Nicole started tearing the cheese into strips. "Did the killer use a knife?"

Holy Mother. How quickly a conversation could turn from mundane to morbid within one sentence.

"So…" Gabriel needed to divert the topic and fast. Amanda looked helpless. Nicole looked near tears. And he didn't like all this emotion. "I'm sure you will get a chance to ride your bike again. Do you ride it only to and from school? I had a friend who cycled. He entered a good number of national competitions. He even won a couple of races."

They both turned and looked at him as if his brain had started leaking from his ears.

Then Nicole stared at a point in front of her. Her breathing quickened, reflected by the rapid rise and fall of her chest. She'd forgotten the pizza and had latched onto the side of the table with claw-like fingers. "Tell me! Did the killer use a knife?"

The unmistakable agitation radiating from Nicole hit him in thick waves. Afraid the girl was about to have a panic attack, he decided to lie. "It was not a knife."

After a moment of awkward silence, Nicole's fingers eased their death grip on the wood edge, but she latched onto Amanda's hand resting near her plate instead.

Amanda fisted her hand over the girl's as Nicole's

agitated breathing eased. "Don't worry, you're safe with me. I won't let anyone hurt you. Ever."

The poor kid. Being in a full-blown panic was understandable with someone being murdered and having the killer running loose, but there was something more. What was it with the knives? Gabriel frowned. What had happened to her? Her fear seemed magnified compared to a normal child's. Had the stepfather threatened her with a knife, or done something even worse? Amanda was hypersensitive to the girl's needs for a reason. At work, the woman was calm, methodical, and not one to overreact, so whatever had happened in Nicole's past had to be some horrific scenario.

Nicole clutched her mother's hand, squeezed it, and then nodded. She took one deep, long shuddering breath and nodded again but with more conviction. Then her chin firmed. "I know. That's why I love you."

A tender smile tipped Amanda's mouth. "As for your bike, you'll get a chance to hang out and ride it soon enough. I know you had problems with it on Monday, but next time, don't let anyone drive you home you don't know."

Wrinkling her nose, the girl finally loosened her grasp on Amanda's hand and started folding her napkin into accordion-style creases. "I know. But she was really nice. Not scary at all, and I didn't know what to do with a flat tire. No one was around, and then she appeared right when I needed her. Like a real angel. And she looked like an angel. She was super pretty. Just what I would think Sleeping Beauty would look like. She was so nice, too, not letting me help when she put my bike in the trunk of her car."

"She's still a stranger."

"Fine." Nicole nodded. "I promise. But she didn't hurt me. She didn't look like she was mean or anything."

"Some of the nicest-looking people can be really mean," Amanda insisted with a frown. "It's a shame you didn't get her name or some more info on her so I could thank her."

"I didn't think about it. She was asking me lots of questions, and I got distracted." She slid a palm across her folded napkin as if to sharpen the crease. "She had this amazing hair. All silver-like, but prettier than mine. And long. Right down to her waist. I've never seen hair like that on anyone else."

Gabriel's breath caught in the back of his throat and a sudden film of sweat formed on his brow. "That is unusual, are you sure it wasn't gray?" He fought to keep his voice casual.

"Yeah. It was really shiny." Nicole's eyes crinkled at the corners. "She asked me some questions and said she'd probably see me again. But she said it depended on certain people."

"Really?" Amanda's brow creased in puzzlement. "That's a bit odd."

Fuck! If he had eaten any of his pizza, he would have vomited right there on the table. "What was she asking you questions about?" His voice was steady, but inside he was falling apart. He ignored the sudden interest in Amanda's gaze. He didn't care. He needed to know. No, he *had* to know.

"Oh, I don't know. What movies I liked."

Amanda asked with a smile, "Boyfriends?"

"No, of course not!" A delicate flush rose into Nicole's cheeks.

"I was teasing. There'll be time enough for that down the road. You've got years yet. Plus, Cade seems to think he's your boyfriend."

"Amand—Mom!" She scowled and crumpled her napkin in both hands.

"Sorry." Amanda chuckled, but her lips twisted into a self-deprecating smile. "Still learning this parenting thing."

Nicole wrinkled her nose.

"They don't give manuals out," Gabriel said.

Amanda frowned, and her head cocked to the side. "What's wrong? You look…"

"He looks sick," Nicole chimed in.

Gabriel shook his head. "It must be the pizza and—"

"But you didn't eat anything…"

Damn it. The kid was too observant. Abruptly, he jerked to stand, his chair screeching backward.

They both stilled and looked back at him in surprise.

"Your bathroom?" He asked for Nicole's benefit.

"Down the hall to the left It's two doors—"

"Thanks." He flung himself from the kitchen. In the bathroom, the click of the closing door reverberated inside the small room and punctuated his racing mind. Why the hell was Nicole being harassed? Why the threat of seeing her again? She was a child. Innocent and completely blameless.

To hide his ragged breathing, he turned on the faucet. He cupped his hands under the water and splashed his face. The frigid temp did nothing to pull him from his panic.

He gripped the lip of the sink and stared at himself in the mirror. Water dripped from his chin and jaw onto the sink and counter. Nausea, fear, and rage roiled and twisted through his gut. He could not shake the panic. He thought he had some time. Damn it. What should he do? What could he do? How could he protect Amanda and now Nicole?

An answer didn't come.

He stared at his reflection. A man with dark brown hair, thick brows over brown eyes, a somewhat stubborn jaw, and... He sucked in a breath. The image in front of him wasn't a man...

A monster stared back at him.

He stood frozen, unable to think one coherent thought. He wanted to give up. Maybe he should have given up years ago. But now he absolutely could not. Not with Amanda and Nicole in the mix. Not unless he really wanted to become a psychopath with no compassion or...soul.

A knock sounded on the door. "Are you all right?" Amanda....

He cleared his throat. "Yes, yes... Just give me a minute."

He didn't move from his place at the sink until the sound of her footsteps disappeared. Then he turned off the faucet. With a hand that still had a distinct tremor in it, he grabbed the towel hanging over the brass circle against the wall by the mirror. He wiped at his face and gently folded the towel back against the holder, all the while consciously taking air in and out in slow, somewhat steady breaths.

But the panic still clawed at his insides.

He should have killed Mayor when he had the chance.

CHAPTER 8

I s something wrong with him?" Nicole asked from the sofa. The muted sounds of the television drifted over the room, masking any noise that might be happening down the hall and in the bathroom.

"I don't know." Amanda frowned as she stood in the doorway leading from the kitchen to the living room. He'd been in the bathroom a long while. Long enough that she'd overcome her embarrassment to check on him.

To say he was acting weird was an understatement. It was almost like a trigger switched inside his head and he'd shut himself off.

She was still upset that she hadn't even rated a text to let her know that he'd planned to skip town. At the moment, the only reason he was under her roof was because of Nicole's invitation.

And she still had to give him his stupid badge back. Damn the man. It was under the bed like he'd suspected. Just her luck, he'd leave it behind again, and she'd have to track him down, or worse, word would get out at the police department that he was leaving things at her house on top of giving her hickeys. And she wouldn't be surprised if he'd planted the badge there just so he could come back. She grimaced. She was reaching there...

At the sound of a step, she turned and folded her

arms across her middle. "What's wrong? You look really pale."

"I'm fine." Gabriel nodded sharply as he stepped from the hallway and into the kitchen, pausing by the kitchen island to grip the counter's edge.

He did look fine. Damn him. No doubt, fine in a completely different context from his way of thinking. There really should be a law against being so ruggedly handsome. Any woman with a dose of red blood cells would consider him drool worthy. Even in her angry state, she still found him nerve-rackingly attractive. The faded jeans slung low over his hips accented his narrow hips, and the black thermal-style shirt clung to his broad shoulders, corded arms, and flat belly.

She remembered just how hard and muscular his back was against her hands as she'd gripped him in the throes of her release. *He* was all hard and… Enough. That was going into dangerous territory, and she didn't dare. Nothing was going to happen between them again, so she had to forget just how hard and delicious every part of his body was. He'd caught her at a vulnerable moment. She just hoped he wasn't around when she got around to having another weak moment. "I'm glad to hear you're fine, because I want answers, like why you left like that and—"

"Later, I promise—when you don't have company," he muttered, nodding to a spot behind her back, no doubt referring to Nicole in the living room. "How about we meet at Wombats during your break tonight? We can talk then."

"Really?" Her arms tightened across her middle. "Sounds to me like you're giving me the runaround."

"No. I'm not going to do that." He rubbed the back of his neck. What looked like exhaustion added shadows below his eyes. "What type of weapons do you have in the house other than the gun you're issued from the department?"

"What?" She stared back at him in shock. "What type of question is that?"

"I just want to know."

"Something is seriously messed up." She narrowed her eyes. "What is going on? Obviously, asking a crazy question like that, you know something far more than I do."

The doorbell rang. Amanda pivoted and moved toward the hall and front door. "Don't you dare leave through the side door while my back is turned, or I swear—"

"Don't open the door!"

She swiveled back around and gaped at him. "You need to calm down, Gabriel. It's only Katie, the babysitter. She's due anytime."

"Still…" He strode past her, walked over to the front window in the living room, and peered outside.

After Amanda snapped on the porch light, she followed him over to the window. She glanced quickly over to Nicole and double-checked if she'd overheard Gabriel's odd behavior, but the girl had a glazed look and silly grin on her face as she stared at the television, enraptured by the latest teenage heartthrob, who must have said something witty because the canned laugh track immediately followed.

As Amanda suspected, Katie stood waiting by the front door, a backpack over one shoulder while listening to something through her neon-green earbuds.

"See," she said over the sound of the television. "A completely harmless college student." She ignored Gabriel's grunt and hurried over to open the door. She bumped into him as she let the babysitter into the house. Although she frowned over her shoulder, the man didn't move. The heat of his body burned into her back, while his breath, scented cinnamon from the gum he usually chewed, feathered against her hair from behind. Any closer, and he'd be pasted to her body. Even though she stepped to the side and away from him, he moved as if he were her shadow. She wanted to smack him. He was acting like her bodyguard, and she didn't need one. She'd been taking care of herself all her adult life.

Katie pulled one of her earbuds from her ear and smiled. Then the girl glanced over Amanda's shoulder at Gabriel.

Ugh. She was going to have to introduce everyone. "Katie, this is Gabriel. He's a co-worker"—*and my one-night stand mistake*— "and Gabriel, Katie comes in and helps me out because of my nocturnal hours. She's been a godsend, watching over Amanda while I'm at work."

As she closed the door after Katie, Nicole twirled into the entryway, eyes flashing with excitement, and immediately asked Katie. "Did you remember?"

Katie's eyes widened as she stared back with mock confusion. "Remember what?"

Nicole laughed. "Nice try. Let's see it."

Katie rummaged through her backpack and retrieved a picture. "This was where he lived until they moved to California. Right next door to *moi*. Who would have thought he would have become famous!"

"That's amazing!" A silly grin formed on Nicole's face.

"And who is he?" Amanda asked.

"He's on *the* show of all shows, *High School Watch*." Nicole stared at her in horror as if Amanda should know. "Every girl in class is crazy about him."

"Oh, like Zach Efron."

"Who's he?" Nicole asked.

Amanda shook her head. "Never mind."

"I bet he was just as cute as a little boy," Nicole insisted, her grin never wavering.

Amanda inwardly groaned. "Don't swoon on me."

"What's swoon mean?" Another confused look from Nicole.

She caught Gabriel's amused smile and almost smiled back, but caught herself in time. "Ladies, how about you take yourself into the living room and say goodbye to Gabriel. He's got to get going."

He raised his brows but didn't argue. "And how about a cup of coffee and a slice of pie when you are on your break later? I seem to remember you like the pie at Wombats. We will talk then. No runaround this time. Promise."

"Fine," she agreed reluctantly. Unlike here, where she felt like she had some advantage—even imagined— the restaurant was in neutral territory. "I've got to get some things done before work."

"Just make sure neither girl opens the door to anyone."

She found the intensity in Gabriel's eyes a bit unnerving. "Of course not. Both of them know better."

"Well, Nicole took a ride from a stranger just this last week."

"But that's different…"

Lips firming, he shook his head. "Just promise me you will stress to her again not to answer, even if that same woman shows up at the front door?"

"Fine." At this point, she'd say anything to get him out of the house. Gabriel hovering nearby was making her agitated and drawing her thoughts inadvertently back to the night they'd spent together—his sweat-slick body, his capable hands, the feel of his mouth… Ugh. Seriously, she shouldn't even be thinking of sex. But the memories of being with him were pretty near impossible to shake off.

Finally, he left. His scent—clean, woodsy with an almost citrus aroma—lingered in the air. Shivering, Amanda closed the door after him.

Then locked it.

More because of a savage killer roaming loose in Spirit Lake than Gabriel's insistence.

Amanda pulled into the parking lot of Wombats. The building was an old brick one-story structure built in the 1950s. Very little had changed from then. Narrow windows ran the length of the front and on each side of the glass doors. The black leather booths and black-and-white checkered flooring had been replaced in the last year, but the style hadn't changed. At one time the place had been an ice-cream parlor. They served very little ice cream now, but Wombats was known for their pie to the point where tourists came up from even Des Moines and Omaha to have a taste.

Thank God they were open 24/7. Otherwise, she

would have been out of luck finding anything to eat during the night shift, unless she wanted a hot dog or stale taco from the gas station. As she closed the car door and walked up to the entrance, Gabriel pulled up in the parking spot beside hers. She waited at the front door as he approached. They'd texted each other about a good time to meet, and he'd shown up at that exact time. He'd always been punctual, and until this thing with him quitting and skipping town without a goodbye, she'd counted on his word.

His hips rolled with each long powerful step. His hands swung easily at his sides. The way he walked spoke of confidence, strength. Not a swagger, exactly; he moved with unconsciously fluid movements, unaware of the gazes he collected from the opposite sex when he walked into a room or in any other public arena. When she'd patrolled with him, Amanda hadn't missed the way women reacted to him. She hated to admit it, but he looked good in uniform.

She wasn't the jealous type. At least she'd never thought herself capable of it. But Gabriel dragged out this crazy possessive feeling that twisted her insides all around. She sighed inwardly; it was damn hard to be detached even though she'd been trained to be exactly that.

"Pretty quiet," was his way of a greeting.

"I'd rather have that than another mutilated body." She made a face. "Quiet makes for a long night."

"Tell me about it." He smiled down at her as he opened the front door to Wombats. "When you were partnered up with me, you made it go fast. Your jokes—"

"Were lame. I know. Everyone tells me. It's called

lack of self-control. I've had to cut way back on my vulgar humor with Nicole." She paused in the doorway. "She's caught me too many times saying things that weren't exactly appropriate for someone under 13."

At her comment, something shifted in his gaze, and Amanda tensed.

Sexual awareness, suddenly thick and unmistakable, filled the air around them.

"I'm not the best when it comes to self-control myself."

Frowning and determined not to think of what he meant by that comment, she quickly stepped through the doorway and said over a shoulder, "You promised me pie along with coffee. I'm holding you to it."

"Pie?"

"Oh, don't act so surprised. These last couple of hours, I've worked up an appetite sitting on my butt in the car, and they do a great pie."

"I actually have not tried their pie."

"Really? I can't believe you haven't. Everyone raves about it, including me." Her lips dipped at the corners. "I'm sure being a sugar addict is going to get me eventually."

She really needed to shut up. She was starting to talk nonstop to hide her nervousness. Now that they were there, she felt like it would be best for everyone involved—especially herself—not to dig up Gabriel's lack of feelings for her and his needing to skip town.

Gabriel scanned the large room. A group of local teenagers hung out in one corner, while in a back booth, a young couple, heads bent, mouths attached, were oblivious of their surroundings. If they got any hotter, Gabriel suspected their table might be used for something other than food. Not an act the owner would appreciate, not to mention the other customers.

Scott, behind the cashier's counter, glanced back and forth between Amanda and Gabriel. "So, any new developments?

"That's not something we can discuss with you," Gabriel snapped back, not in the mood for Scott's one thousand questions.

The other man's eyes widened. "Something's happened. I can see it on your face. Has someone else been murdered?"

Amanda's lips thinned, but Gabriel didn't give her a chance to reply. "Cut it out, Scott. Fishing isn't going to get you anything."

"I'll find out soon enough." He nodded and rocked back on his heels.

"I'm sure you will."

"I bet someone got their chest ripped out again. Amanda looks a little green in the face. Did you just leave the scene?"

Gabriel glared back.

"Fine." Scott made a face at him then glanced over at Amanda. His brow creased, and sudden interest flared in his gray, watery eyes. "Hey, Amanda. You're a woman."

She arched a brow. "Last I looked, I was."

Scott rolled his eyes. "Well, my brother-in-law bought this cross on the Internet, and I bought it from him for my wife. She's always been into crosses, but I wanted to get your opinion. I think it might be a bit too bulky and over the top. When Eric sent me the initial pic of it, I thought it was a lot smaller. I asked Jared, a jeweler in town, but I don't really trust him. He's got his eye on a possible profit on his end."

He ducked under the counter and came up with a large silver cross and placed it on the glass counter. A large ruby rested on top of a raised circle the size of a quarter in the middle. Even though the medallion was worn with age, the elements hadn't yet eliminated the etching of a primitive face above the ruby and several vines as they twined a path around all four arms of the cross.

Gabriel sucked in a large breath. "Where did you get this?" he bit out. "It looks rare. Something that should be in a museum."

Scott frowned. "Calm down. From the look on your face, you'd think Eric and I stole it. Well, neither one of us did. He bought it online on one of the sites that sells pretty much anything."

"Who did he buy it from?" Gabriel demanded, then realized how he was sounding and snapped his mouth shut.

"I'm sure it doesn't matter where he got it from," Amanda murmured, looking at Gabriel oddly before turning back to the necklace. "It looks very old. That or someone tried to make a replica of an antique cross."

"So..." Scott slid the medallion across the counter closer to Amanda. "I'd be interested in what you think."

Amanda lifted the cross in one hand and rested a hip against the side of the counter. "It's pretty large. I'm not sure it would be a piece your wife would wear too often. The ruby is large and attractively cut, though, and the design is unusual. It looks like an antique. I've never been up on what's fashionable, but it does look old and worn in places. Do you have any idea how old?"

"I haven't a clue, but I was thinking the same thing. We're pretty sure it's an antique." He glanced over at Gabriel as if he expected him to launch over the counter at him.

Amanda frowned. "It seems familiar, for some strange reason. I haven't a clue why, but…" Her gaze cleared. "It looks like a replica of the one you have, Gabriel, hanging from your rear-view mirror which—"

"You are mistaken." Gabriel cut her off abruptly.

"But…" Amanda stiffened and frowned up at Gabriel.

Scott glanced at both of them, suspicion growing in his eyes. He crossed his arms over his belly. "Hmmm. You're both acting a little odd."

"It has been a long week," Gabriel replied smoothly. He could not take back his behavior but seeing the cross had been entirely unexpected. It was not some random cross. He had held that particular medallion in his hand at one point. He was well aware of its small, interior compartment, but what was hidden inside was more alarming than anything else.

The radio at Amanda's shoulder broke into static, and then dispatch said, "We've got an 11-82 at the four-way at 71 and 9."

Gabriel inwardly groaned. The last thing he wanted to do was help Amanda take care of a fender-bender. Thankfully, Jacobson's voice came on the radio. "10-4. I'm over in that area right now."

"Hey, look at this," Amanda said. "There's a latch."

"Don't!" Gabriel cried out.

With a jerk of her hand, she snapped open a circular, coin-sized lid beneath the ruby at the center of the cross.

A vial flew out.

Amanda tried to catch it but missed.

The glass tube smashed onto the concrete floor.

Glass shattered, and the contents sprang free.

Gabriel jumped back but not fast enough. Two beads of liquid silver connected to his exposed right hand. Pain slashed through his flesh and stabbed into his body.

"What in the world is that?" Scott peered over the counter.

Amanda bent down.

"Don't touch it!" Despite the pain, Gabriel lunged and grabbed her arm to haul her up to her full height.

Amanda pivoted and gaped at him. "Why?"

"It's mercury," Gabriel managed through gritted teeth.

"Mercury?" Scott's face paled. "Why the hell would someone put mercury in a cross? That's not only stupid but dangerous. I bet you it's some sick person getting a thrill at making someone ill."

Amanda's expression darkened. "It doesn't make any sense. Why turn a cross into something deadly and poisonous?"

"Poison…" The white around Scott's pupils widened. "It can't be mercury!" A hint of hysteria climbed into his voice. "Do you know what the hell something like that will do to this business? They'll close the place down. I'll lose my job."

The mercury seeped deeper into Gabriel's body.

There was nothing he could do. He stumbled back as pain leached deeper into his body, and he tried to straighten but couldn't get his body to function. He clutched at Amanda and dragged her toward him. "I need you to get me out of here," he growled into her ear. "Now. If I don't know it does not make leave in a couple of seconds, I am liable to cause a scene you will not soon forget. No one in this town will want to deal with it."

The alarm in his voice must have kept her from asking questions in front of Scott. Instead, she grabbed Gabriel's arm and backed toward the restaurant's front entrance. "Sorry about that, Scott, but we've got a possible hit and run." She blatantly lied. "We'd like to help, but there could be a number of casualties, and probably a drunk driver involved. I need Gabriel with me for backup. All I can suggest is using a dropper from somewhere to get it off the ground. You'll have to shut down the place and have someone out of town deal with it."

"Deal with it? Deal with it?" Scott's voice rose. "I'm not dealing with this. You're the one who opened the damn cross."

"But you're the one who bought it," Amanda argued. "It's a good thing you found out about it before your wife started wearing it. Poison around her neck for an indefinite period probably could have made her ill. If not worse."

"Amanda." Gabriel slurred her name as images faded along his peripheral vision. Things weren't looking good. He listed to the side and bumped a hip against a menu stand. Before crashing into the podium, he grabbed the counter's edge, but he knocked over a container of business cards.

"What is wrong with you!" Anger flashed across Scott's face. "You're—"

"Drop it," Amanda demanded. "Deal with the mercury. We've got a call to take care of."

Gabriel got to the parking lot unassisted—barely. He slumped against the side of Amanda's patrol car. Any minute and he might land on his face on the concrete.

"Here, get in," she urged after opening the passenger door.

He crumpled into the seat and barely heard the slam of the door as he slung his head back against the padded rest and closed his eyes against the pain.

Behind the wheel, Amanda asked in an urgent voice. "What's wrong? You were perfectly fine five minutes ago."

"Just get me to a Catholic church."

"What? A church?"

"Yes."

"Are you sure? That would be the last thing I would think—"

"It's the only thing that can save me."

"I don't understand. Are you having some type of seizure or something?" She inhaled with a loud hiss. "My God! Your hand."

He opened his eyes but didn't lift his head and look to see her reaction. He heard it all in her voice. He slipped his hand from his thigh and dropped it between his seat and the door, but the parking lot light had illuminated enough of the interior's shadows to reveal its ugly state.

"A hospital. I've got to get you to Lakes Regional Hospital."

He laughed at the absurdity of the statement. "No

hospital, damn it. I know what's wrong with me. I need to get to St. Augustine's Sacred Heart."

"That's not a good idea—"

"I know what I need. Just do it. Please…" The last word came out strangled.

"Sure." She sounded like she was getting a couple of teeth pulled.

The car rumbled to life, and she sped from the parking lot, hitting the curb and the street with a hard bounce. "Other than the church, is there something more we can do? Something I can do?"

"Nothing."

"There's got to be something." A distinct edge entered Amanda's voice. "It looked like the flesh was melting off your hand. I can't take you to a church. How is that going to help? We're going to the hospital."

She changed lanes and hit the lights. Red and blue flashed into the night.

"Damn it. Turn them off." His voice rose in panic. "I know what I am talking about. If you take me to the hospital, I will be dead within the hour."

Amanda didn't argue, but she didn't turn the car around, either. "Is it getting worse?

"Probably." He had a good idea the flesh along his forearm was disappearing. With each moment, death crawled closer. "It's the mercury."

"Mercury doesn't do that. It's got to be something else."

"Amanda. Trust me. I know it doesn't make sense, but if you don't get me there, I am going to end up dead." Shifting, he winced and then tried not to move. The pain was unbearable. "Just get me to Sacred Heart."

He slumped deeper into his seat. Talking and thinking drained what little energy he had left.

"I've never been much of a churchgoer, but even I know it's going to be closed. It's too late at night," Amanda argued and then muttered a couple of four-letter words under her breath. Her next words melded into nothingness

He came to with Amanda peering at him by the open door of the passenger side of the car.

"We're here," she murmured, her breath clouding the frigid air around her. The car's interior light illuminated the worry in her brown eyes and the strain of the night's events across her delicate features. "The church doors are locked."

"I need you to go ask Father Henry to open it for us. I can't do it in the state I am in now. His house is to the right—the one with gray siding. Make something up. Just make sure you can get that door open."

"Gabriel. This is crazy. What can a church do that a hospital can't?"

"It has holy water."

"You can't be—"

"Just do it," was all he was able to manage.

She frowned, spit out a couple of swear words, but disappeared from view, the crunch of snow beneath her shoes echoing in the night.

Not looking at the remains of his hand and arm, he grabbed the side of the roof with his good hand and struggled to pull himself up, but slumped back against his seat, his limbs vibrating and ineffective. He hated needing Amanda's help. He had already put her life in jeopardy, but she was the only one he trusted in Spirit Lake. Even her assistance might not be enough, though. It was questionable if he would even make it once they got inside the church.

A new wave of pain-like pressure closed in around him. Death was not far away. He had managed to escape it several times before. What an ironic twist that a couple of minuscule drops of mercury would be his final undoing. Any moment, he could expire, leaving nothing behind but pain and anguish. There would be no heaven for him.

Hell—not some metaphor or mythical world conjured up from Dante, but the physical realm on the other side of this earth plain—terrified him. The thought of no hope, or faith…the idea of a place filled with complete despair…

Enough.

Voices carried over the air, Amanda and Father Henry's gruff, rapid replies, then momentary silence, and finally the sound of Amanda's steps returning. Grappling for renewed strength and not accepting failure this time, he used an elbow against the headrest of his seat to leverage himself out of the car as Amanda reappeared with a keychain dangling from an index figure.

"I lied and told him there were possible vandals in the area causing trouble. He didn't need any encouragement to stay inside and keep his doors locked." She flipped the key into her hand and frowned. "I don't think I can get you inside on my own. I'm going to need some help from you. Do you think you can do it?"

"I'll try." He draped his good arm over her shoulders, struggled out of the vehicle and immediately bled over the ground as they stumbled toward the front door. He hoped to God Amanda, too occupied with keeping him on his feet, didn't see the pieces of flesh melting into the snow along with the blood.

Even though shallow, the stairs were a bitch to climb. He looked down at his hand and forearm. His blood-soaked sleeve covered much but didn't shield the damage to his hand. The mercury had melted away more flesh from his body. Skeleton fingers gleamed beneath the overhead entrance light.

As he rested a shoulder against one side of the double doors, Amanda fumbled with the lock. Much to his relief, it didn't take long for her to unlock and open it. As he draped an arm again around Amanda's shoulders to keep himself from pitching to the ground, she trembled but kept from buckling beneath his weight as they stumbled into St. Augustine's main vestibule.

Moonlight through the stained glass along the upper tier of the building illuminated the gleaming wooden pews in front of them.

"Where would the holy water be? I didn't want to alert Father Henry by asking."

He ignored the skepticism in her voice. "There. To the left. The marble baptismal font with the statue of Mary. You should be able to slide the top part open."

"I thought for sure it was some type of bowl or something."

"Many churches use dispensers now." A strange pin-and-needle sensation crawled across his flesh and burrowed into his legs and chest. He hoped to God he wasn't too late. "P—prevents the chance of spreading flu or infection."

As they stumbled toward the font, Amanda slammed a hand against a switch on the wall and flooded the church with light. The white marble with gold accents shimmered and beckoned them forward. She staggered beneath him, and they pitched forward. Somehow they managed to keep from landing on the floor.

"Sorry," he muttered.

Sweat gleamed against her brow, and a flush clung to her cheeks.

He hated being powerless.

"A couple drops of water aren't going to do it," he managed through numb lips

When they reached the font, Gabriel clung to the wall to keep from falling while she fumbled with the latch and thrust the top to the side with such force the marble smashed against the wall, the noise reverberating through the otherwise hushed room.

"I need to get this off." He struggled at his long-sleeved shirt and forestalled her questions. "I don't want it woven into my arm. My T-shirt underneath can stay. It's not touching my injury."

Thank God, Amanda didn't demand answers but helped him pull the hem up and over his head with shaking hands. Questions could come later—if he lived. Between the two of them, they removed all of it until the sleeve clung to his injured arm. "Just yank it off. Fast. Don't worry. I can take it."

She hesitated, her jaw taut, her lips white with tension.

"Now."

With one swift jerk, she pulled the sleeve from his arm. Strips of skin and flesh peeled away with it, leaving bloody muscle and sinew.

"Oh, God. Oh, God." Amanda sucked in a loud gasp. "I'm so sorry."

He shivered. Strange. He'd never felt cold before.

"Here. Hurry. You look like you're about to pass out." She urged him toward the water.

He lurched forward and stuffed his arm into the interior.

And screamed.

The pain. He felt like he was dying all over again. It sucked him under, drowned him with suffocating pressure.

Gabriel lost his balance, pitched sideways against the font. The marble shuddered as he caught a hip against the stand before he slammed to the floor with Amanda beneath him. He barely managed to crawl off her and curl into a fetal position.

Steam rose from his arm. Skin bubbled and dripped onto the floor. Another scream ripped from his insides.

The pain. Holy Mother of God. The pain.

"Jesus!" Amanda cried out. She peered down at him. Her ponytail dangled over one shoulder, its tip dripping holy water onto his cheek.

He met her gaze, unable to respond, as the smell of his burning arm permeated the air around them. It was worse than the stench of melting plastic.

"Don't you dare die on me," she ordered from above him.

Gabriel swore he heard tears in her voice and saw the gleam of moisture in her eyes. He wanted to believe they were because she cared for him and not because if he died, she would be left to explain his dead body and why they'd broken into a Catholic church.

But then, all needs and wants disappeared as a new wave of pain washed over him.

CHAPTER 9

He'd passed out.

But had he? Amanda didn't know at first glance. He could just as easily be dead. He'd stopped responding to her. Still on her knees, she stared down at Gabriel. His wet, short-sleeved, navy T-shirt clung to his belly, the indentations of his ribs, and his chest—a chest that lay still as death.

Who was he? Better yet, what was he? To expect to have holy water cure him spoke of something not quite human…or someone truly crazy. Maybe she shouldn't have listened to him, should have instead taken him to the hospital. But the desperation, the fear in his voice and eyes had made her relent. But for what? To have him die instead?

She'd completely lost her brain when it came to Gabriel. Holy water? Really? Had she become some idiot during these last couple of weeks?

She ran a palm over the biceps of his injured arm. Her fingers encountered unblemished skin, cool to the touch. It was below the elbow where it got ugly. Sections of the meaty part of his arm had melted away to reveal the bone, while much of the flesh around his hand had vanished to leave skeletal digits.

There was no way anyone or anything could live without medical intervention after succumbing to such massive bodily damage. The sudden sense of loss caught her at the back of her throat. Oh, God. She'd gotten attached to Gabriel far more than she'd ever imagined…. For the briefest of moments, there'd been possibilities of something more than sex, more than a fleeting relationship.

Wait, something strange was happening…

Skin, sinew, and flesh shifted and moved above Gabriel's wrist, forming new tissue where there was none before.

He might survive after all…

But if he survived… What did that say about him? He couldn't be human. Mercury was dangerous, but she'd never heard of it eating away at someone's body. Unless that body was otherworldly…

She shivered and looked up at the statue of Jesus Christ above the doorway leading from the vestibule to the main prayer area. His silhouette gleamed against the mix of artificial light and stained glass windows. A wave of unease crawled up her spine. Her heart rate kicked up. She shivered as a feeling of being watched inched across the nape of her neck. She'd never been a very spiritual or religious person. She'd talked the talk but never really focused on faith or hope. It was a detriment to herself, and especially Nicole, she was now realizing.

Gabriel stirred by her knees. His eyes snapped open.

Amanda tensed, edging closer to his prone body.

He lay there as if frozen, his chest still, his gaze on the ceiling. Then a shudder rolled through him, almost as if his entire body was about to convulse. But as suddenly as it started, it stopped. He blinked once, twice, and his brow dipped. He opened his mouth as if to say something.

A wave of relief flooded her to the point where her entire body shook. She was having a hard time dealing with the intensity of her feelings for Gabriel and how quickly they shifted from joy to sorrow and back again. His name was becoming synonymous with chaos. She couldn't mask the fear in her voice as she stared at his hand. "I thought I lost you."

The skin continued to knit together. The bones of his wrist slowly disappeared beneath new muscle, tendon, and skin.

Her heart continued to crash against her ribs. She was seeing something that didn't belong on this earth. *What was he?*

Memories of the times they'd shared together flashed across her mind. Those meals at Wombats. The evening he'd stayed for pizza at her house. He'd been served coffee, even pizza. But had she seen him eat anything? Had she just assumed he'd touched his food because she'd been so self-focused?

Horror movies flooded her head. Zombies, werewolves, aliens…

Zombies didn't eat normal human food. But they didn't talk either. And Gabriel had a working, coherent brain.

Werewolves…?

There'd been two savage killings in Spirit Lake, the likes she had never seen before… Gabriel had shown up moments after she'd discovered Clark Swanson in the large meadow north of the Jeffersons' house. She really didn't know how strong Gabriel was or what he was capable of in a rage. What if there had been a full moon at both killings?

No, that didn't work. The two murders weren't a month apart.

Werewolves, really? She stared down at Gabriel. Other than his mangled hand, he looked human enough.

But she'd never seen him during the day. Never. Each and every time had been during the night. He'd always worked the night shift, was her understanding. Her mind veered back to the impossible.

Flashes of horror movies raced inside her head again. *Salem's Lot. The Lost Boys. Let Me In...* Vampires. But the cross hanging from his rearview mirror and the holy water didn't make any sense. He would have been terrified of both if he were...

No. Impossible.

But was it? She'd just witnessed the impossible.

Crap. Paranoia was setting in. She was getting way too carried away and imagining things that were just not there. She had seen him during the day. That time when he fixed Nicole's bike and stayed for pizza.

He struggled to sit up, using his uninjured hand. His other one still looked like he'd shoved a good part of it into a garbage disposal. "I didn't think I would make it this time."

"This time?"

"Yes. I've had it happen a couple of other times."

"When?"

He shook his head. "It doesn't matter."

"Are you..." Amanda stumbled over the words. "Will you be okay?"

Shifting, he flexed his injured hand, looked down

at his arm, and winced. "I must have scared the hell out of you."

She frowned. That was a given, but she didn't bother stating the obvious. "Does it hurt terribly?"

"No. Just aches a bit, now."

"How did you know that holy water would work?" She stared at his arm with a mix of amazement and trepidation as the skin continued to knit together inch by slow inch. It wouldn't take long for the flesh to mesh together completely. "Isn't it supposed to kill you? That's what's always been in the movies and books…"

Had she really just said that aloud? But she couldn't retract her words. They hung in the air like some dark, ugly stain.

He flexed his hand again. "It's amazing how rumors and superstitions are fanned by fear. Fear kills, rots not only humanity, but the soul."

She frowned. "What is that supposed to mean?"

He shrugged. "Just an observation."

Her frown deepened. *What was Gabriel?* She really needed to know, but at the same time she was afraid to ask the question aloud. Because once he answered, there was no going back. Hell. Who was she kidding? Everything had changed. She couldn't pretend. Gabriel had some sick, twisted secret. But the idea of asking if he was a vampire, werewolf, or zombie seemed surreal and outlandish. Then she looked at his hand.

Everything about the night was surreal.

In one rapid and smooth motion, he stood. He offered his undamaged hand to help her up.

For the briefest of moments, as he loomed over her, she hesitated, conscious of his power and masculinity. There was a flash of pain in the harsh lines of his face, in the shadow of his eyes.

Then he shifted, and the expression vanished as he smiled. But sadness still lingered in his eyes.

It was a sadness she'd never witnessed in him before. What was beyond the façade he presented to the people around him? His hand engulfed hers as she rose to her feet. She immediately slipped from his grasp and stepped away. In her hurry to put distance between them, she skidded on the wet floor.

Gabriel caught her elbow before she landed on her butt.

She took another step away from him. She was acting like an idiot but couldn't stop herself. His nearness was driving her crazy. She'd witnessed a vulnerability to Gabriel, but she would be a fool to believe he was as frail as any human. He could be dangerous in ways she couldn't begin to fathom.

To hell with her fear. She needed to know. "What are you?"

His gaze latched onto hers. Again, there was that flash of pain in his eyes for the briefest of moments. "I don't know."

"You don't know?" she parroted.

His gaze dropped as he splayed the fingers of his injured hand. The bone had disappeared beneath flesh and skin. His hand looked normal again. "I haven't a clue. All I know is that I'm different from you and everyone else."

"Since you were born? Or after?" She raked shaky fingers across her skull to move her hair back from her face. Several strands had escaped her ponytail.

"After. I was twenty-eight. Thirteen days after my birthday, my life changed."

"What happened?"

His lips firmed, and he shook his head. "Not now. We don't have time. Father Henry is going to think we have been murdered and call for backup."

She wanted to argue but he was right. "I told Father Henry to stay inside because there'd been reports of vandalism happening in the area. But it looks like we're the vandals."

The wall was dented where she'd rammed the top of the marble font against it. Nothing she could do there, other than pay for the damages.

"It shouldn't take much to clean up." Gabriel leaned down and grabbed his shirt from the wet floor. "I'll donate a healthy amount to the church for what happened."

After Gabriel helped her fix their mess as best as they could, she disappeared inside Father Henry's home for a bit to calm him down. Gabriel met her back at the patrol car but placed a hand on the top of the driver's door to stop her from slipping inside.

"I'll follow you home after we're done at the police department," he murmured.

"Not my house. Yours. And it can't be today. Nicole's got a field trip that I volunteered to help chaperone. And I'm packed with other school projects. How about three days from now? You're not working then, right?"

"Correct."

She folded her arms across her middle. Yeah, she was champing at the bit to know the details. But Nicole came first. Always would. "And you're not following me home. That's ridiculous. It'll also look odd and only confirm to Bill we're having an affair when we're not."

"And what would you call what we were having, if not an affair?"

The question floored her.

Before she had the chance to get her mouth around the right words to answer, he told her, "Forget I said that." A crease formed between his brows. "How about I join you on this field trip."

"What? Are you serious?" She didn't like that stubborn look in his eyes. "That's ridiculous."

"I think it would be safer if I were with the two of you."

He really was serious.

There was no way she was going to get his imprint off her body and out of her head with him hovering around her. It would drive her beyond nuts. "That's not happening."

"Is the idea of me being around you that distasteful?" He eased away from the door, his gaze on her face far too intent for her liking. He lifted his uninjured hand to graze her cheek with a thumb. "The other night you didn't seem to mind me near you."

Amanda grunted, making a herculean effort not to show how much his touch affected her. "That was before you decided to skip town without letting me know."

"That was really inexcusable on my part. I will apologize again, which I know is not enough."

Lips firming, she looked over his shoulder at a sky slowly turning from midnight to gray. Soon the sun would hit the horizon. "I better drive you to your car. The sun—" She bit her lip. "It's getting late."

Gabriel glanced over his shoulder and then faced Amanda with an odd look on his face. "You don't still think…" His voice lowered to a husky whisper. "Amanda. I am not a vampire."

Heat crept into her face. "I never said—"

"But you were thinking it."

"Well, what the hell am I supposed to think? Your arm looked like it was something from a horror movie just a while ago."

"Are you repelled being this close to me?" His gaze intensified with a mix of concern and another emotion she couldn't discern. "Me being this close to you gets to you, doesn't it? It's in your eyes."

Damn him. It seemed like Amanda couldn't hide one stupid thing from him. He was making her flustered, unsure, and vulnerable.

"Do I frighten you? I can understand if I do, after what you witnessed."

"No," she lied, easing backward. The cold, winter air added to the chill that raced across her skin.

He dropped his hand and angled his head to one side. Moonlight highlighted the cool marble of his cheekbones while deep shadows clung below his brow, masking his expression. "I wouldn't hurt you. You do know that, right? You trust me on that at least, after having been partners these last couple of weeks?"

Did she? She thought back over the time she'd worked with him and how he'd interacted with the people in Spirit Lake, not just by words but through his actions.

He couldn't fake something like that for that long. Having been in the town for five years, his real character would have shown through. People there seemed to trust him.

She'd always thought of herself as a damn good judge of a person's character—her job demanded that of her. If some dark force drove him, she was positive he would have slipped up at some point.

"I'm sure you wouldn't intentionally hurt me," she finally admitted. Yeah, physically Gabriel might not lay a hand on her, but it was the emotional upheaval…and the thing with the holy water and mercury did have her rattled.

"But I already have." He frowned. "I think it's a good idea for you to take a couple of days off."

"With a crazed killer roaming the town?" Amanda asked in disbelief. "Even if I wanted to, it sure as hell won't go over well. We need every officer in the department right now." Also, she lived in a world where walking away from responsibility didn't exist. Never had and never would. "I need to work, feed Nicole, keep a roof over our heads. I'm already in jeopardy with my job. Taking time off would only incite Freer. He wants an excuse to fire me right now. No thanks to you." The last came out harsher than she intended.

"You don't understand."

"What don't I understand?"

A muscle on one side of his jaw pulsed. "You need to be safe. You *have* to be safe."

She was appreciative of his concern, but the intensity of it hinted at something more profound. "Something's going on that you're not telling me. Give."

A door banging shut echoed in the night, probably from Father Henry's house.

"Later. In three days, like you said. Take care of

Nicole's field trip and the other things you've got lined up with the school. We can meet up then."

"Amanda? Are—are you out there?" Father Henry called out.

She so wanted to argue, but the alarm in the priest's voice stilled those words. So instead, she muttered, "Fine."

After soothing Father Henry's fears, she came back and slipped into the driver's seat beside Gabriel. She kept her mouth shut during the drive back to Wombats. No arguing. She'd given her word, but that didn't mean it wasn't tough.

"Talk to you in three days," Gabriel murmured before slipping from her car.

Nodding sharply, she stared through the windshield and strangled the steering wheel with both hands as he moved across the parking lot, his gait smooth and powerful. Assured he would be fine—at least physically—she pulled onto the street toward the precinct.

While Amanda didn't think she'd be *fine* ever again. After that night, the way she looked at life would be forever changed.

CHAPTER 10

Wee have a problem." Gabriel twisted the wand of the living room blinds, shutting the neighboring houses from view as day crept into dusk. Although he hated to call Luys, the man deserved to know what was happening in Spirit Lake.

"Mayor?"

The question hung heavy between them. Gabriel closed his eyes briefly. Failure pressed hard against his shoulders, chest, and brow. "Yes."

"Are you sure?"

"We've had two brutal killings within the last two weeks. Before all this, the last murder here was over 30 years ago." Gabriel paced the confines of the living room. "After doing some digging, I discovered there has also been a sighting."

Luys swore savagely. "I had thought...hoped."

"Same," Gabriel managed. "Mayor's out for revenge. When done with me, you'll be next. I thought you needed the warning."

"Give me two days, and I'll get down there."

"How about a week? If I can't contain the situation, I will need your help. Hopefully, no one else will be killed. Mayor is in hiding. Where, I don't know yet, but given time, I will find out."

"Can you do that? Are you strong enough? Neither

one of us was before. What makes you think you're capable now?"

"I have to be. There are people involved, people I care about." Gabriel thought about Amanda.

"And Mayor knows this?"

"Yes."

"Jesus, Gabriel. I'm sorry."

"You know it's going to come down to them or Mayor. I chose Mayor last time. I can't do it this time."

"I don't like it, but I understand. Keep me posted?"

"I will." Gabriel rubbed the back of his neck. "Are there any new developments?"

Luys sighed. "Nothing. I have had to scrap the latest project. My first hypothesis might be the way to go after all. I am back to thinking of it as a virus. I swear I am running down rabbit holes. I don't think the technology is there yet."

"What about medications?"

"I need a subject. I can't test on just anyone. And if I push it too much, people are going to get suspicious. Baxter has already been asking me questions."

Gabriel closed his eyes against Luys' words. Not something he wanted to hear. He rubbed the back of his neck again and continued to pace across the living room floor, unable to throw off the sense of suffocation engulfing him. Panic. He didn't need it or want it. "Don't give up."

"Trying not to." A pause of silence followed. "But I am tired… Sometimes I think it would be best for everyone, including Mayor, if I walked away."

"I know. Still…" Gabriel looked up at the ceiling. "You have got to focus on…"

"Hope?"

"If not that, what is there?" Gabriel didn't expect an answer. He hung up after agreeing to let Luys know if or when he needed help. When his phone chirped, he glanced down to see a text from Amanda.

Come over in three hours. Nicole should be settled for the night.

He texted back, then tossed his phone on the end table to where it butted up against the lamp's base.

Great. In a few hours he would have to confront Amanda and reveal things about himself he had never shared other than with his family. It would be like slashing his wrists wide open.

He glanced down at his right hand and flexed his fingers. Looking at it now, no one would guess the hand had been only bone. He had almost died. Probably better if he had.

He had to get that vial from Scott at Wombats before meeting Amanda. At the moment, Amanda was safe. But he didn't know how long Mayor intended to play around with him before turning savage. After rummaging around in the garage, he grabbed a pair of gloves. He would have to hunt around for a syringe and other material. First, he needed to drop by Wombats. Then after that…

The only person who could help him was Jared, who owned a jewelry store in town. Unlike Scott, he hoped the man could keep his mouth shut. He did owe Gabriel a favor for not busting his son for underage drinking.

After grabbing his jacket by the door, he rushed from the house.

When Gabriel showed up at Amanda's house later that night—three days since they'd parted at St. Augustine—she opened the door with a guarded expression and left lots of space between them. In the foyer, he moved left, she moved right. He moved forward, she moved backward. He stuffed his hands into his coat pockets and sighed. Could it get any more awkward?

The main light in the kitchen was off, but a light from above the sink cast a warm, cozy glow over the counters and round maple table. No intimate places if she could help it, as Amanda waved him into the living room instead, where two lamps on either side of the navy sofa chased all the shadows into small, dark crevices.

Amanda dropped into the chair by the side of the sofa and rubbed both hands against her jean-clad legs.

He caught her glancing at his hand before averting her gaze. First he shrugged out of his jacket. Then he draped it against the arm of the sofa before he sank down on the cushion to the right of Amanda. "I don't know if I thanked you for what you did the other night." He could not remember much, other than the pain, the flash of Amanda's face over his own, and the need to get away from her and the mistrustful and repulsed look on her face. "I wouldn't have made it without your help."

It had been a long time since he had needed to thank anyone. He had never let anyone get that close.

She scowled at him, bit her lip, and nodded sharply. "Yes, well, I didn't want you dead. I've had my moments when I've been furious at you, but I would never want you to be in pain, especially after how you have suffered."

Her eyes softened. He was drawn into their depths and how the gold flecks circling her pupils darkened into deep, warm chocolate. Her lips parted, lush, kissable. He frowned. Now wasn't the time. The time was never. Not with what he was about to explain to her.

Gabriel dug inside his coat pocket and retrieved a 3-by-4 inch metal box. "I need you to take this."

"What…"

"Open it. You will see soon enough." He had no clue how she was going to react. She could be stubborn.

Frowning, she took it from him with a tentative touch.

He rose quickly and backed up until he stood a safe distance away from her.

She twisted the metal clasp and opened the lid. Her frown deepened. The shadow of her thick black lashes shielded the expression in her eyes as she glanced down at the cross, its thick chain snaking into a coiled circle beneath the old and worn metal.

After a long moment of silence, she looked back at him, uncertainty flashing briefly in her eyes. "I can't take this. I saw it dangling from the rearview mirror in your SUV. It must have some importance."

"No. This is a duplicate, the one Scott had. I went back to Wombats for it."

"What about the mercury? How can you even touch it after-after—"

"It's been cleaned. And then cleaned some more and sterilized. I went to the jeweler in town. There's a new circular vial inside with several drops of mercury. I had to do some bribing. Jared soldered the hinge and made it a tighter fit, so this time there's little chance of it escaping by accident and breaking open. Plus, it's in a thick metal case. Another safety measure in case there were any remnants of mercury, and I haven't had it near me for any length of time."

When she stared at it and didn't move to take the medallion from inside the box, he insisted, "I need you to wear it."

"Why?" She looked at him as if he'd gone crazy. "It's dangerous having poison wrapped around my neck."

"It will be more dangerous if you don't wear it."

"I don't understand. How can a cross with mercury keep me safe?"

"Trust me. It will protect you."

"Trust you? I don't think so." Her gaze narrowed as she placed the cross and metal container on the end table beside her. "Do you seriously think I'm going to blindly do what you ask when I have no clue who or what you are? And the cross part has me thinking super crazy things. Not once have I seen you eat anything or walk around in the light."

"I told you I am not a vampire."

"Really? Then what's the importance of the cross? It's got to have some type of meaning. Why else would you have it hanging on your rearview mirror?"

"I was raised Catholic. I used to be very religious."

Her frown deepened. "But there's more."

"Yes," he managed to say, but the admission tasted like bile. His entire life, as far back as he could remember, had been one lie after another. But he could not lie anymore. At least not to Amanda. She deserved more. More than he could ever give her.

"It has power not just over me," he finally admitted.

"Because of the mercury?"

Gabriel walked over to the television mounted

against the wall to delay his answer. Such a simple question, but nothing about his situation or life was.

A high-pitched scream startled him. Loud, terror-filled. Then another, followed by wailing that quickly disintegrated into sharp, rapid shrieks.

Amanda jumped from her chair and raced from the room toward the main hallway. The sounds came from deeper in the house.

There was so much pain and fear in the cries.

After grabbing the cross from inside its container, he rushed into the bedroom after Amanda. It took him a moment to adjust to the darkness. Light from the hall spilled across the floor and onto the ruffled bed where Nicole sat rigid in the middle of the mattress, hands clamped against both ears.

The girl was alone in the room.

"It's okay. It's okay," Amanda soothed. She crawled across the mattress before sliding a hand over the girl's cap of blonde hair.

Nicole violently shook her head from side to side. "He's got the knife. HE'S KILLING HER. Tell him to stop. STOP. PLEASE MAKE HIM STOP."

Gabriel stood in the middle of the room, unsure of what to do. There was no man. There was no knife. But there was terror. He had seen such fear before. He had felt it himself.

"MOM!!"

Amanda dragged the girl onto her lap. "I'm here. I'm here! Shhhh. It's okay now. It's over. Brent will never touch you or anyone else again.

He flinched. Now he understood. Nicole had witnessed her mother's murder. His chest tightened.

The poor child. Holy Mother, the girl had been through hell.

Amanda looked over her shoulder at him. The light from the hall shimmered against her tear-filled eyes. "Can you give us a minute?"

"Of course." He retreated quickly from the room, feeling an interloper on the raw and intimate scene.

Guilt gnawed a path into his stomach as he walked back into the living room and set the cross with its container back on the end table.

Nicole and Amanda had fought hard to start a new life—a safe life—and he had fucked that up royally.

She sat in the middle of Nicole's bed and held the girl against her breast, all the while running a gentle hand over the silken strands of her hair. Nicole had calmed somewhat. Her violent shaking had subsided to mild trembling and an occasional shudder when she grappled for air. Still, the thump of her heart didn't seem to slow down as it pounded against Amanda.

Amanda hated feeling hopeless. She couldn't take away her daughter's pain, make the nightmares go away, erase her horrific past. Holding her seemed so inconsequential.

Finally, when Nicole seemed sufficiently calmed, she eased back a bit until the light from the hall illuminated her daughter's blotchy face. She gently slid a thumb across the girl's cheek, smudging a tear against her skin. "I've got to go for just a minute and talk to Gabriel."

"Don't!" Nicole twisted her fingers around the sleeves of Amanda's shirt until the material cut into the skin.

"Give me two minutes. Max. Promise. He's waiting in the other room. I've got to tell him to go home."

After a while, when her daughter nodded with a jerk, Amanda rushed from the room and found Gabriel standing in the middle of the living room.

He turned when she entered the archway into the room. "Is she going to be all right?"

"Yes, I think so." She hugged her middle.

He frowned. "Does Nicole have nightmares often?"

"She hasn't for a while. Probably the last one was a couple of weeks ago, but I'm sure word is all over the school about the killings in town. It's got to be rattling her even more than someone with a normal upbringing."

"Let me know what I can do."

The deep concern in his eyes made her soften. Yeah, he might be a lot of things, but he did care for people. She'd seen it time and again while working with him. "Sure." She nodded toward the hallway behind her. "I should be getting back…"

"Yes, of course. I'll check up on you and see how she is doing tomorrow."

She backed up a step and hesitated in the doorway to the hall.

He stepped toward her, lifted a hand, hesitated, but then clasped her upper arm gently and kissed her brow.

She blinked at the unexpected and tender act. Her heart rate stuttered for the briefest of moments as his scent wrapped around her, and memories of his body, the weight of him against her flesh rushed through her. She took a stumbling breath.

"I am only a call away. Remember you are not alone," Gabriel murmured, his breath whispering against the hairline at her temple before he turned and hurried from the house.

With the touch of his lips still on her skin, she hurried back to Nicole's room. For just a moment she didn't feel completely alone. Taking a deep breath for calm, she stepped into the room.

Face buried against her knees, Nicole still sat in the middle of the bed hugging her shins tightly to her chest.

Amanda snuggled up to her and wrapped an arm around her shoulder. She pulled her daughter's hair back from her brow and asked softly, "Same dream?"

"Yeah… but different."

She froze with her hand still on the crown of her daughter's head. "How so?"

"It didn't finish."

"Because you woke up—"

"No— No. It just stopped, and then I was falling, and it was all black." Nicole pushed away and looked up into Amanda's face with wide, fearful eyes.

"Maybe that's a sign that your nightmares are fading. Or maybe you're getting stronger and able to stop them." Amanda was far from an expert on dreams.

Nicole sniffed and wiped the back of her hand against her nose. "But the knife—" She sniffed louder. "It was black and just as weird looking as all the other times. But bigger. Huge. He went after me. He's never done that before. He was about to stab me when I woke up." She dove back into Amanda's sheltering arms and latched onto her with a fierce, painful grip.

Several bruises were undoubtedly going to appear in the morning. Amanda's shoulders slumped. She'd always thought the dreams replayed the actual murder of Nicole's mother, Joyce, by Nicole's stepfather. Now, she wasn't so sure. As far as knives went, the usual kitchen variety hadn't been used. In this case, Brent had used a black obsidian blade. One from his weapons collection. The guy had been a freak.

Doubts assailed her. Maybe they should have stayed in Chicago. Nicole had a good therapist there. Amanda didn't have any recommendations for a child psychologist in the area. Something she needed to research immediately. She rubbed Nicole's back. "How about I stay here for the night? Will that help?"

Tension eased visibly from Nicole's slight frame. "Please."

Amanda snuggled under the covers with her. "I was thinking." Probably not a good idea, but hell, she wanted her child happy and distracted. "Maybe it's time we adopt that dog you've been wanting. We've got the big backyard. It's all fenced and ready to go."

"Really?" A shudder raced through Nicole's body. From excitement, thank God.

"Yep, but small. Nothing over twenty-five pounds."

"I'll take anything!" Nicole laughed and rubbed the rest of the tears from her face.

Amanda crossed her ankles and stared up at the ceiling, wondering if she'd made a stupid mistake. But as she shifted and looked over at Nicole's face, the hall light revealed unmistakable happiness in the girl's blue eyes, and nothing was a mistake if it brought pleasure to her daughter's life.

CHAPTER 11

Gabriel stepped through the entrance of Jimmy's Joint. Country music throbbed from the jukebox in the corner of the room, while a couple danced in the middle of the dance floor—if it could be called dancing. Bodies draped over each other and barely moving to the music, they looked shitfaced and close to passing out. If they let go of each other long enough they probably would both land on their asses. No one else was dancing, but a couple of people sat at the bar and in murky booths on the other side of the room, and a few other groups hung around the jukebox and pool table.

The faces of the people within the shadowed booths looked familiar, all locals. Tourist season was long dead. That was one advantage of living in a small town. One might not know everyone, but a person pretty much would recognize them. Then again, it could be a disadvantage if a person wanted to avoid someone.

He didn't go out to bars much. He had lost interest long ago, but there was no mistaking the atmosphere. Even this late at night with alcohol in everyone's system, no loud voices or raucous laughter filled the room.

People were afraid.

This was his fifth bar that night. He hadn't gone

home after leaving Amanda's house but had hit the bars instead. Jake Blunt was known to frequent this place and three others. There were no sightings of Mayor or any suspicious out-of-towners. He had casually questioned the staff at each bar, but they had not seen anyone or anything out of the ordinary either.

Things were too quiet. Mayor liked to shock, frighten, and thrived on the power of fear, liked to drag out everyone's terror. Still, Gabriel felt confident Nicole and Amanda were safe for a little while longer. Maybe two weeks and Mayor would tire of the current game and turn on him.

When he sank down on a stool, Alex, behind the bar, draped a towel over his shoulder and tilted his head. "What are you wanting tonight?"

"I'll have something on tap. A lager. Surprise me."

"You got it. Just got to take care of this guy's tab over here."

When the bartender paused long enough to set a mug of beer in front of him, Gabriel asked, "How's the place been? Seems kind of quiet."

"With this last murder, the crowds have definitely thinned. Plus, everyone knows Jack used to come here. I guess they're thinking of death by association. No one wants to take their chances if being in a bar makes you lose your body parts. I'm sure they want their heart inside their chest."

Gabriel took a swallow, frustrated at how quickly details of the killings were being leaked out. It was apparent someone in the department couldn't keep their mouth shut. "So, you haven't seen anyone new or anything unusual this week?"

"No, just the regulars." Alex leaned over the bar and nodded toward the couple. "Shit. When Ron's wife gets wind of what's going on, someone else might end up dead. That, or he might lose his balls if Janie has a say."

Gabriel glanced over his shoulder and arched a brow. The man was now grinding into the woman's hips. She seemed to like it from the loopy smile on her face. He turned back around and rolled his eyes at Alex. "Even though I'm off duty, I don't want to call it in either and have them charged for indecent exposure. It will be on their record for life. If it gets any wilder, though, they might be doing it on the floor, and I'll have to step in."

Alex sighed. "Won't be happening on my watch. I'll smack him with a damn pool stick before it gets any worse." He made a face as if realizing who he was talking to. "Just talking. I wouldn't hit the guy, of course."

"Of course." Gabriel smiled as Alex ambled off to take care of the two men farther down the bar. He ran a finger absently along the side of his phone, then pressed the button to check the time. It was a little past midnight.

He sighed. Why should he be surprised at Mayor not showing up at this bar or anywhere else in town that night? Mayor would show up when and only when *Mayor* decided it was time.

Gabriel took a long drink of his beer and thumbed the condensation on the side of the glass. His thoughts turned to Amanda as they always did since she had moved into town. He needed to protect her. At all costs. No repeat of the last time. He would rather kill himself.

A message popped onto the phone's screen. He slid the phone closer and looked down.

I AM GOING TO HAVE A PRESENT FOR YOU TONIGHT. HOPE YOU ENJOY IT.

He didn't recognize the out-of-state number.

Mayor…

The front door opened with a loud sigh, and a couple walked into the bar. A sharp winter breeze followed them inside. Its talons crossed the room to scrape across his flesh.

Gabriel shivered. A chill of dread burrowed into his skin.

Shut the fuck up.

I am going to rot in hell.

No, you're not.

Yes, I am.

Shut the fuck up.

I am in the middle of a forest. Pines surround me on all sides. The scent of it is suffocating. I press both hands against my ears and look to the sky, but pine branches shade me from the stars and moon.

The thoughts do not go away. Relentless, they slice, cut, and batter at my brain until I grow raw with fear. I need to stop the voices, rip out my ears, but no matter how much I distract myself, they always come back, sly, lying voices, urging me to do things I do not want to do.

He wants you dead.

I am not going to hell.

But I am already living in hell right now.

Alone. Always alone.

The deep throb of music rises through the night,

distracting me. The unmistakable strum of a guitar. Its rhythm beckons. I move toward it as a frigid breeze whispers across my skin. I love the cold. It numbs my skin, my cheeks, my lips, my fingers. I want the cold to go deeper. I want it to seep into every fiber of my being until my heart is no longer beating. So deep I no longer feel the pain or the rage.

The sound urges me forward. I have always loved music, no matter the type. I close my eyes and let the soothing melody calm me. I find my lips curving into a smile. An elusive emotion stirs inside my chest. It takes several moments to recognize it. Pleasure. I let it wrap around me and warm me. I chase the feeling, clutch at it.

A hoarse voice breaks into the night.

My eyes snap open, and my fleeting pleasure shatters into icy shards and scatters into the night like rabid bats. I am left with nothing but the cold.

Another emotion, this one far stronger, roars through me.

Rage.

My constant companion, my lover, my friend. It fills me with a heat I recognize immediately. Familiarity does not breed contempt. Without the rage, I am nothing. I forget the brief respite of pleasure. The feeling is too alien, and it brings only weakness and despair.

As I move closer, the trees and brush thin, and a building comes into view where a spotlight illuminates a sign that reads, *Barry's Bar and Grill.*

The shadows of a man and woman stumble from the exit. The man grabs the woman.

She jerks her arm from his grasp. "Get the hell away from me."

"Don't be flashing your tits at me and walk away. You want it."

"I want you gone!"

"Bitch!"

He smacks her across the face. The sound of flesh against flesh explodes into the quiet night.

The woman's head jerks back from the impact. From here, I can see the tremble of her hand as she touches her mouth. She shakes her head but remains silent as she backs away from him.

I step closer, but the man stays in place as the woman retreats to a vehicle several car lengths away. Her car rumbles into life. Tires slip on ice, then catch on gravel as she turns the car sharply onto the road. Taillights disappear.

The man still stands in the middle of the parking lot. But then he stumbles forward and lurches to another car. This one is blue with big fat tires. He fumbles with his keys as he stands by the door. He is too focused on his keys to notice my approach. The building's light glimmers off shoulder-length hair, a profile that looks somewhat attractive. And familiar. Blond hair. The thick waves remind me of another.

For a second I contemplate trying to make him like me.

He must sense someone watching him. He stills and turns. His eyes widen as he stares back at me.

I move forward until I am only two yards away from him.

Then he smiles, not bothering to mask the predatory gleam in his eyes.

He does not deserve to live. He does not deserve my gift.

"Hey, can I help you?" The stench of alcohol erupts from his mouth.

I wrinkle my nose in distaste. Even so, saliva forms in my mouth. I flex my fingers. I start laughing. I can't stop. I want to. But I continue to laugh.

He stares at me. The predatory gleam in his eyes fade. Now he looks at me with uncertainty.

This predator will now be a victim. He will not slap or speak unkindly to another. Tonight is the last time he will hurt anyone.

I will kill him. I am kinder than I should be. Because I know if I make him like me, I will infect him. Once infected, he will become as crazy as me.

Because I have no gift. I only have a curse.

I stop laughing. My lips spread into a large smile. I let the rage fill every pore of my being.

CHAPTER 12

Carrying five bags of groceries between both hands, Amanda struggled with the side door of the house, leading into the kitchen. Finally, she got the knob working and nudged the door open with a knee. The clock above the microwave read six. Damn, she was running late. She'd hoped to have dinner done by now. It looked like she might have to pop some ready-made meals in the oven. With the heel of her boot, she closed the door to keep the frigid air outside, then dropped the bags on the kitchen island and managed not to break anything.

Look at that. No broken glass or spilled milk. Maybe things were finally starting to look up. She hadn't been worth much most of the day. Working nights always got her body out of whack, and Nicole's night terrors hadn't helped earlier. She'd spent the night staring at the ceiling, reassuring Nicole and herself everything was going to be fine. But was she lying to them both, considering the savage killings in town, witnessing Gabriel's near death, and Nicole never seeming to shake off the horror of her mother's murder?

Brain foggy, slow to respond, mood far from cheerful, she'd kept close to home after dropping Nicole at school. She hadn't called Gabriel since he'd left after Nicole's violent dream. At the church and later when he'd shown up at her house, she'd wanted the truth, but now…

Now, she was afraid of the truth. Sometimes oblivion had its useful qualities.

"Hey, Nicole, can you give me a hand here?" Amanda shrugged out of her jacket and hung it up on the coat rack by the door.

When Nicole didn't appear immediately, and the television's laugh track was the only response, Amanda walked over to the living room and stopped in the arched doorway.

Nicole wasn't alone. And she wasn't with Katie.

A woman with long blonde, almost-white hair sat in the middle of the sofa with Nicole. Both were huddled together and staring at the tablet in Nicole's hand. The woman casually brushed away several strands clinging to Nicole's cheek.

Amanda didn't recognize the woman, and she particularly didn't like the familiarity with which she was touching Nicole. Then she felt stupid for feeling that way. Maybe she was reading too much into a simple gesture. "Hello."

Both looked up. Nicole smiled, while the other woman regarded her with interest. She was beautiful, unusual, and quite stunning. She didn't seem to be much older than Katie, mid-twenties at the most. Her white-blonde hair framed a face of smooth, pearl-like skin. A dusting of rose clung to her cheeks, and her thick, generous mouth was the perfect shade of pink. Her winged brows were a far darker hue from her hair. And her eyes… They were her most unusual feature. Blue ice, the color of a glacier at sunset, but deeper, even more penetrating.

A little unnerved at the intensity of the woman's gaze, Amanda was the first to look away. Stuffing her hands into the back of her jean pockets, Amanda rocked back on her heels, feeling awkward standing in her own living room. "Can I help you?"

The woman smiled. "I wanted to check on how my new friend was doing."

Nicole tapped the tablet to her knee. "We were just looking at this new game. It's supposed to help me with my math."

"I didn't know you were struggling with math." Amanda stepped farther into the room.

"Oh, I'm not." Nicole hugged the tablet against her chest.

"I thought it was a good tool to help her get further ahead in her classroom." The blonde smiled down at Nicole.

From Nicole's previous description, this had to be the woman who'd helped her with her flat tire. "Nicole told me what you did for her when it came to her bike. Thank you."

"It's nothing. I am just pleased I was nearby to help. It's never good to have such an innocent so defenseless. You can never be too safe."

Amanda frowned. The words hinted at some type of accent, but she couldn't identify it. "That's true."

"Well, I think I better leave the two of you. I do not want to intrude. I am sure you both have many things to do that I am interrupting." The woman uncrossed her legs that were encased in black leggings. A bright, flowy long-sleeved blouse in emerald, aqua, and black swirled around her as she jerked to her feet and moved from the sofa. The carpet muffled the heels of her black ankle boots. She stopped abruptly as her gaze flicked to the end table. Something shifted in the back of her eyes. "Where did you get that?"

Amanda glanced at the table and the medallion Gabriel had given her. Uneasiness etched a path up her spine.

"A friend." Amanda crossed the room toward Nicole and the table.

"Really?"

Amanda sensed a change in the woman, even though the blonde's expression remained polite and interested. Maybe it was Amanda's own hyper imagination, but tension, thick and palpable, snapped into the room.

"Yes." She grabbed the necklace from the table and quickly slipped it around her neck before standing in front of Nicole, legs braced, uncaring how strange her behavior appeared. Gut told her she wasn't overreacting. Her gun was in the safe in her room. Too far, and she suspected too inadequate. What or who the hell was she dealing with?

The woman's eyes. That glacial stare kicked up Amanda's heart rate. Damn it. Was this what Gabriel had been talking about? Were the medallion and its mercury a deterrent against this woman? Was she like Gabriel? Oh hell, she didn't know how dangerous Gabriel was. She'd been so concerned about Nicole the other night, she'd let her questions wait for another time.

It was a delay she was sincerely regretting at the moment.

She started to think she was turning paranoid and

letting Gabriel, the bloody corpses, the savage killing distort her judgment until the woman spoke.

"You will regret associating with Gabriel."

Stiffening, Amanda released her hold on the necklace and forced her hand back to her side. "Is that a threat?"

"I do not threaten." The woman's gaze locked on the necklace.

Amanda couldn't read the woman's expression. But even so, her unease escalated, and she didn't get the feeling it was going to dip any time soon.

"Gabriel is a bad man."

"Bad?" Amanda asked at the odd description. "What do you mean by that?"

"You do not know him. No one knows Gabriel. He has seen and done horrible things. He is not what he appears. He has dark secrets."

Amanda already had a good idea what some of Gabriel's secrets were, but she asked anyway. "What things are you talking about?"

"I do not need to explain myself further to you." Impossibly, her irises seemed to shift in color and texture.

Amanda could only describe them as faceted ruby stones. They didn't look human. She fisted her hands. Damn it. A gun in her hand would feel really nice about now. When she looked back at the woman, her eyes looked normal again. *Get a grip. You're losing it.* "And why is that?"

Her lip curled. "You are a fool."

The doorbell chimed.

Amanda clutched the cross in one hand, but didn't

move from in front of Nicole and the sofa as she called out, "Come in."

The woman wouldn't do anything crazy with a witness, would she?

The door opened. Katie stood on the threshold, a smile on her face. "Hey, sorry I'm late, but my mom needed some help with the nurse, and in between, I was trying to study for a midterm. I never can get stuff done at home. More distractions there. Don't ask me why..." Katie caught sight of the platinum blonde. "Oh, hi."

Amanda had hoped someone burly and muscular, not Katie, was at the door. The last thing she wanted was for the woman to go off on the girl. Katie was really a kid, used to small-town life, willowy and with not much strength or street smarts to fight in a dirty battle.

The woman pivoted, brushed by Katie, and slipped from the house. The screen door slammed behind her.

"What was that about?" Katie glanced over her shoulder and back at Amanda with a frown.

Amanda shook her head. "I honestly don't know, but don't let her into this house."

"Of course." Katie closed the door

Amanda muttered a few choice words. "I don't even know her name. Nicole, what do you know of her? Do you know her name?"

"No, I forgot…"

"I've told you before not to open the door to strangers. You should know better."

"But Mom, she's fine."

"No, she isn't." Amanda looked out the front window but didn't see where the blonde had disappeared to. There wasn't an unfamiliar car parked on the street. The woman had walked outside in below-freezing temperatures with no coat. "We don't know anything about her."

"I know I remind her of her daughter. She wouldn't hurt me. Not if she loves her daughter."

Rather than easing her fears, Nicole's words only stoked them that much more. Who knew what the woman was capable of. Her growing fascination with Nicole wasn't something that made Amanda feel warm and fuzzy all over.

"Trust me on this." She knelt on one knee by her daughter. "Please, don't open the door to her again."

"But she seems so nice—" Nicole started to argue.

Amanda frowned.

Nicole finally gave a sharp but grudging nod. "I won't."

The sound of a car's engine and tires on the drive brought Amanda to her feet. The sun had dipped and faded with the approaching night, but that didn't stop her from immediately recognizing Gabriel's car through the front window.

Great. Just great. Amanda wasn't ready to see him. She was exhausted and she had a full shift at work to get through. What could be so important that he couldn't hunt her down while she was on duty?

She edged back from the window, wanting to watch Gabriel walk up to the porch unobserved. Her lips dipped. He really was an attractive man. The bulk of his jacket didn't disguise the long length of his legs, the breath of his shoulders, or his imposing height. Why couldn't he be ugly? Maybe then she wouldn't have jumped at the chance to get his clothes off.

"Who is it?" Nicole asked.

"Gab—Mr. Martinez."

"Hey, how about we hit your room and study?" Katie asked Nicole. "I could use some company, and that will give your mom some privacy."

"If you promise me you'll watch that show with me later tonight," Nicole bargained.

"You bet."

The doorbell rang.

Heart thumping inside her chest, Amanda rubbed her palms against her jean-clad thighs, then took a breath before opening the door. She shouldn't be surprised Gabriel had shown up at her door. He had promised to check on Nicole.

She looked up and searched his face. His dark hair looked like he'd stepped into a wind tunnel for a good hour, while exhaustion and something else, something dark and haunted, radiated from his brown eyes. Her heart thumped even louder. "What's wrong?"

"Where's Nicole?"

"In her room with Katie. Why?"

"I didn't want her to overhear what I had to say."

"How bad is it?"

"Bad," he muttered. "We've got another dead body."

CHAPTER 13

Gabriel's stomach twisted as guilt gnawed into him. The moment he had found out about the killing, he had raced over. The relief at seeing Amanda fine and hearing that Nicole was safely in her room hit him like a plank of wood. He'd had to physically come over and see for himself that she was all right. A text or call wouldn't have been enough.

The relief didn't last. Neither knew he had staked out Amanda's place every day since he had heard about Mayor showing up with Nicole. He didn't intend to tell them, either. Amanda would only get frustrated at him for sticking his nose into her life, and he would have to explain why, and every time he tried to get the courage to face her, he had backed down. A cowardly act, but he had never professed to himself or anyone else that he was a hero.

"Who? I pray to God the person isn't someone I know." She backed up to let him in, biting down on her lower lip.

"Andy Jakes..." He then noticed the medallion around her neck. Some of the vise-like tension clamped around his muscles eased. He was surprised, knowing how stubborn she could be, that she had listened to him about wearing it. Distancing himself from the cross and mercury inside, he took a step back. "I don't know him. I heard he'd moved to town about a year ago."

"I don't think I've ever met him." She cocked her head to one side as she closed the door. "Is he another white male?"

"Yes."

"Same MO?" She wrapped both arms around her middle and shivered visibly. "Were there markings on the body? Tattoos of any type?"

"I'm not sure. I think it might be similar to Blunt. I don't have all the details yet, other than it was a pretty ugly scene. Travis Perry took the initial call. We'll hear more tonight."

"Jeez, I would never have moved here if I'd known some sick freak was going to start offing innocent people here. Why is this nut taking their heads or cutting them open?"

"I don't know," he lied. Another death on his hands. He might have just as well murdered Andy himself. He hoped to God a part of Andy's body didn't end up in his sink like Blunt's had.

"What's wrong?"

He sighed. "Just getting sick of it."

"We all are." She frowned. "Shoot. Come in. I've got to get these groceries into the fridge."

Unzipping his jacket, he followed her into the kitchen where she slipped a hair tie from her wrist and scraped her hair back into her familiar ponytail. "Need any help?"

"No." She rummaged inside a grocery bag and pulled out a couple of packages of frozen vegetables. "Just need to get these put away and get some type of food into Nicole's stomach. I'm sure Katie can whip something up too."

After closing the top freezer door, she turned around. Face flushed, she stared back at him with those luminous eyes of hers.

His chest tightened painfully. Shit. He needed to leave right now. He felt like a bastard.

She glanced at his hand and nodded to the area where he'd lost a good part of his flesh. "How is your hand?" she murmured in a low voice, no doubt mindful of Nicole and Katie within earshot. "I feel awful for not asking sooner. You haven't had problems with it since, have you?"

"No." He flexed his hand. "No scars or anything. Good as new."

"You said you've had it happen to you before. What is it because of the mercury?"

With his hands tightening into fists at his sides, he tried to brush the question off with a shrug. He hated everything to do with those years. "There have been a couple of situations, mercury being one of them."

She must have sensed he didn't want to talk about his past or decided it was not the time to ask fifty questions because she nodded and changed the subject. But as she pulled out more food from a grocery bag, her brow deepened, and her eyes clouded with concern. "There was a woman here today. It took me a bit to realize she was the one that helped Nicole. Something was off about her. She was interested in the medallion, and—"

"Why didn't you mention it before? Right when I came in?"

"Well, I kind of forgot after you told me someone was *murdered.*" She stressed the last word in a harsh whisper while waving a box of macaroni and cheese at him. "I was getting around to it, believe me. I wasn't about to forget the woman. She had some choice words about you. Hate might be a good word to describe what she thinks of you." Her gaze narrowed. "She's like you, isn't she?"

"Hey, Mom! Is dinner done?" Nicole appeared in the doorway from the hall and rushed into the kitchen.

"Um, not yet. Sorry."

Katie followed at a more sedate pace and hovered in the entryway. "I probably could put something together. I'm not the best cook, but I know how to boil water."

Amanda laughed, but Gabriel wasn't fooled by her lighthearted smile. Her white-knuckled grip on the boxed meal said it all. "Don't worry, I've got a couple of frozen dinners I can stick in the microwave. If not that, I've got macaroni and cheese with some fresh broccoli if there are any takers."

Nicole leaned over the kitchen island. "What type of frozen?"

He cleared his throat. "I better let you take care of Nicole. Meet me at Wombats at the end of tonight's shift. I'll explain about—I'll explain." He wanted to elaborate but he could not with Nicole and Katie right there and looking like they weren't going to move any time soon. She obviously wanted to argue, but with an audience, there wasn't much either one of them could discuss.

He pivoted and strode from the room and out of her house.

〜◎〜

With the box of macaroni and cheese in one hand, Amanda watched him go. What the…? She'd never understand men. She scowled at the spot he'd just vacated. One minute he was overbearing and the next he couldn't run fast enough away from her.

"Don't worry about dinner," Katie interrupted her thoughts. "I can put together mac and cheese with broccoli while you get ready for work."

"I seriously don't know what would have happened if I hadn't found you." Amanda shook her head with a smile.

"Right back at you!" Katie grabbed the box of macaroni from her and motioned with it to the hall. "Go get ready. I've got you covered."

She gave Katie a quick hug and hurried to her room, and then chucked her shirt and jeans in the hamper before running a shower.

Amanda managed to get ready, eat, and help clean up with fifteen minutes to spare before she needed to get to the department. She grabbed her gun from the safe in her room, holstered it, and pulled her hair back into her standard ponytail. Maybe one day she'd cut it all off and wear it short, but she was vain and liked her long hair.

Before she rushed from the house, she hugged Nicole and warned, "Remember—"

"I know, don't open the door for anyone."

"We'll be fine, Amanda." Katie smiled at her. "I've got Nicole taken care of. Anyone will have to get past me to get to her."

"Thank you, Katie." The young girl's words were touching. And she believed her. Katie had a great work ethic, was fiercely loyal toward her mother, and had a deep fondness for Nicole. "I'll call to check up on you a little later."

When she stepped from the house, Amanda locked the door and jiggled the knob to make sure it was secure. Yeah, she was worried about leaving both girls with that woman hanging around. But Katie had a good head on her shoulders, so she felt pretty secure having them behind closed doors.

The shift was quiet, boring, and exactly what she'd wanted when she moved to Spirit Lake, but it was long. By the time she walked into the department at its end, she was tense, irritable, and not liking the idea of being social.

Travis Perry was leaning against the edge of his desk, arms folded. With his collar askew and the remaining strands of hair on the top of his head tossed about and over his bald pate, it looked as if he'd been hit by a microburst and lost. Beside him stood Josh McKinney with boats for shoes and hands at odds with his lanky frame. He was probably one of the nicer cops in the department and had a massive crush on Katie. He'd graduated from the academy three years ago.

The lead detective on the case wasn't around. She didn't really know either man well. She was sure, though, they'd overheard her very public conversation with Freer and the hickey/curling iron incident. No doubt hickeys and her name were going to be synonymous for years, she thought in disgust.

But no amount of embarrassment or desire to rush

from the department was going to stop her from asking a couple of questions. "Hey, Travis. I hear you were—"

"You and everyone else." He grimaced, his thin lips disappearing into a flat line.

"How bad was it?"

"Never seen anything like it, and I have only a couple more years before retirement." He rubbed at his jowls. "Andy didn't deserve that. Hell, no one does." Travis searched her face. "Your luck's worse than mine. You came across two ravaged bodies."

Josh rubbed the back of his neck with a large, knuckled hand. "From what I've heard and seen, they weren't any better than Scott's call."

"It's not something I want to repeat," Amanda admitted. "Were there any missing body parts?"

"His fucking heart." His brows drew into one dark slash across his sizable brow. "There was blood everywhere. Did they write on the wall in Blunt's case? I didn't hear or read anything like that on the others."

"No." Amanda wrapped a finger around her ponytail, twisted the strands around several times before letting go. "What did it say?"

"'This one is for you.'"

"A revenge killing?"

"Who knows? All I know is that we need to get this sick bastard, and soon. We can't afford to lose someone else." Travis's lips dipped at the corners. "Who does that type of stuff? I'll never get it."

"Maybe we're not supposed to," Josh murmured. "We're here to protect, not ask questions."

"Yeah, like we've been doing a hell of a job doing that," Travis muttered.

"We'll get him, or them," Amanda assured before retreating to her desk. The cushion groaned with her weight as she rolled her chair over to the phone. She stared at it for a long moment and then decided to hell with it. She dialed Jennifer's cell.

"You're even worse than everyone else," Jennifer said the moment she answered. "I stopped answering the office phone long ago. At least the others don't contact me on my personal phone."

"Would you believe I'm calling to see if you want to get a drink on your next day off?"

Jennifer laughed. "Not bloody likely. But I'll take you up on it. I need a freaking break, even if it's just an hour. I've got to check to see what slot I can put you in. Seriously. Between band practice, work, hockey practice, work, and volunteering for the school dance..."

"I'm sure you're buried. No pun intended with these killings."

"Never. Ever. Been this busy. Not even in Detroit." Jennifer sighed. "So give. What do you want to know about this latest killing?"

Amanda ran a thumb along the medallion's chain resting along the back of her neck. The cross lay hidden beneath her uniform, the weight of it a continual reminder of things she had little knowledge of.

She thought of that strange blonde who'd taken a liking to Nicole. The woman was somehow tied to Gabriel. She'd been thinking of it from the moment the woman noticed the medallion. "Do you think a woman could do it?"

"Attack and kill three strong white males? We're not talking a gun, but knife victims. These are men who could have easily fought back. Even a woman on steroids and/or a champion weightlifter would have had trouble murdering the latest victim. Andy was over 6 feet and a good 250 pounds. Also, there are only a few contusions on his body. He was either taken by surprise, asleep, or a willing victim. But…"

"What?"

"He was none of those things. He was found in the middle of the kitchen. There was an open beer bottle on the counter. From the contents, it looked like he took one or two swallows from the bottle. Also, preliminaries show he did have alcohol in his system. It was almost like he had company, but no one could find fingerprints outside of the family's."

"Do you think someone in the family—"

"Not from what I hear. Resnick knew the guy. Andy wasn't married, but he had family in town. They're good people according to Resnick. There's no motive—no insurance policy, no strange or recent changes to his will."

"I swear, you're a walking encyclopedia. You have more information than even Resnick or anyone else in the department has."

Jennifer chuckled. "It's called being damn good at what I do."

"Modest, eh?"

"Hell, no."

"What about markings? Anything similar to the others?"

"Yeah. Another symbol. Also Jakes' heart is missing like Swansons'. Blunt so far is the only one who didn't have his chest ripped open."

"Do you think it's a ritualistic killing?"

"No. Not with the way the body was found. Granted, I'm getting thrown as to the reason why they're taking the heart. I guess it could be some type of trophy to them."

How about you come down and check it out? I've sent you pics of the others, but maybe if you come down in person, it might jog your memory of any of the gangs you've worked with in Chicago. Plus, I know you're dying to get a look. Just keep your mouth zipped."

Amanda glanced at her cell. She hadn't yet seen Gabriel come in after his shift. She'd text, let him know she needed to run an errand before meeting up at Wombats, and give him a time she'd show up. "I just need a minute to finish up here, and I'll be right over."

It took her fewer than 10 minutes to get to the morgue. When she popped her head into her friend's office, Jennifer got up from the chair behind her desk with a groan.

"Ugh, 38, and I feel like I need to retire. I swear I've been living here 24/7. If my face gets any paler, they'll think I've escaped from the morgue."

Jennifer's usually vibrant red hair seemed faded, while it looked like the long hours had leeched the normally rosy hue from her cheeks.

"Hopefully, we'll get this perp soon."

"Someone better. My family life is in the toilet." Jennifer led the way from the office to the elevator. "Adrian is getting sick of being a soccer mom, taxi driver, and all-around daycare center with me out of the picture much of the time."

Amanda grimaced. "I can only imagine. It's good you have Adrian."

"Well, hopefully, I keep having him around. But who knows if things keep going with my workload."

She gave Jennifer a sharp look as they stepped into the empty elevator and the other woman pressed the button for the basement. "You're not having any problems, are—"

"No—No, not at all. He's been perfect. The guilt is getting to me, though." It was Jennifer's turn to grimace.

"Well, I'm sure your schedule will ease up soon. The killer is too brazen, too angry. All that emotion will get them caught or killed." Amanda encouraged her friend as the elevator dinged and swished open. Stepping into the hallway, she waited for the other woman to go first. "Did forensics find out what the knife was made of?"

"Not yet. They're swamped. I should know within another 48 hours."

"Let me know as soon as you find out," Amanda urged. She wanted these murders over with. She wanted to move on, to have a normal life, to have Nicole free of fear. Damn it, she wanted to run away, but she'd already fled Chicago. Moving to another city or town wasn't going to stop Nicole's night terrors, or keep crazy people from acting out.

A crease formed between Jennifer's eyes and she sent Amanda a curious look as they walked down a long corridor. "Do you know more than you're telling?"

"No." Which was pretty much the truth. Amanda didn't know a damn thing, but she had her suspicions. Suspicions that sounded crazy and ones she didn't dare voice to anyone until she talked to Gabriel.

She followed Jennifer into a large refrigerated room with light-gray linoleum from wall to wall and white unadorned walls. Five gurneys rested at the side of the room. Two were occupied.

Amanda shivered even though she'd left her winter jacket on. There was something about a morgue that gave her the creeps, although she'd stepped into a number of them. Probably too many horror movies as a teenager. The two bodies on the gurneys weren't going to magically pop up, unzip themselves from their body bags, and jump onto the floor to go after her.

There were no such thing as vampires, zombies, or anything remotely like that. Take that back. There was Gabriel. Gooseflesh raced over her arms and neck again.

"We had a car accident earlier today," Jennifer was saying. "It's pretty gruesome. I hated to do it, but we had to have someone come in and identify the victim. That's never fun for both sides. Andy Jakes is over here." She moved to the gurney closest to the wall, then unzipped the bag, the noise sounding far too loud in the sterile room. She peeled back the plastic enough for Amanda to get an unobstructed view of the victim's face and upper torso.

Amanda flinched. She'd expected ugly, but actually getting up and personal with a savagely mutilated body was worse. Even the last couple of killings hadn't prepared her for another brutal slaying.

"We have another tattoo. The same as the others. The carvings have various differences, but for all intents and purposes, they're the same design."

Amanda leaned over the body, quickly looked away from where his heart had been ripped from his chest and stared at the circle carved into the flesh below the breastbone and by the shoulder of the victim—Andy. She needed to remember he'd been alive days before. No doubt, family and friends were now grieving for him. This time, though, she really looked at the carving.

It was a circle like the others. She peered closer. Wow, there was a face, large eyes, and a tongue cut into the flesh. Dragging air into her lungs through clenched teeth, she narrowed her gaze to hide the shock that roiled through her.

"Something the matter?"

"Nothing. Nothing at all." Amanda shifted, then shifted again. The loud rush of blood pulsing against her ears drowned out much of Jennifer's words.

"What do you think?" The other woman looked at her, brows raised.

Amanda managed to catch the tail end of her conversation and took a stab at a reply. "I don't know what to think." Her voice sounded tinny in the large room. "It looks like the same carving as the others. Yeah, there are similarities to those in Chicago, but the tattoos I saw were far more intricate than this. This one's primitive and childlike. It reminds me of prehistoric cave etchings."

"They're primitive because carving someone up takes time and a creative hand. A tattoo with a complicated design can take 5 hours or longer."

Amanda looked away from the body and met Jennifer's rueful gaze. She wanted to escape but had to make some small talk. If she didn't, the other woman would know something was off. She forced a smile and lifted an eyebrow. "Is that experience talking?"

"'Fraid so."

"I didn't know you had any tattoos." Amanda shifted, and smothering the urge to crack her knuckles, stuffed her thumbs into the front pockets of her pants.

Her friend's lips curved into a half-smile. "I was smart enough to put it in a place I can hide. But it's bigger than shit on my back." She made a face. "No, I'm not going to tell you what it is. You can just imagine."

Amanda smirked. "Must be pretty bad. At least you escaped a neck or face tattoo."

Jennifer wrinkled her nose. "Not effing likely. I can't even imagine having something like that for the rest of my life."

"Well, one of these days I'll get it out of you." Amanda joked as the medical examiner covered the victim's body.

"Maybe after a half dozen shots," Jennifer countered as she led them out of the room and back to the elevator. "Which reminds me, we still have to meet up for a drink."

Amanda sighed. "Oh, how about after we get these killings solved?"

"Sounds like a plan." Jennifer waved a hand at her as they exited the elevator on the ground floor and parted, moving in different directions.

Amanda nodded, then headed for the main entrance and opened the door. Cold air rushed inside and hit her in the face. Shivering, she pulled her collar closer to her jaw, then stuffed her fisted hands into her jacket pockets. Mindful Jennifer might be watching, she walked across the parking lot, while taking slow measured breaths. *Easy. Calm.* But inside she was a mess.

Once inside her car, she struggled to pull the medallion's chain from around her neck, but the clasp caught on her ponytail.

"Shit!" She ripped the chain from her hair, pulling out several strands from her scalp in her hurry. With a trembling hand, she palmed the cross and stared down at the carvings within the metal circle.

She'd never paid attention to the design, thinking that it was too worn and old to really see any type of pattern or design, other than some kind of face with vines branching out from it. But now…now, the circle, the design…the etching of the face with its tongue sticking out and bulging eyes screamed back at her.

The same design that had been carved on Andy stared back at her. Yes, there were some differences. The lines on the body hadn't been so precise. But they were the same crude image.

She tightened a fist around the medallion and closed her eyes, but the design burned into her mind. Just what the hell was Gabriel into? He couldn't be involved in the Mexican Mafia, could he? That didn't explain the sister.

Was he the killer all this time and laughing at her and everyone around him?

Amanda glanced at the clock on her dashboard.

Shit. Shit. Shit.

She was scheduled to meet him in 10 minutes.

CHAPTER 14

S o?" Amanda stared back at Gabriel with narrowed eyes, rigid jaw, and pinched brow. She wrapped her ponytail between a thumb and forefinger. "Where did you want to start?"

He hated the coolness in her brown eyes. But what did he expect? She could have left him for dead the other night, called for backup, or done several other things. But instead, she had been patient and waited to hear him out. He owed her more than an explanation, but at the idea of reliving a time he had barely survived—if he could call it that—a clammy sweat crawled between his shoulder blades and down his spine.

Gabriel sat across the table from Amanda in a booth at the back of Wombats. He should have picked somewhere different, but few people frequented the restaurant at that time of night, and he didn't see her agreeing to meet somewhere other than a public place. The only good out of the week so far was the state had tested for mercury poisoning, they had found none, and the owner was able to keep the doors open. "A fire in the kitchen" had been the owner's excuse for the place closing down briefly.

He leaned over the table, mindful how his voice could carry. Did she have the medallion on? There was a good chance she did. He needed to make sure he didn't remain too close to her for any length of time. Otherwise, the mercury inside the cross would drain his energy.

Where did he start? The beginning? The end? At this point did it matter? All of it was pain. A festering wound that had never healed.

She flicked her ponytail over her shoulder, opened her mouth to say something, but snapped it shut. Something in her eyes shifted. Fear? Something different? He could not tell. Did it even matter? After he spilled his guts, he would never be able to touch her again. Which was crazy to even think. Like he'd had a chance since nearly dying at her feet in the church…

He slid his cup of coffee closer to himself on the Formica table. "We had left Spain—that is, Mayor and her family, our brother Luys, and me—along with others wanting a new life. We had barely made landfall less than thirty days before we were captured." His words sounded rusty and unused, even to him. "Or I should say, sold."

Amanda's brows arched. "As in slavery?"

"Yes." He dipped his head briefly and cupped his coffee in both hands, letting its warmth seep into his chilled palms. Right then, he didn't think he would ever get warm again.

"That just doesn't make sense. I've never heard of whole families being forced into slavery. Not in this day. Something like that wouldn't go unnoticed. Yeah, I know there's human trafficking in the US, but that's more the sex trade. You're talking about sisters and brothers, and you don't fit the image…"

"Of what?"

"I don't know." She shrugged.

"A victim?"

A flush darkened her cheeks. "Well, you're male, strong, capable of taking care of yourself more than many."

"It's called being jumped in the middle of the night." He rubbed the back of his neck to ease the stiff muscles. He should be offended, but he was not, because he could have easily made the same assumption, looking at a man of his size. "Let me explain…" He cleared his throat. He needed to appear calm, lucid, because everything he intended to disclose was beyond anything normal. "The others in our group hated us. More so, my sister. They found her odd and labeled her a witch. Even though we tried to allay everyone's fears, we could not stop the rumors from spreading. By the end, they considered us worse than the dirt they walked upon, and no better than the locals they despised."

He frowned down at his coffee as the light from the ceiling gleamed against the dark liquid. Holy Mother. By vocalizing the words aloud, they gave the past power, concrete form.

"My family and I, along with a dozen others, were sold to the Tlaxcalans. Or, I should say, were given. They hated Mayor, feared her, but I didn't think they would ambush us and drag us from our home. It was stupid of Luys and me to think we had more time to smother the growing allegations and soothe everyone's apprehensions."

"That's awful! And who are the Tlaxcalans?"

"They were allies. They hated the Mexica and

wanted them slaughtered. The two races had been at war with each other for years. But we never reached Tlaxcala. Pedro de Alvarado had provoked an open revolt by massacring 600 nobles, and we were in the crosshairs. During the siege, they captured us for their next festival, Tlacaxipehualiz. A quick death would have been better. But it was Mayor and her strange coloring. They had never seen anyone with such blonde hair, and because they realized we were related by birth to Mayor, they considered us, like Mayor, unusual, and decided to use a different sacrificial ceremony."

"I'm getting really confused here. This sounds like we're in the medieval ages. Who are 'they'?"

"The Aztec."

Amanda snorted. "The Aztecs? You've got to be kidding if you think I'm going to buy that."

Gabriel met and held her gaze. He waited as she stared back. After a moment, the fierce light in her gaze dimmed.

"That's impossible," she insisted.

"But I am here. Living in spite of what the Aztecs did to us."

"That would mean you're hundreds of years old." She shook her head, her words rising in volume. "That's not possible." Glancing around the room, she lowered her voice, insisting in a harsh whisper, "It can't be possible."

Gabriel looked over his shoulder to see if anyone might have heard. The murmur of a couple on the other side of the diner drifted toward them, but they looked absorbed in their own drama, while the waitress had disappeared in the back, and Scott sat behind the front desk area, too far away to hear. Even if someone were close enough to eavesdrop, they would think he and Amanda were crazy or high on some illegal substance. "But it is. You know it's true. Your gut is telling you it is. The signs are all there."

She leaned her head back against her cushioned seat and stared up at the ceiling in silence.

His jaw tensed. He waited. And he waited some more. He could not remember a time he had felt this raw or exposed. He wanted Amanda to look at him, to show him that she didn't hate him.

"Would you like me to stop? Walk out of here and pretend I didn't say a word?

She dropped her head back down and met his gaze again. She swallowed audibly, the motion of her throat visible above the collar of her uniform.

His chest eased. She hadn't looked at him with horror, jumped up, or raced from the restaurant. At least not yet...

"The symbols," she said in a hushed voice, "on the cross you gave—on the bodies. The Mexican Mafia has nothing to do with the killings."

"No. This is all from another time. A place of violence and brutality. And of fear."

"What happened after you were captured? Obviously, you weren't sacrificed. I don't know much about the Aztecs, other than they were a bloody tribe. Why didn't they kill you? From what I've read of the period, there had to be a good reason…" She cupped her coffee and took a sip.

"When Fernand de Brusa sold us off to Xicohten-catl and his fellow tribesmen, he warned them of Mayor being a witch."

She cocked her head to the side and placed her cup back on the table. "Why did they think she was a witch?"

"Her blonde hair." He didn't like mentioning the other reason, because it was more complicated. A label didn't describe the complexities of Mayor.

Amanda nodded. "It's incredibly pale to the point where it looks more like it's from a bottle than anything natural. With everyone else having dark skin and hair, I'm sure she looked very unusual. But I can't see someone's hair getting them in trouble. Unless she spurned the advances of a powerful man?"

"There was a don in Spain. Alonso Rodrigo de Avila was his name." He could not keep the hatred from his voice. He'd thought he'd gotten over it long ago. But the sudden rage inside his chest was too powerful to deny. "He took a liking to Mayor and a deep dislike of her husband."

"She's married?"

"She was. I am not sure it was a happy union near its end. Mayor has always been a bit fragile, and I don't think Juan understood how to deal with her." Gabriel shook his head at Amanda's raised brow. "Mayor was a different person when she was younger. She was also naive and full of life and love. But Alonso decided she would be better off widowed. He murdered Juan to get to her. Then he raped her. I'd been gone from the village, traveling, and could not get to her in time. We had no means to fight him, no money, no power, being little more than peasants. But abusing her physically was not enough. He hated her rejection and retaliated. He started accusing her of witchcraft, of killing the livestock in a nearby village, and causing one of the locals to have a stillborn child. It didn't take much for the villagers to turn. They had always considered her strange to begin with. We fled, leaving everything behind, and managed to escape from Spain. We colored Mayor's hair with brambles, but we ran out of the dye, and soon her hair returned to its natural color. We had fled one horror only to find ourselves in a far worse one."

He glared down at his coffee. A pulse throbbed by his temple. By all that was holy, going back was painful. The futility, the powerlessness...

"But you're not telling me everything. This followed you to a different country. I would think you would have found others who would keep silent even if they discovered the truth."

He rolled his shoulders to expel the tension across his neck and shoulders. It didn't help. When Amanda tilted her head to the side and he read the genuine concern and intelligence in her eyes, he decided that it was best she know the entire truth. She deserved it with his sister arriving in Spirit Lake, and he wanted her to realize why Mayor was doing what she was doing. "She developed a condition on the voyage... You have to understand, times were different. They were filled with superstition and fear. Science..." He shook his head in disgust. "At times, I was no better than the others, I was fearful a demon had overtaken her body.

"A doctor was on board. He was far worldlier than any of us. When I think back, he was the one who opened my eyes to other possibilities, of knowledge, of science. He convinced Luys and me that Mayor had some type of disease. He tried numerous methods of bloodletting. Leeches, cupping, extracting blood through an artery in her arm. He finally concluded she had a mental disorder."

Amanda frowned. "I have an idea I'm not going to like what you have to say." She carefully placed her coffee back on the table. "What type of disorder?"

"They didn't have a name for it then. She would have been either burned as a witch or locked away in an asylum."

"Can she get help now for it?"

"Yes, if she was normal. But she's not. They did something to her, Luys, and me. We tried long ago to help her with medicine." He sighed. "None of it worked."

"I'm sure there's got to be some developments since then."

"Luys believes with cognitive therapy and the latest medication, Mayor would be able to function as an adult, but she does not consider herself sick, and she is not going to listen to either one of us. Right now, her hate blinds her. She refuses to acknowledge she has schizophrenia. Unlike some cases, she can be highly functional."

Amanda glanced down at her coffee as she bit down on her lower lip.

Gabriel tensed. He had seen Amanda's expression before she banked it and was surprised—he had expected more from her, but he should have known. She didn't understand. Few did unless they had a loved one with the condition. "She was never dangerous or violent before."

"But you said yourself that she's dangerous—"

"Not because of her illness. She's dangerous because of what she went through. I'm surprised she can function fully at times. But it's her rage and hatred that fuels her and makes her act out."

"Why? I mean why the hate?"

Gabriel shrugged. "Why does anyone hate? Fear, I think. Maybe fear of being alone for the rest of her life. Of never having children."

"But there has to be more of a reason." Amanda stared back, her gaze far too shrewd.

"Her daughter. They did things to her daughter no mother should ever see." His throat tightened with emotion. He hated the past; he hated the horror, the memories, and everything to do with it.

Amanda grabbed her ponytail and tugged at the end before she twirled it between her thumb and index finger.

He shuddered as he cupped his coffee with one hand. "Did you know the Aztecs had their own form of a zoo? For humans? We had our own pen. But we were treated worse than their livestock. They would use sticks and—"

"Gabriel. Don't. Don't do this to yourself. I'm sorry." She started to rise but sank back down in her seat. Instead, she reached across the table and clutched at his free hand.

He took her fingers in his grasp. Welcomed them, welcomed their warmth, their pressure. He also welcomed the sympathy, empathy in her eyes. But not the pity. He didn't need pity.

"They took her," he whispered as the years tumbled away. "They took her right from Mayor's arms."

"Who?"

"I couldn't stop them. I could not do a damn thing to save Maria."

"Gabriel…"

"They killed her. In front of Mayor, in front of Luys and me. They sliced her chest open." He covered his mouth. Shit, the pain. The guilt. Even now. It wrenched at his gut, his battered heart, his soul—if he even had one. "She was more fragile than Luys and me. After they murdered her daughter, Mayor cracked."

Memories of their capture flooded his head. Too many of them. They swirled and pecked at his brain like vultures on carrion. His hand on his coffee tightened. Dark liquid sprayed onto the table and across Amanda's cheek and brow. Jagged pieces of pottery cut into his palm.

He jerked his hand back. "Shit!"

Amanda jumped to her feet.

Gabriel brushed at his bleeding hand. Then he snatched a napkin to clean up the blood while growing aware of stares from the other diners.

Amanda rushed around the table, sank on the cushioned bench beside him, and grabbed at his wrist. "You need stitches."

He frowned at his hand and lowered his voice. "I've had worse. I'm fine. I have caused enough of a scene."

"Gabriel."

"See." He dipped the corner of his napkin in his ice water and wiped more blood from his wound. "It's superficial."

Her grasp on his wrist tightened, and she tugged sharply until she captured his gaze. "But what did they do to you, since they didn't sacrifice you? They must have done something—something that makes you different than the rest of us." She didn't let go of his wrist. "Tell me."

"Mercury. Liquid silver. They found it fascinating. They used it as a symbolic representation of water when they worshiped their god Quetzalcoatl. The ceremony was cloaked in secrecy and performed by one of the highest priests in their hierarchy." Gabriel stared down at his hand and the stained napkin. The blood from the cut to his palm had congealed.

"And?"

He glanced back at her unflinching stare. "They killed all three of us."

CHAPTER 15

They killed you?" She released his wrist as if scalded

He crumpled the napkin in his fist. "Yes."

"But how?"

Holy Mother. How did he answer that? He stared at the ruins of his coffee cup and swept the shards into a small pile with another napkin. Finally, he glanced up and met her gaze. "Do you really want to know?"

"I…" Her gaze softened. "I don't want you to relive something you find excruciatingly painful. I know you've had a hard time talking about this so far."

His cell phone dinged with a text. Then two consecutive chimes quickly followed. He pulled his phone from his pocket and thumbed the security button.

Are you enjoying yourself with your new girlfriend?

Setting the phone on the table, Gabriel frowned down at the phone's screen.

Do you really think she is safe after Teresa?

Are you a fool?

Have you not learned?

"Not again…" he whispered.

"What's wrong?"

"Nothing," Gabriel murmured, careful to keep his voice neutral and his hand from strangling his phone, as another text chimed.

"Let me see."

"No. You can't—"

Have you been in your home recently? I have been promising you a present.

Amanda pulled the phone from under his palm. When he moved to grab it from her, she sprang from the bench, jumped back from the table, and looked down at his phone. "She's talking about me, isn't she?"

He pressed his fist against the side of his neck until his knuckles cracked.

"And who is this Teresa?"

"My wife."

"Your wife? You're *married?*"

"No. Not anymore." He couldn't rid himself of the pain. It kept ramming him in the chest again and again. "She died a long time ago."

Amanda paced to her side of the booth and pivoted back around to face him. "Son of a bitch. She's going to try to kill me, isn't she?"

He rose to his feet.

She didn't wait for his answer but strode toward the restaurant's exit. He flung a ten on the table and hurried after her. He caught up with her outside.

Snow feathered the night and caught on her hair.

"You don't know how much I want to hit you right now." She pointed his phone at him, her gaze mixed with horror and fury. "You're a stinking bastard. You knew that sleeping with me was going to make me a target, didn't you? But you went ahead anyway."

"I didn't know Mayor was in town. At least, not that first time."

"You should have stayed the hell away from me."

"I tried, but could you have stayed away from me?" he asked gently. "Can you honestly tell me that?"

"I thought you were normal!" She shook her head, her ponytail whipping to both sides. "I really, really seriously want to hit you right now." She clutched his phone in both hands and glared at its face. Suddenly she stilled. "What does she mean by present?"

"She likes leaving things for me." Holy Mother, admitting everything was killing him inside. He should have ended everything when Teresa had died.

"What's that supposed to mean?"

"Body parts."

"Are you freaking serious?"

He rubbed a palm along his jaw and chin. "I need to check my place now just in case Mayor has left something—"

"We need to call this in. She's killing these people, and you're not doing a damn thing."

Gabriel tamped down his anger. Amanda had a reason to be upset, but she didn't know everything. "It's not that simple. She's an expert at keeping herself hidden. She is not like a normal person. The elements don't bother her. Freezing temps, storms. They don't faze Mayor."

But Amanda wasn't listening to him. "I need to turn you in. Go to the department and report her. You should report yourself as an accomplice."

"Listen to yourself, Amanda. Think this through. What are you going to tell them?"

"I'm sure I can think of something."

"Like what? How would you explain Mayor to Freer and everyone else? Do you think they're going to believe you? You're not Freer's favorite person right now. And do you think anyone is going to take you seriously once you start talking about a fragile-looking woman as a serial killer? Especially when they know the killer is strong enough to take down a man so efficiently there are no signs of a struggle?"

She scowled at him. "There's a way. I just need time to think this through."

"We don't have time. It will take weeks for them to wrap their brain around what Mayor is, what I am. They don't know her. They have no idea what rage will make her do. I need to stop her myself."

"When? When someone else dies? For all I know, I'm next!" Amanda threw his phone at him. Ducking, he caught it before it smacked him in the head. "Well, we better go check what's she left you. I might be next, and I want to know exactly what I'm up against. Better to face her now than when I'm distracted by something else."

She jumped into her car and kicked the engine into gear.

Gut twisting in panic, he hurried to his own car, but by the time he started the engine, she had already raced from the parking lot. Holy Mother. Amanda had no clue what she was up against with Mayor.

Five minutes later, Gabriel crept his car along Lake Street. Then he turned off onto Gary Avenue. Fortunately, Amanda had enough sense not to park in front of his property. Instead, she'd parked before the rise in the road beside a large stand of bushes and trees, though still visible from his house. She was already out of her car by the time he slammed to a halt behind her vehicle. He closed his door with a heavy hand and caught up to her on the sidewalk.

When he grabbed her arm, she tried to shrug off his hand, but he didn't let go.

"Seriously?" She glared up at him. "Do you mind?"

"Yes, I do mind. You can't rush around like you're invincible. Mayor's dangerous. She's not like everyone else. She's strong. Stronger than you, than me." He grunted. "I don't want you going inside. Period. I can't protect you from her."

"I don't need your protection!" Amanda muttered while eyeing Gabriel's property through a patch of dense bushes. "Let. Go. Of. My. Arm."

He glanced down at her hand on the butt of her gun strapped to her belt. "A gun is not going to do anything to her."

Her gaze gleamed in the darkness. "What do you mean?"

"They're useless."

"What else is useless?" she asked, her voice harsh with displeasure. "So are you saying that if I shot you now, right in the heart, nothing would happen to you?"

"It would hurt like hell, and I would be out of commission for a while, but it wouldn't kill me."

"But mercury will?"

"Yes…"

Her chin lifted a notch.

He briefly closed his eyes and rubbed at his nose. "There *are* a couple of other things."

"Like what?"

"Beheading."

Amanda winced. "So chopping her head off will do it. Great. Just great. It sounds like I'm pretty useless." She tugged on her ponytail with one hand. "I'm starting to feel like I've stepped into a horror novel. Next, you'll be telling me I need to wear cloves of garlic around my neck. To top it off, we've got holy water to add to the mix. Seriously?"

"There's a reason behind the holy water. When the Catholic church settled in the area, they performed rituals to rid themselves of what they considered savages. They had their own primitive spells under the guise of prayer. They knew the Aztecs were playing around with mercury and working with the 'devil.' Somehow they found a way to fight back."

"That isn't what killed them off, was it?"

"No, but—"

She lifted a hand in protest. "This is all too much. I can't think. My head is already spinning with everything else."

"The medallion. Do you have it on you now?" He didn't release his grasp from around her upper arm even though he suspected she did, given the sluggish feeling of his body and mind.

"Yeah." She tugged at the chain around her neck until the silver cross slipped from beneath her uniform. The metal gleamed beneath the street lamp.

"Don't hesitate to use it against her. All you have to do is break the glass vial. A drop on her skin will stop her. Getting the metal on her clothing will keep her at bay. But I don't think it will come to that."

"And why's that?"

"Simple. Mayor does not want to die. Not really. Otherwise, she would have found a way to end her life long ago." He eased his hold on her arm, stepped closer to her, and peered down at her angry face. "If we check my place out, promise me that you will always be within a couple of yards of me? You might not think it, Amanda, but I do care for your welfare. I would have left immediately if I had known Mayor was behind the killings. Do you understand?"

For a long moment, Amanda stared up at him in silence. Finally, she nodded. "Yeah, but it doesn't make me feel any better. I like control, and right now, everything around me is out of control."

Gabriel let go of her arm and nodded toward his house before turning and leading the way. With Amanda within reach, he picked his way through the shadows. The snow against the soles of their shoes crackled into the night, while a small dog barked from a neighbor's yard. Everything seemed magnified as they reached the side door to his house. Since he had found Blunt's head in his sink, he had made a point of keeping all his doors and windows locked.

The knob turned easily in his hand and listed to one side. He'd locked the door earlier, but now wood frayed from around the door's faceplate. The damaged deadbolt hung drunkenly from the wood frame. The wood and metal looked as if someone had used a hammer or ax to get the door open. Mayor, of course...

He had not faced Mayor since they had captured her and put her away decades ago. And if he came across her after all those years...what would she say? What would *he* say when he finally confronted her? A wave of sadness and something deeper he could not decipher washed through him.

He glanced over at Amanda with her back against the wall, one hand holding the medallion around her neck and the other hovering near her gun. Moonlight reflected off her pale face with its fierce expression. To have a woman fight for him like that...he could only dream.

The door opened with a sigh as he stepped through the threshold and into the kitchen. A rustle of clothing indicated Amanda was right behind him. The streetlight by the road pierced through the window and onto the kitchen table and floor. Shadows clung to the corners, but they weren't thick enough to hide Mayor's platinum-colored hair. He inched toward the sink and shuddered in relief. Both sinks were empty.

Systematically they searched each room from the main floor to the second floor, and also into the basement. No sign of anyone. The only vandalism was the broken lock and door. Finishing back in the kitchen, Gabriel turned on the kitchen light.

Amanda blinked against the sudden light as she leaned a hip against the kitchen counter.

Gabriel stood several yards away, a hand resting against the corner of the refrigerator. The color had leached from his face. A good five years or more seemed to have etched lines on the sides of his mouth and across his brow.

Her anger dissolved, and she couldn't help feeling some sympathy. "She likes playing with you, doesn't she?"

He glanced her way, and it took a moment for his eyes to clear. "Yes. I would think I would learn."

She dreaded the answer but had to ask. "What did she leave you last time?"

"Blunt's head."

"Damn it, Gabriel. That's evidence. All this time you've known and not mentioned anything to anyone! What about his family? They deserve to have all his body buried and—" Then it hit her. "Where is it? His head."

He grimaced. "Taken care of. You don't want to know." Gabriel pushed off the fridge and stepped toward her. "And what would you suggest I do? It's all very well to think in black and white. But life's not that way. You should know that. What would I have accomplished, other than getting myself behind bars?"

"That's not true. You have a reputation for being a good cop. But I'm sure they would wonder what someone has against you and—"

"And tie me to the murders," he finished for her. "Which is something Mayor wants. I'm surprised she's not framed me in some way, but then she's probably waiting, biding her time for the perfect opportunity."

"If they find it on your property—"

"They won't." He folded his arms across his middle. "I'm not proud of what she's made me do. I've disregarded my ethics, lied, let her get away with murder. I've also protected her when that was the last thing I should have ever done. But I can never erase the memories of who she once was and the horrors she endured. And then there is Maria. Her child. She adored her. We all did." Unshed tears gleamed in his eyes until he blinked them away.

Amanda softened even more. She always was a sucker for lost causes, lost people, and couldn't turn away from someone in need even if she wanted to. Her mother's DNA was too deep inside of her. "Why is she so angry?" she asked gently. "It sounds to me like she wants to get even and has a vendetta against you from what you've been saying. What did you do to her?"

"Here." He turned around and pulled a bottle of wine from a rack on the counter. "How about I spill my guts with a glass of red? Or do you like white? Or beer? I might need to finish a bottle or two by the time I'm finished."

"No, red's fine."

After uncorking a bottle and filling two glasses, he handed her one. "You might want to sit. But then you might be fine with what I have to say after what you have already learned."

She followed him into the living room and sank down on the sofa as Gabriel turned on a floor lamp with muted lighting and then closed the blinds.

With a wine bottle in one hand and a glass in another, he sank down into a chair on the opposite side of the room from her and the medallion. He drank deeply, paused a moment, and then finished his glass before pouring himself another. He set the bottle on the coffee table in front of them.

"Okay, let's see." He frowned and wiped his mouth with the back of his hand. "Your medallion"—he paused, his expression suddenly guarded—"it used to be Mayor's."

Amanda stiffened in shock. "No wonder she was staring at it so oddly when she was at my place."

Gabriel twisted his mouth into a grim smile. "She was looking at the medallion oddly because she thought she had left it behind or destroyed it."

"What do you mean?"

"Luys and I were the ones who made her wear it."

"I don't understand how you can make anyone wear a necklace, never mind Mayor with her inordinate strength."

"As you've seen yourself, mercury is dangerous to me. It's just as dangerous to Luys and Mayor. The metal can kill within hours, if not minutes, if it comes into contact with our flesh, but it also has this strange ability to render us impotent, to the point, that it knocks us unconscious if it's encased in lead and on our body for any great length of time."

"But what about the medallion in your vehicle? Why doesn't that do anything to you?"

"Because there is no vial in it. There never was. Luys had three medallions made after we fled the Aztecs."

"So, if I've got this right, you forced the necklace on Mayor, which in turn rendered her unconscious. Something like Sleeping Beauty."

"Not quite. We knocked her out with a drug Luys formulated, and with the necklace on her for several hours, it eventually had enough power to immobilize her."

Amanda took a sip of wine. The liquid—rich and bold—slid down her throat. Somehow, one glass wasn't going to be enough. She was probably going to need the rest of the bottle—or a couple of Xanax—to get her through the next couple of days until they stopped Mayor. All the info from Gabriel was hitting her brain like a swarm of angry bees. She didn't know what to think, what to feel. "For how long was she unconscious?"

The room stilled. He took another deep swallow of wine as if to delay his answer.

"How long, Gabriel?"

CHAPTER 16

Finally, Gabriel admitted how long Mayor had been entombed. "Decades."

"Oh, my God." Amanda's hand tightened around her wine glass. "That's horrifying! And she survived all this time?"

His gaze darkened in what looked like shame. "You don't understand."

"Then make me understand."

"She has killed before. Many times. Not just strangers, but people Luys and I cared for. People I loved."

Amanda was beginning to understand. "She murdered your wife."

He finished his glass, set it on the coffee table with a distinct tremor in his hand, and rose to his feet. He paced the room with measured, controlled steps. "Yes. We needed to do something to stop her. Everything we had tried before had never worked—the two of us reasoning with her, Luys' numerous attempts at a medical miracle that might cure her. But she continued on a destructive path."

"Why didn't you just kill her?"

He pivoted and faced her, his expression stark. "Killing someone you love—a person you once adored? A woman who was once a beautiful, innocent child? A person you have shared horror after horror with, only to escape with what was left of the ruins of your life? We had a shared past and at one point a deep love for one another." He looked down at her with intense eyes. "Can you understand how difficult that is? Can you?"

Amanda thought back to all the family dynamics she'd come across as a cop. Her friend Danielle, working in social services, and all the stories she'd relayed—siblings, parents, and children vying for some twisted semblance of a relationship. All for what they considered love when love really had nothing to do with it.

Then she thought of her own relationship with her mother, who'd passed on a year after Amanda had graduated from college. She'd succumbed to cancer at such an early age, less than a year after her diagnosis. Amanda had considered her not only invincible, but a woman who could do no wrong, and had worshiped her as only a daughter could. But her mother had her own failings. Years after her father's death, Amanda had discovered a box of letters between her mother and a lover. Why her father had kept them, she didn't know and never would. But even with that blemish, Amanda would have moved heaven and earth to save her mother, would even have taken on her mother's cancer if she could. Love did that. It could turn a person into a hero, but that same love could make someone vulnerable, weak, or blind.

"I'm sorry, Gabriel. But you must see she's not only ruining your life, but the lives of innocents. She's a serial killer, highly dangerous, irrational, and a threat to anyone who comes into her path."

"I know. Holy Mother, I know. Both of us finally decided to put a stop to her when everything else failed."

Amanda's heart softened at the look of horror on Gabriel's face. How could it not? She was human and had experienced her own moments of fear at her mother's death. She whispered, "What happened?"

"I tried to end her life. We both did. When it came to finally acting on it, neither one of us could finish the job. Mayor escaped and went into hiding for years."

"And that's why she wants revenge."

"No. That's not the reason. After the death of her daughter, she hated the idea of either one of us being happy. If she thought for a moment we were getting close to being content with our lives, she would crush it—like a child destroying another's toys out of a fit of rage."

"So what is the reason?"

"When she surfaced again, she learned from others that I was happy with a wife and a life I enjoyed. She decided I was undeserving of both and killed Teresa."

"I'm so sorry!" The words felt insignificant and inappropriate.

"Teresa was the one who pushed and pleaded with us to kill Mayor. When Teresa revealed that to her, my sister, feeling betrayed, retaliated by murdering my wife.

"After that, I wanted my own revenge. I had lost all love for Mayor and grew to hate and despise her. We had discovered what mercury could do to us centuries before. What better way to stop Mayor than by immobilizing her and keeping her from killing anyone else? Why not keep her in an unconscious state until Luys or I learned of a way to heal her?

"We captured her. The medallion you are wearing now is the one we placed around her neck. It incapacitated her, rendering her helpless and fully unconscious. We then placed her deep in a cave, so she would no longer harm another soul."

"But she escaped…"

"Yes. Somehow someone found a way into the cave. Thinking the necklace valuable, they must have removed it from her neck. From there…I'm sure the victim didn't have the strength to fight against her."

"And now she's loose to kill again…"

"Because of me. I was too weak. We should have killed her. I hated her, but at the same time I couldn't find the strength to end her life, even knowing others would suffer because of her." His eyes darkened to almost black. "And crazy as it might seem, it never occurred to me that she might escape until we came across the medallion at Wombats. I don't know how long she's been roaming the streets killing or how she found me…"

Amanda stared up at Gabriel. Pain and anguish etched lines across his rugged face. Seeing both cut at her heart. She could imagine how hard it was to live with the guilt, the anger, the helplessness of dealing with a family member both loved and despised. She should be angry, filled with indignation, but who was she to judge and be so self-righteous when she'd turned her back on and closed her heart toward her father without hearing him out, without giving him a chance to love her? How would she have acted if she'd been given Gabriel's choices? Probably no better.

"Stop." She hated to see him so tormented. Setting her glass down by the wine bottle, she rose swiftly to her feet. "How were you to know? Nothing you did was deliberate. I understand now why you left without saying anything. You've dealt with the pain of your sister forever. How long was she hidden away in the cave?"

"Since before the Revolutionary War."

"I'm sorry." Again, such feeble words couldn't convey all she wanted to say. She moved toward him and placed a comforting hand on his arm. When he made a move to step backward, she tightened her grip. "I never knew what you were going through. All this time you've dealt with this alone."

"I had my brother."

"But no one else to share your burden," she whispered. "I know how it is to be alone. To be the one who has to be the strong one when all you want to do is crumble."

"Don't." He shook his head.

"Don't what?"

"Look at me like that."

"I can't... I...."

"I'm not strong." He edged toward her until her breasts pressed against the hard planes of his chest. "I have weaknesses like every other person. You already know that after tonight. I can only bend so much before I crack. Holy Mother, if you haven't realized it yet, you are one of my biggest weaknesses...or strengths."

She sank against his body as his hand cupped her shoulder and he dipped his head. The touch of his lips against her brow caught at her heart. Such a simple but tender gesture. Then she completely lost all ability to voice her thoughts. Savoring the warmth of his body beneath the knitted fabric of his sweater, she didn't look away from the heat in his gaze. Breathing suddenly became difficult, while awareness whispered through her body until it settled low in her belly. Her breasts grew heavy, and the room seemed suddenly warmer.

"Tonight…I want to forget for a little bit. To lose myself in your arms and pretend we're a normal couple. The moment you walked into the department, I knew I was in trouble." He tenderly slipped a loose strand of hair around her ear.

The whisper of his finger against her lobe sent a delicious shiver racing down her spine.

"But I can't get close for long with the mercury you have around your neck."

"That's easily remedied." Inching backward, she pulled the medallion from under her shirt, tugged it off, twisted around, and tossed it on the sofa. After she turned back, she met his dark, hot gaze and shattered just a little from the desire in his eyes. He cupped her cheeks in his large hands as his mouth grazed hers, soft like the sweep of a feather against her over-sensitized skin. His breath smelt of wine, while his lips… she could get drunk beneath their touch.

Memories of the previous time with Gabriel's flesh against her naked skin flooded her thoughts. The hardness of his body inside her. How his hands would clench her hips as he came into her… He'd made her feel feminine, powerful, and sultry all at the same time.

She gasped into his mouth as his lips turned suddenly demanding. She slid both hands up his arms and over his shoulders to wind her fingers in the sable texture of his hair. Sinking into his kiss, she pressed deeper against his body. Suddenly the clothing between them was too much. She wanted to feel his body—the heat, the silk, the hardness, all of him—against her. Her tongue eagerly met his as she continued to play with the strands of his hair. She swiveled her hips, needing to get closer. Someone groaned. She didn't know or care who. He felt so good.

Gabriel drew back for a moment, his breath sawing into his lungs. The rough texture of his jaw scraped against her cheek, her neck as he reached around and fumbled with her ponytail holder. With shaking hands, he released her hair and dragged his fingers through the locks.

Then he kissed her again, more thoroughly than before, deeper, hungrier, until she was shaking with need. The heat of desire rushed through her limbs and pooled low in her belly as she pressed harder against his chest. His body was tight. That was the only way to describe it. Every inch of him was hard. That idea weakened her legs even more, and she latched onto his shoulders for fear her legs would give from beneath her.

"Holy Mother, you taste like heaven," he whispered against her mouth. He delved beneath her shirt. "I want to savor every blessed inch of you."

His fingers felt like fire as they trailed across the small of her back and slid just below the waistband of her pants. The uniform's thick shirt and bulletproof vest were too confining. She wanted to rip everything off both of them so she could feel the heat of Gabriel's skin. He started tugging at her belt, and she was right there helping. Her hands shook so badly she was surprised she managed to pull at the zipper without it snagging in her rush to get her pants off. But then the material caught around her ankles and her clunky shoes.

"Here." Gabriel swept her up in his arms with ease

and carried her down the hall to his bedroom. He hit the bedroom light with an elbow. "I want to see every part of you this time."

A floor lamp rested beside a lounge chair in the corner and threw the room into deep shadows. Amanda glimpsed dark furniture and a painting of a wooded landscape, but little else as he set her gently on the edge of the mattress, then kneeled and unlaced her shoes as she pulled off her shirt and yanked at the Velcro ties of her vest. When everything was off except her panties and bra, she helped Gabriel with his clothing. She forced herself to slow down and enjoy his body as she helped strip him of his uniform, vest, and T-shirt, all the while touching, stroking, and kissing his body at every opportunity.

With them both fully naked, he dropped back onto the bed, taking her with him in one fluid motion.

Sucking in a breath, she lay on top of him, momentarily stunned at the feel of his naked body beneath her. He nibbled on her neck, and she arched involuntarily against the caress, her heart racing like crazy as he swept his tongue along her throat to nibble on her jaw and ear before turning to her mouth. She groaned as he palmed her ass and ground his cock against her belly.

Before she lost it right there, she pushed off his body, though somewhat reluctantly, and settled to his side while running a palm over his thick muscled chest. Moonlight caught against the lines of his body. A jagged mark ran from nipple to nipple, while another mark cut a swath from just below his collarbones. Six inches of scars. Her hand stilled on his stomach, which quivered beneath her fingers. Their last time together at her house, she'd seen some type of marking on his chest but hadn't really paid attention; she'd been so caught up in their passion.

"How did... who did..." But she knew, she knew. She tried to keep the horror from her voice, but she didn't think she'd managed it. She'd been too shocked.

"They cut me open during one of their ceremonies." He reached over and caught her wrist. "There is no pain now."

"But it must have been horrifying. I can't imagine what you went through."

"It's done and in the past."

But Amanda didn't believe him. How could something that traumatic not touch him on a daily basis? One day, maybe he would have enough trust in her to tell her the whole story. At least she hoped so. God, she wanted to take away some of his pain, if only for a short time. But for the moment, she would focus on the rest of the night.

She bent and pressed her lips to the scarred tissue below his right nipple and caressed the horizontal line with her tongue and lips. He stiffened for a moment, and she paused, her mouth hovering just above his skin.

Then his grasp on her wrist eased, and he shuddered, sinking into the mattress.

Touched and pleased by his capitulation, although his surrender was more mental than physical, she was encouraged. She eased her body over his, straddling both legs over his thighs. Loving the feel of his hair-roughened skin against her body, she continued to kiss a path across the horizontal mark. Once done, she moved upward and started on the vertical scar and moved slowly downward, not stopping at the end of the marking but continuing, ever so slowly, past his belly button. She paused along the hollow of one hip, finding pleasure in the silken texture. A quick glance showed he had one arm flung to one side and the other cradling his head as he stared back with hot, hungry eyes.

His erection quivered beneath her head and his deep shuddering breath filled the quiet of the room.

While keeping her gaze locked to his, she dipped her chin and licked him, a long wet stroke of her tongue, once, twice. Then she—

"Enough!" Gabriel grabbed both her wrists and dragged her up the length of his body. His hard planes and indentations fit beautifully against her.

She gasped as his cock nudged at her opening. The hunger, so crazy painful, caught her off guard. She couldn't remember feeling such a deep passion for another man. But Gabriel… she craved him like no one before him.

Sweat broke from Gabriel's brow. He wanted to dive into Amanda's body that second, take her right away, and to hell with being slow. At the same time he wanted those moments to last, he wanted to drag out every sensation, prolong the passion until it hurt. He used his weight and twisted around until she was beneath him, cradled in his arms with his hips resting between her thighs.

Closing his eyes, he twined his fingers into her hair as it draped over the pillow, buried his head, and breathed in the scent of lilac and an earthly, sensual fragrance he could not place. He'd always associate that smell with Amanda. Everything about her was sexy, confident, and mind-numbingly intoxicating. He was drunk on the taste, the scent, the silk of her skin as he ran his other hand over her forearm, the dip of her elbow, and up across the curve of her shoulder.

Her flesh quivered beneath his mouth as he licked and kissed both breasts, laving the tips until they were hard buds. He wanted her coming hard, long, and more than once. He wanted her to remember this night. He wanted her to forget everything but him and how he felt with his mouth on her and his cock inside her. He probed between her legs, and his fingers quickly became slick from her body. She was deliciously tight. Groaning, he got on all fours and backed over her body until he sank down between her thighs. He buried his head and flicked his tongue lightly over her clit.

Grabbing his skull, Amanda cried out and jerked off the mattress, but he held her hip down with one hand, forcing her to take his tongue and mouth. He licked, nibbled, and tongued her, then probed deeper into her slit. He used fingers and tongue, all the while searching, touching, delving. She started whimpering, bucking under him, but he didn't let up until she stiffened and cried out her release.

Wiping his mouth with the back of his hand, he rose on his knees and looked down at Amanda. He reveled in the flush on her cheeks, her body sprawled across his mattress, and her hand clamped around one side of the headboard. His chest tightened with emotion. If he wasn't careful, he was going to fall head over heels in love with her. Seeing her fully sated hardened his cock that much more, and all patience fled. She was wet and ready for him, so he caught her ass cheeks in both hands and arched his hips, embedding his cock into her body, fully seated. She was hot, wet, and perfect. Holy Mother, she was tight.

Beneath him, Amanda gasped, wrapped her legs around his waist, dug her fingers into his back, and arched to meet each one of his thrusts. When her bucking quickened, he lost it, coming hard and long, jerking into her until he was spent and unable to move. He collapsed but had just enough energy to twist to the side so he didn't crush her. He closed his eyes, brushed his lips against her damp brow, all the while running a palm up and down the curve of her hip as she lay on her side and inside the crook of his arm.

He brushed a stray strand of hair from her brow and curled it around her ear as he met her gaze. For a long moment, they silently stared at each other. There was a softness, a tenderness in her gaze he'd never seen from her before. The intimacy between them caught at him.

She snuggled against his side, and he nudged her closer with his arm. As the remnants of the moment dissolved, reality intruded and a new form of dread pressed hard against his chest.

"What's wrong?" Amanda lifted up on one elbow.

He had not realized how transparent he had been and frowned. "This time with you has been… I have a hard time explaining what I feel."

She placed a finger against his lips. "Don't. Let's just take one day at a time. This is new for both of us."

He nodded, but her words stoked his unease even further. "Mayor will not go away. That's not like her. By being with you again, I have again jeopardized your life.

I need to ensure you're safe. The only way to do that is to have no further contact."

She looked over at him with sober brown eyes and argued with a humorless laugh. "It's too late for that. She knows there's something between us. I saw it in her eyes the day she came to visit."

He had made far too many mistakes over the years—too many to count. He already knew what he must do, but it killed him to say the words aloud. "Then there is only one solution."

"And what is that?"

"My sister is too dangerous, too irrational to reason with. I have no choice. I made a mistake last time, but this time, I will not do that to you or anyone else."

Amanda searched his face, her gaze far too keen for his liking.

Finally, he forced the words from his mouth. "I have to kill my sister."

CHAPTER 17

The shrill ring of the school bell screams into the barren afternoon as clouds, dark and belligerent, crawl across the sky.

I wipe my palms against the linen of my pants as I wait. I breathe again and again and watch how plumes of fog swirl, then dissipate in front of me. It is a simple act. Breathing. But living is not so simple. Living is hell. Death is even worse.

Children erupt from the doors of the school. A hundred voices buzz like the drone of bees from the boys and girls rushing from the buildings. Many disappear into those things they call cars with their mothers and fathers. Happy families. Happy homes. Happy lives.

I see her now. She leans against a waist-high brick wall that runs parallel to the sidewalk along the length of the school's parking lot. I hover by the thick trunk of an oak tree, its leaves long dried and dead. My white clothing blends perfectly with the snow. She has not noticed me yet. But I saw her the moment she stepped away from the building. Her blonde hair is a beacon against the other children.

She is a beautiful child.

I don't deserve a child. I am unholy. A demon. Dirty. *Shut your stinking mouth, you stupid fuck.*

I flinch. I know I am not stupid. I shiver and refocus on the girl.

Nicole is her name

I do not like that name.

Isabella is better. It is a beautiful name. Much prettier than the ugly name of Nicole.

Rage roils through me. The woman is not with the child. She is not taking care of and protecting the child from evil people. Anyone can run over to the child and harm her. This woman is not deserving of such a pretty girl. An innocent.

Gabriel has picked another ugly woman. This one has brown hair and wears dark, unbecoming clothing, hiding the shape of her breasts and hips. She even walks like a man. This—this Amanda is not worthy of a child as beautiful as Isabella.

I know this Amanda is innocent. I have watched and listened to how she behaves. She is not like some others who look innocent. Some are cruel and hateful. Some throw stones, pull hair and spit on you. Some even like to smear your own blood on you.

I shiver again. I do not want to think of the bad. The bad gets me in trouble.

I step toward the girl. She still does not see me. She reminds me of Maria. My heart shatters. The sudden pain in my chest takes my breath away. The sting of tears burns my eyes.

I move closer but pause as the girl steps away from the wall and hurries to the sidewalk. A maroon car drives to the curb and stops behind another doing the same.

The girl opens the door and disappears inside. As the car turns away from the building, I glimpse its windows, but I am unable to see inside because they are too dark. But I know. I know. The ugly woman is taking the girl away. The same woman Gabriel is interested in.

My lip curls and hatred bubbles up inside of me, so much so, that I think I am going to vomit. I do not like to think of Gabriel as my brother. He lost that name long ago. Now he is only my enemy. A man who is worse than the dung I walk on. Again and again, he betrays me. And each time I want him to pay again and again. But death is not enough. He would only welcome it.

I will do as I have always done before. I will hurt what or who Gabriel admires and loves. It is fitting. It is just.

Before the rage takes complete control of me and I go to the bad place, I step backward and turn away from the school and the children still milling on the grounds. I need to leave before I kill an innocent.

Now is not the time to kill anyone, but soon.

Soon.

CHAPTER 18

I wish you had told me sooner you had promised to spend the night at Megan's," Amanda grumbled while she hunted around in Nicole's closet for her sleeping bag.

It had been three days since she'd left Gabriel's home and managed to get into her house undetected. She would have had some explaining to do to Nicole with her hair a complete disaster and her usual crisp uniform in disarray. She managed to jump into the shower before either Nicole or Katie had woken up for the day.

During that time, another body had shown up. This one had the same M.O. as the others. Tattoo carved on the body and missing heart. She'd forgotten to ask about the body part to Gabriel. Or maybe she hadn't really forgotten. Perhaps she just didn't want to know. Many a time she wished she'd never stepped into Gabriel's world and learned about Mayor, but then she remembered their shared passion, and her heart and body warmed and quickened and won over her mind.

She needed to let her brain take over and focus on what was happening to the town. Yeah, she thought of going to her boss with what she knew, and Gabriel probably knew she'd mulled it over, but he was right. No one would believe her. She was starting to see a platinum blonde-haired woman in her peripheral vision every-where when there was none. That she might be a target only fanned her anxiety. She really wanted to stay alive, and that included keeping Mayor's hands away from any of her body parts. She liked her heart inside her chest, thank you very much.

"I forgot to tell you about spending the night," Nicole said from behind her.

"That's fine."

Having Nicole away from her probably was a good idea. She didn't want her daughter being in the cross-hairs of Mayor. But it was a big step having her leave the house, and Amanda, for any length of time. Nicole was branching out, taking a huge leap when it came to socializing and becoming independent. She'd been such an introverted soul a year ago, almost to where she could have been easily diagnosed with a severe case of sepa-ration anxiety disorder. It looked like having them both take a chance on each other just might be working out.

If she didn't consider Mayor....

Amanda frowned and renewed tension snapped across her shoulders. Nicole staying somewhere other than Spirit Lake until Mayor was gone was tempting, but Amanda didn't have a family to send her off to, and if she disrupted Nicole's life now, it could quickly bring the girl's healing back to square one.

Ugh. There was no easy solution.

"Did you find it yet? Megan wants to leave soon."

Nicole's friend was watching television while waiting for Nicole to get her things together. From there she was driving both girls to Megan's house. Amanda wasn't about to let Nicole out without some type of adult supervision. At least her daughter hadn't noticed Amanda hovering around far closer than usual, or if she had, she hadn't commented on it.

On her knees now, Amanda shoved a box on the floor to one side and pulled a sleeping bag from its hiding place. "Found it!"

"Thanks!" Nicole grabbed it and then asked, "Can you get that game up on top? The blue box? Also, Scrabble if you can find it. Megan wants to play both games tonight."

Amanda scrambled to her feet. "Sure, but don't forget to get your toothbrush."

Her daughter groaned. "I'm not a little girl."

Amanda dusted her hands with a smile. Nicole sounded like a pre-teen and so normal. Something she was doing must be working. For too long, her daughter had sounded decades older than she was.

The doorbell rang as Amanda rose on her toes and caught one of the games wedged between several others with the tips of her fingers and slowly slid it forward. Just a couple more inches and she'd get a good grip on it.

"Amanda there's a woman at the door!" Megan called out.

"What the hell—" She dropped back down on her heels. The game she'd tried to pull out from under the others tilted and tumbled off the shelf. It landed with a crash at her feet as alarm exploded inside Amanda's chest.

Nicole moved toward the doorway, but Amanda clutched her shoulder and whispered in a voice raw with panic. "Stay here."

"But why?" Nicole stared back in confusion.

"I'll explain later, but right now stay here. And whatever you do, don't come out."

"What's going on? You're acting really strange." Nicole's brow dipped, and she looked about to argue.

But Amanda didn't care about anything other than Nicole's safety. "Damn it. Just do it!"

Unable to bear the reproach in Nicole's eyes, she stumbled over the game and hurried down the hall. In the bedroom, she grabbed her gun from the safe, checked the safety, and stuffed it in her waistband behind her back. From the kitchen, she rounded the corner to the living area and the front door.

Oh, shit. Her foot momentarily froze in midair as Amanda recognized the woman silhouetted in the doorway.

"Megan get away from the door!"

"What are you talking about?"

"Now!"

Megan backed away from the doorway. She stared back at Amanda, unmistakable hurt flaring in her eyes.

Amanda softened her voice. "Please go to Nicole's bedroom."

Megan pivoted and rushed from the room.

Amanda didn't relax. How could she? This woman, Gabriel's sister, was a killer. She had no clue how strong the other woman was, but Mayor had downed much heavier and stronger men than herself. Not to mention the woman was crazy enough to dig out human hearts from a person's body. Chin raised, as fear scratched its way up her spine and across her back and shoulder muscles, she faced Mayor.

Standing in the foyer, the woman's blonde hair

gleamed beneath the hall light. As before, she wore no coat, jacket, or gloves.

"Why are you here?" Amanda asked.

"Are you going to invite me in?"

The question made Amanda pause, and for a wild moment, she thought back to all those horror movies she'd watched as a child. But Mayor wasn't a vampire. Still, even though she looked innocent and hardly strong enough to assault someone, never mind a six-foot and two-hundred-pound man, she was dangerous as hell, and Amanda needed to remember that. "No. I want you out."

The woman didn't move from her spot in the foyer.

Amanda stiffened, stepped back and grabbed her gun from her waistband as Mayor brushed past her into the living area.

"I do not think so," Mayor murmured as she turned and faced her. The woman's ivory skin glowed beneath the lamp from the end table beside her, while her eyes, a strange violet and blue shade, glowed an eerie incandescence, almost as if they radiated from something deep inside her.

Drawn into the woman's eyes, Amanda couldn't look away for a moment. Then she blinked, and the strange spell shattered. Still, the feeling left her equilibrium off.

Mayor smiled, or more accurately sneered as she eyed the gun. "That is not going to do anything to me. You do know that, yes?"

Amanda's hand turned slick as she tightened her fingers around the gun's grip. "It can slow you down."

"True, but then I would still be able to easily

overpower you." The blonde cocked her head to the side. She stepped over to a floor vase holding metal flowers in shades of yellow, pink, and mauve. Picking one from the vase, she twisted the thick metal—a good half-inch of copper Amanda couldn't bend even if she'd tried—into a coil with ease. Not one flinch or pause from the woman as she held Amanda's gaze. "Try it. I'm sure Gabriel would love to find you like the other dead men in Spirit Lake."

Amanda stood rooted to the floor as she looked at Mayor's eyes. The irises altered, then transformed into white. It was almost like she'd rolled her eyes back into her head, but no, it wasn't like that...they'd changed to silver, the color of the mercury inside the vial in the medallion.

Mayor had sounded articulate and rational until she'd just pulled that stunt. And her eyes. Those eyes... Gabriel hadn't lied about her. The visible proof of the woman's actions dried Amanda's mouth and punched her in the gut. Just what was this woman capable of? But she wasn't about to ask for fear of Mayor wanting to demonstrate.

"Why are you here?" Amanda asked instead, voice firm, violently hiding the fear from her voice and face, since the other woman would only use it to her advantage. Strange to have faced murderers, drug dealers, ex-convicts, and to have never been nearly as frightened as with this woman facing her in her own home... Then again, none of them had gone and torn or cut out someone's heart from their chest, or stood in front of her with little concern over getting shot with a bullet or two.

Mayor tossed the metal flower on the carpeted floor. "Gabriel, of course. He is my family."

"Family? You lost the right to call him that long ago. You have no clue of the meaning."

Gaze narrowing, Mayor stepped toward her.

Quickly, Amanda grabbed the necklace from around her throat, yanked it from beneath her shirt and over her head. Clutching it in one fist, she thrust the cross at the blonde.

Mayor stiffened. "Do not threaten me. You will lose every time."

"Then don't *threaten me*. You need to keep away from my daughter and me."

Something in the back of Mayor's eyes flickered. "You do not take care of your daughter. You let Nicole walk around alone. Anyone can hurt her."

At the mention of Nicole's name, sudden panic twisted at Amanda's insides. "You keep away from Nicole! She's a child. She has nothing to do with your vendetta with Gabriel."

"I would not harm her unless I choose to."

"What the hell kind of answer is that?"

Mayor shrugged. She glanced around and picked up a piece of pottery on the end table.

Nicole had made it in a craft class last year during the summer. Amanda kept the gun trained on the woman's chest and tightened her hold on the cross. She wanted to pull the trigger; she wanted to hit the woman. She'd never felt such rage as she did the moment Mayor had picked up Nicole's work of art or spoken her name.

Gabriel's sister turned the cup around in her hands. "This must be Nicole's. This is well done. My daughter used to—" Abruptly, she set the piece of pottery back on the end table and turned her focus on Amanda. "He told you about his wife, yes?"

Unease crawled across her spine. Some gut instinct told her to lie. "No."

Surprise flickered in Mayor's eyes. "Really? Then you must ask him what happened to her, yes? Nothing personal, you understand, but your fate will end in the same way." She brushed at the sleeve of her blouse. "His treatment of me is his biggest mistake. For him to think or act as if I do not exist? He has turned into a fool. For too long because of him, I have been alone, banished from his and Luys' lives and lacking any semblance of a normal life. It only fits that he experiences how it feels to be alone. What is that word people like to spout off? Karma?"

With the medallion in one hand and the gun aimed at Mayor's chest, Amanda backed away to make room as Mayor walked past her to the front door.

"You really are an ugly woman," Mayor shot over her shoulder as she opened the storm door.

Icy air burst into the house and chilled the sweat along Amanda's neck and brow.

The woman disappeared outside, the door slamming shut behind her.

For a long while, Amanda stood rooted to the floor. Then mentally berating herself for being an inept fool, a coward, and everything in between, she strode over and shut the front door and snapped the lock home. Only then did she ease her grip on the gun.

"Is she gone?" Nicole whispered.

Amanda turned to see Nicole peering around the

doorway leading into the kitchen. "Yes." She closed her eyes, ashamed at how harshly she had spoken to her daughter. "I'm sorry I yelled at you like that. But she's a dangerous woman."

"She looks sad and lonely."

"Jack the Ripper was probably sad and lonely, but he liked to kill people." Then Amanda realized what she'd said and wished she could take it back. The stress had made her thoughtless and stupid. Shoot! Nicole must have been watching and listening. "I told you to stay in your room."

"That was before you started yelling."

"I wasn't yelling."

"To me you were." Nicole ventured out of the kitchen, her brow furrowed. "Are you angry because they haven't found the killer? I know you've been really upset lately." When Amanda didn't immediately answer, she asked, "Has he killed someone else?" A look of panic flared in her eyes, and the color drained from much of her face. "Why haven't they found the killer?"

"It's not so simple." Amanda bit her lip. How could she explain?

"The knives. Where are the knives?" Nicole held her hands together at her waist, fisted them, opened, and fisted them again. "Where are they?"

"They're hidden."

"Are you sure?"

"Yes."

Nicole pivoted and rushed back into the kitchen.

Amanda hurried into the room after her.

Nicole jerked open drawers, threw open cabinets. "I need to find the knife. I have to have the knife."

"Nicole." She caught the girl's elbow and pulled her away from the counter. "Stop it!"

Her daughter twisted from her grasp and rushed around her. She then grabbed the handle of one of the drawers from the kitchen. She yanked at it with such force, spatulas, tongs and other metal utensils tumbled from inside and clanged on the ceramic floor.

"Listen to me!" She pulled Nicole away from the drawer, wrapped both arms around her. She held on fiercely as Nicole squirmed and bucked against her. Stumbling, Amanda hit the wall with her back. With nowhere else to go, she sank down along the wall with Nicole in her arms. After a couple more minutes of struggling, Nicole slumped into her arms and cried bitterly against her shoulder.

Eventually, Nicole's breathing calmed enough to ask, "When is it going to stop?"

Amanda's throat tightened with anguish. She cupped the girl's elbows and urged her backward until enough distance separated them so she could look down and meet her wounded child's eyes. "I don't know. I thought time would help, but tonight has only opened old and barely healed wounds."

At the sound of rustling, she looked over Nicole's shoulder.

Megan stood uncertainly in the doorway, a thick sheen of tears in her eyes. The fear in the girl's face was unmistakable.

What could Amanda say? How could she explain what tormented Nicole without revealing the girl's dark, tortured past? And even if Amanda were to speak up, explain why her daughter acted the way she did, Nicole would never forgive her. So instead, she held her tongue and remained silent, hoping Megan knew what friendship was at this early stage in her life... Because right now, more than ever, Nicole needed a friend.

Amanda could do only so much...

CHAPTER 19

With the sleepover postponed for another night and Megan home with her mother, Amanda sat on the sofa as the soft murmur from the television in her bedroom drifted into the living room. For a good hour, they'd watched a silly program to keep Nicole's fears at bay. When Nicole finally drifted off to sleep, Amanda had slipped from her bedroom, unable to sleep herself. She needed time to wrap her head around the evening's events. But she hadn't accomplished much other than staring at her cell phone in her hand for a good long time while holding onto the metal chain of the medallion around her neck. She didn't care if she got mercury poisoning if it meant Mayor kept away from her and her daughter.

With Nicole hopefully asleep for a good while, Amanda left the living room for the office. Maybe paying bills might keep her mind occupied on something other than the crumbling mess of her life. Sitting at the desk, she powered up the computer and put her cell to the side of the monitor. While waiting for it to load, she might as well clean out the desk's large drawer. She'd stuffed a good amount of paperwork inside and hadn't done much to it since they'd moved. Old calendars, envelopes filled with previous tax returns. Her fingers stilled on one plain manila envelope absent of any label. Her mood darkening yet further, she pulled the envelope out from the others and slipped the flap from its metal clasp.

The contents consisted of newspaper clippings about the murder of Suzie, Nicole's mother, her stepfather's death, and Amanda's involvement in the attempted murder-suicide. The poor woman never got a chance to see her daughter grow up. Sighing, Amanda upended the envelope.

An old picture of Nicole and her mother and a faded image of Brent tumbled onto the desk but nothing else.

She shook out the envelope and looked inside, just in case the newspaper articles were stuck, but there was nothing else inside.

Nicole.

Did she take them? But why? And why hide them? It seemed strange. Could she have hidden them away and kept referring to them as she relived the events of that day again and again? That could be the reason why Nicole's nightmares weren't going away.

Amanda shoved the pictures back inside and stuffed the envelope on the very bottom of the drawer. The monitor's light tinted the office walls blue, but given the way her mind was, she was liable to do something stupid with bill pay and transferring to and from various online accounts. The silence in the house turned deafening. Even with Nicole down the hall in her room, she felt alone.

Amanda always prided herself on being an independent, modern woman. Hell, she was a cop. She was supposed to be strong, take it when others folded. But right now, she felt fragile, uncertain, and yes, frightened. Since her mother's and then her father's death, she'd been without family the last five years and hadn't realized just how dependent she'd been until she'd had only herself to count on. Since the loss of her mother, she hadn't had anyone to confide in, to lean on. Yeah, there'd been guys, but no one special, no one she found herself drawn to on more than a physical level until…

Sighing, she stared at her phone for another full minute before breaking down and dialing his number.

Gabriel answered on the first ring.

"I—" Amanda began, unable to find the right words. "I was hoping…" She cleared her throat. She couldn't seem to find the right words to ask. Maybe it was pride. Maybe it was something else.

Gabriel must have sensed her struggle, because he said, "I'll be right over."

"Thank you," she muttered and hung up. She pulled the medallion from around her neck and put it on top of the refrigerator. She suspected wearing it would only cause Gabriel physical discomfort even though he'd hidden it well while they were together.

The rumble of Gabriel's car announced his arrival.

She opened the front door as he stepped from his SUV.

Wind tossed the dark locks of his hair and flung wide his open jacket, while the street lamp illuminated the rugged lines of his face and the breadth of his shoulders as he hurried up the driveway.

Her breath stuttered. He was a physically handsome man, but she was coming to appreciate his personality, his moral compass. Yeah, he was gray. No one was black or white. She'd found that out long ago when she first joined the police force.

She was learning just how much he cared about her.

Stepping inside, he shut both doors and frowned down at her as he shrugged out of his jacket and hooked it up on the coat rack. "What's happened?"

"She was here." Amanda didn't need to elaborate.

"Holy Mother."

She gasped as he suddenly swept her in his arms. She latched onto his neck with both arms as he strode into the living room and sat down with her on his lap.

With shaking hands, he touched her face, neck, arms. "She didn't hurt you, did she?"

"No." She met the intensity in his gaze and tension eased from her shoulders and back as she settled into his embrace. Yeah, Mayor hadn't touched her or Nicole, but Gabriel's sister had scared the hell out of her, far more than she liked to admit. She wasn't as unflappable as she'd thought.

He kissed her brow, his breath fanning her skin. He smelled of cinnamon.

She closed her eyes and let his strength slowly calm her racing pulse. "She's going to kill—"

"No, she is not." Gabriel was adamant. "Not while I am on this earth. She has ruined my life again and again. I will not have it this time."

"You might not have a choice," Amanda pointed out.

"Listen to me." He placed his palms on each side of her face and forced her to meet his gaze. "I will not let anything happen to you or Nicole."

She wanted to believe him. She really did. The fierceness of his expression, the hard light in his brown eyes spoke of his resolve. But she was a realist, and pretending he was her savior would only end in heartache, and maybe even her death. The only person she could rely on was herself. And she'd be a fool to think differently.

"That's impossible," Amanda scoffed, pushing his hands away, rising, and moving away from Gabriel and the sofa. She needed clarity, and she wasn't going to get it by sitting on his lap. He shouldn't look so damn good. The wind had tossed his hair to where it looked like she'd run her fingers all over his scalp. "Don't promise something like that. Not when you know you can't protect Nicole or me every second of the day."

She walked over to the discarded metal Mayor had twisted into a crazed-looking pretzel. She lifted it from the carpet and waved it at Gabriel. "She wanted to scare me, probably hoping I'd pee my pants. And I hate to admit it, but she succeeded in putting the fear of God in me."

Gabriel shook his head as he leaned forward and placed both elbows on his knees. "I'm sorry. You're right, I have only so much control. All I can do is try."

"Trying isn't good enough. Trying might get me killed, and you know that." She tried to shove the metal stem back into the vase, but the flower tumbled onto the floor. She picked it up and turned back to Gabriel. She ran a hand over the twisted metal. Of course, she'd assumed Mayor was the only person with incredible abilities. "Can you do that? Bend metal?

His eyes widened before a guarded expression slid across his face.

"You can, can't you?" She strode over and offered him the flower. "Show me. I need to see for myself."

For a moment, she didn't think he would take it.

Finally, he reached over and eased the metal slowly from her hand. Lips grim, he straightened the copper with slow, measured movements. But the stem lacked the original straight, vertical line.

Kind of like twisting a paper clip and trying to put it back to its original form. No matter how hard you struggle to rework the metal, it would never be the same unflawed design. It was like her life. From the moment she met Gabriel, even if they survived Mayor but went their separate ways later, her life was forever damaged. "There was never any sign of your strength. I never knew…"

"You and everyone else. But after today, you, along with Luys and Mayor, are the only people who know."

She was surprisingly anxious at being given that much power. It made her feel like running, but she couldn't run mentally or physically. She needed Gabriel's help. Even though she should be furious at how he'd pulled her into his life, he had taken action by trying to leave to protect her. But he'd been too late.

He offered the flower back.

Amanda took it, amazed at just how much he was trusting her not to reveal his superhuman strength to anyone else. As she put the flower back in the vase, she looked over her shoulder and asked, "What else can you do?"

"Other than die a normal death?" He gave her a rueful smile. "Nothing."

She grabbed the hair band she had around her wrist and scraped her hair back into a ponytail. "And Mayor? What about her?"

"She's stronger."

"Even with her size?"

"Yes."

He looked as if he was getting uncomfortable with her questions, but that didn't stop her from wanting, needing to know. "So she's stronger, which would explain how she can take down a full-grown man. But she's elusive. No one has seen her at the scene."

"What did she want?"

She knew what he was doing. Distracting her with his own question. She would let it go for the moment, but she needed to know more about Mayor and what they were up against. As she paced the room for a bit, she reviewed her conversation with Mayor before turning back to Gabriel. "Nothing, which is strange in itself. She mentioned you, but not in any depth, and threatened me with the flower. When she started touching Nicole's things, I wanted to punch her, and I'm sure she knew that."

His gaze narrowed. "I'm sure Mayor did and liked how she received a reaction from you. That was probably her whole purpose. It's her way of finding out a person's weaknesses."

"Shit." Panic bloomed in her chest. "I swear if she comes near Nicole…"

"We'll stop her before that happens," Gabriel insisted.

"And how do you propose to do that?"

He rubbed at the bridge of his nose and sighed. "I don't know. Not yet. An ambush isn't going to work. Tricking Mayor isn't going to work, either. Luys and I have tried too many ploys as it is. She isn't going to walk into any trap unless it's ingenious. She has too much experience from Luys and myself, and she is intelligent. But I have a good idea where she might be hanging out. I found out today there was a sighting of a woman with her description in Estherville. A neighbor's friend saw a woman with her hair color at a bar a couple of nights ago."

"Estherville? There haven't been any reports of murders or robberies. We would have been notified."

"Mayor usually keeps away from the place she is wreaking havoc on."

"We need to check it out tonight. I'm sure we can…" Her words drifted to a stop as she thought of leaving Nicole on her own. She couldn't do it. Not when her daughter was having such a hard time.

"And Nicole?" He frowned. "Did Mayor do anything to scare her?"

Amanda made a face. "No. It was me who got her worked up." She pulled at the tip of her ponytail. She felt powerless. She felt trapped. She felt beyond frustrated. At least for the time being. "Katie's with her mother tonight. She planned her mother's birthday for months. I can't ask her to watch Nicole, who isn't in any condition for me to leave her."

"I don't think it's a good idea for you to go off running to Estherville."

"Oh, don't you start getting all he-man on me."

"I'm not, but you don't know what Mayor is capable of."

"You can't say that anymore. I've seen all I need to know what Mayor's capable of in Spirit Lake. Dismembered body parts, decapitated civilians. She's crazy. That's all I need to know!"

He winced. "There's more than that."

"Well, then tell me!" Her words were harsh with emotion.

"Mom?"

Nicole's voice drifted into the living room. Fear and uncertainty were unmistakable in that one word.

"I'll be right there!" She balled her hands into fists as Gabriel rose. Right that second, she felt like a failure as a mother. She couldn't even keep calm enough to make sure Nicole didn't get frightened again that night.

Gabriel walked over and cupped her shoulder.

She looked up, and her heart thudded against her rib cage. This attraction was crazy. How could one man momentarily blind her to everything but this wild fascination she had for him.

His head dipped, and he kissed her hard, deep.

She latched onto his arms and gasped into his mouth at his unexpected onslaught.

Just as quickly, he lifted his head and started to ease backward.

But she lifted herself on her toes and whispered against his mouth, "Don't go without me."

He inched further away and shook his head. "It's best I go on my own."

"Damn it, Gabriel."

"You need to be here for Nicole. She needs you safe."

Her jaw tightened in frustration. Gabriel was right, but it sure didn't feel good knowing it. She watched Gabriel leave and felt hopeless, ineffective, and frustrated as hell. But Nicole's well-being was too damn important for her to risk it by running off and chasing after Mayor. Some sacrifices needed to be made when it came to protecting and loving other people, and she'd known that going in with Nicole. "Tomorrow…." She breathed. "Tomorrow."

She walked back into the kitchen and pulled the medallion from on top of the fridge. With it around her neck, she didn't feel so vulnerable. She thought of making Nicole wear it, but if Amanda wasn't safe, she wasn't going to be any help in protecting her daughter.

CHAPTER 20

Gabriel walked between two parked cars. A single streetlamp did little to illuminate the parking lot. Still, he recognized the maroon economy car and license plate. He had seen it too many times not to. Plus, the vehicle didn't look like it belonged with the others. No rust along the body's wheelbase or frame, or mud and film on the windows. His pace quickened.

He stepped into the bar and scanned the large room. When he didn't see Mayor's silver-blonde hair, he strode farther into the room, the music from overhead speakers masking the sound of his feet against the worn-wood floor.

A woman with a ponytail sat in a shadowed booth in the corner of the room. If he could so easily recognize her, Mayor would pick her out in seconds.

Jaw clenched, he sank into the booth opposite of Amanda. "What are you doing here?"

For a brief second her eyes widened, but she quickly masked her surprise. Shrugging, she nodded at the beer in front of her. "Just having a drink and brushing off advance after advance. A couple of times I had to be a bitch to make a couple guys realize I meant no. That or show them what I'm packing." She grimaced and edged her jacket to the side to reveal the gun on her belt. "The place is reeking of testosterone and bad attitudes, and alcohol isn't helping. It's been way too long since I've been in a bar with a couple of friends, never mind alone. I forgot how some guys can be real asses when they don't get their way."

"What the hell, Amanda! You're not supposed to be here. I told you, I didn't want you coming with me." He tried to bank the anger but seeing her scared him. Yes, she could take care of herself when it came to the opposite sex and any lowlife, but they were dealing with Mayor.

"Hey, I stayed home last night with Nicole while you were probably here and scouring the other bars in the area." She smirked back at him. "And, I didn't come with you. You're the one who showed up after me."

"This is no time to be funny. When I saw your car out there... Holy Mother. You frightened me."

Her gaze softened. "Sorry. The last thing I want to do is upset you. Things are crazy as it is already." She leaned over the table toward him while rolling the beer bottle between both palms. "This is the place, right? There weren't too many choices. 'Dive' was screaming at me as I drove by. The inside didn't disappoint." After she took a sip, she asked, "You're sure she won't try something in a place like this?"

"She's smart enough to know her limits. This public a place will get her in trouble. She can't stop a mob. Where's Nicole?"

"Safe with Katie and Josh McKinney and that new kid who just graduated from the academy. I talked to both guys and asked them to drop by after their shift and hang out with Katie and Nicole until I got home. I mentioned Nicole being really scared of the killings.

It didn't take much to convince Josh to babysit, what with Katie there. He's got it bad for her. I'm pretty sure he didn't want anyone else hanging out with the two of them, though. Mayor wouldn't touch the place with that big a crowd. I was also careful about leaving the house. Checked for a tail and for any suspicious activity."

Gabriel grunted, wanting to argue, but he was not going to win any argument with Amanda from the hard gleam in her eyes.

"So… It looks like you didn't find anything yesterday. Otherwise, you wouldn't be hanging around this place."

Wild Willy was a dive bar with drunks, tweakers, and other lost souls who came there to self-medicate because they couldn't handle what life had dealt them. Mayor always gravitated to places like that, no matter the decade. Lost or tortured souls who suddenly turn up missing don't usually have family or friends asking questions or filing missing person's reports. Often they were abandoned long before.

A reed-thin waitress, with a mouthful of bad teeth and looking like she might be an addict herself, stopped by their booth. "Hey, honey. What'll it be?"

"Water." He ignored the waitress' raised eyebrow.

"I'll have an Ultra Light," Amanda said.

"Drinking might not be a good thing," he said after the woman left.

"Oh, believe me. Another beer right now is probably going to steady my nerves."

"Beer might also mess with your judgment." He was coming across like a controlling ass, but he hated the idea of her facing off with Mayor. Amanda might think she could outwit, outfight his sister, but Gabriel knew what Mayor was capable of, and he was not just thinking of the carnage she left behind.

"I know what I'm doing," she insisted. "And I'm not completely vulnerable. I do have this." She pressed a palm against her chest, drawing his eye to the form-fitting sweater clinging to her breasts. Memories of how she looked naked briefly distracted him. The silken skin, the weight of her breasts in his hands, her gasps of pleasure, then a cry of release as he caressed each breast and drove into her. More images rushed into his head. Entwined limbs, entangled sheets, bodies moving as one.

Enough. He mentally shook himself. Holy Mother. It was not the time.

Amanda then pulled the medallion from beneath her sweater. It looked worn and old even with the dim lighting from the bar.

The waitress paused by their table long enough to serve their drinks and mutter, "Here's your *water*."

Ignoring the woman's snide comment, he leaned over the table and argued, "The mercury can only do so much."

She wrapped her fingers around the cross and twisted her lips into a grimace. "I know. It's only as good as a quick mind and body."

His hand tightened on his drink. "It will slow Mayor down, and she'll be more careful when she knows you have that. Breaking the vial and getting the metal on her before she's on you requires quick reflexes. But I wouldn't have given it to you if I didn't think you were capable."

He reached over and cupped her hand. She quickly withdrew, leaving his hand empty on the table between them, making him feel at a loss and far sadder at her rejection than he'd envisioned.

The silence turned suddenly awkward. And the distance between them was far larger than the table between them.

"How about we try another place?" Amanda rose and tossed a couple of bills on the table.

Gabriel swore as he followed her out of the bar. "Amanda, we really need to formulate a plan."

"And what is your plan?"

He ignored the bite to her voice. "I was going to try to communicate with her."

"Has that worked before?"

"No, but people change."

Amanda muttered a four-letter word as she zipped her jacket and pulled her collar up against her neck. "It doesn't sound like she's changed to me."

"I need to know for myself before I do something irreversible." The idea of killing Mayor haunted him. His hatred goaded him forward, but familiar ties clung to the cobwebs of his mind and made him hesitate and question himself.

Amanda grasped his arm. "She might be your sister, your family, but she's a serial killer."

"You don't have to tell me something I don't already know." This time he was the one with a bite to his words.

"You've already told me a bullet doesn't do it, but other than mercury and a beheading—something I might not be able to pull off—is there anything else that will kill her?"

He followed her to the car. "If you want her dead—"

A flash of white hit his peripheral vision as Amanda reached for the car handle.

Mayor.

He shoved Amanda behind him. Legs splayed, he lifted his fisted hands.

Mayor stopped several yards in front of him.

Facing Mayor sent a cascade of emotions roiling through him. Rage, fear, uncertainty, love, and time separated them.

The lone parking lot light illuminated her pale features. The wind tossed the silver-blonde tips of her hair into the air and across her face, momentarily masking her expression. She brushed the strands aside and wrapped them around one ear. The act revealed the rage in her eyes and the rigid line of her jaw. Her hands balled at her sides as she stepped toward him on bare feet.

She had always loved the feel of the earth on her soles.

"Plotting my death, yes?" She cocked her head to one side. "Again?"

"It's called protection."

"Oh, yes. Protection. You did so well protecting Teresa."

He flinched. He hated revealing how much Mayor's words cut.

He advanced toward his sister, conscious of Amanda a few feet behind him. "Amanda is not Teresa. She has nothing to do with you."

"I can smell your fear. Are you afraid I will snap her neck like I did your *wife's*?" Her lips curled in disdain.

"You have no empathy, compassion, or decency

anymore," he said in disgust. Mayor had been a bane to his existence for far too long. But he'd been responsible for her and had failed. He'd failed all of them. "You lost your humanity long ago. It's good Alonso isn't around to see your sickness. Your husband—"

Roaring in rage, she launched herself at him.

He stumbled back as she hit him with her full weight. He grabbed her wrists as she tried to claw at his eyes. The shock of her strength left him momentarily stunned—he'd forgotten how much an adversary she was. The back of his legs hit the grill of a truck, and he bent over the hood, his head hitting the metal with a thud. Before she landed on top of him, he swiveled and shoved her aside.

Scrambling off the vehicle, he landed on his feet as she pulled herself up and faced him across the hood of the truck. This time he was prepared when she launched herself over the top of the hood and flung herself toward him, hands stretched out, face twisted in fury. Legs braced, he met the force of her body full on and used all his physical strength to fling her away.

She flew backward a good ten yards and grunted as she hit the trunk of a tree. She screamed, spilling out obscenity after obscenity. "I will rip her heart out. That ugly face will be torn from her body! I will drink her life's blood and dine on her heart. I will enjoy draining the life from her. Do you hear me? Do you? And her little girl—I will—"

"Enough!" Roaring, he charged forward and back-handed her in the face.

Her head snapped back, but she didn't stumble at the force of his attack. Instead, she used a right fist to his stomach and a left to his head. Then she twisted and snapped her heel into the back of his leg.

He crumpled, landing in dirt, snow, and grease. It was stupid of him to think he could beat her. Mayor had been only playing with him at the beginning, testing him, seeing how strong he was. And he had played into her exactly as she wanted.

He grabbed the side of a car and pulled himself up, glancing quickly over his shoulder to find Amanda, jaw taut, eyes narrowed, aiming a gun at Mayor. "Amanda, go. While you have a chance."

"Are you crazy? I can't do that."

It was a mistake to turn his attention away from Mayor even for an instant. The force of her body smashing into his back launched him into the air. He hit the ground on his stomach, stunned and brain rattling. He struggled to get up, but Mayor landed on top of him, both legs straddling his hips while her hands grabbed at his hair, twisting her fingers into the locks and yanking his head backward, then smashing his face into the ground, again and again.

With one hand, he tried to grab at her from behind him, but her teeth caught on his fingers and bit down into his flesh.

He grunted as her teeth hit bone. Holy Mother.

This could not end like this.

Somehow, he managed to yank his hand from her mouth and shove both palms under himself and against the ground. He struggled for strength, for the drive to fight back. The thought of Amanda and her daughter was all he needed. He drew an elbow back and hit Mayor. Her gasp rushed past his ear. He'd surprised her. Again and again, he used an elbow, keeping her off-balance. Twisting, he flung himself to the side and from beneath her, hit his back against the truck's tire, and then used it to propel himself toward Mayor.

But she had already scrambled to her feet.

Before she had a chance to land on him, he rose, backed up a few steps to get his bearings and eyed her warily. He'd never won when it came to any type of battle between them. But what should he expect? He'd never followed Mayor in her quest, in her need for power.

He was only half-conscious of a cry that broke into the night. It faded, grew louder, and then faded again as he stared at the smear of his own blood on his hand and how it clung to his sister's lips and chin as she sneered back at him.

"This has been fun, yes?" She laughed, a full-bodied sound. "But I grow tired of watching you flounder around like the weak fool you are. Enough."

She smiled, the light in her violet eyes darkening to nearly black as she flexed her fingers before shoving a wave of silver hair over her shoulder. "You forget how strong I can get, yes?"

A shot rang out. Then another.

CHAPTER 21

Flinching, he stared at Mayor, wondering for a wild moment if he had been shot. But no, it was Mayor.

His sister's eyes widened in surprise. The light from the parking lot illuminated a dark stain against her dress and by her shoulder. Another wound bloomed on her chest where Amanda's bullet had struck.

The wail grew stronger this time and formed into a siren as it drew steadily closer.

Gabriel didn't have a clue how he was going to explain this... That is... if he survived long enough to have police backup arrive in time. Someone from the bar must have heard the noise from the parking lot and called the police.

Mayor didn't notice the sound or didn't care.

But he didn't plan on waiting for her next move. Before Mayor thought to turn on Amanda, he charged at his sister, hitting her with his body weight.

This time, though, she held her ground, the force of her strength jaw-dropping. Legs splayed, she grabbed him by the throat and squeezed.

The pressure closed off the air to his lungs. A low roar drummed into his ears as he grabbed and pulled at her wrist. His peripheral vision faded. He struggled not to pass out. He didn't dare lose consciousness. Not with Amanda nearby to protect. With his other hand, he dug his thumb and fingers into the juncture between her shoulder and arm. Digging, digging....

"Get. Your. Hands. Off. Him." Amanda ordered in a nearly unrecognizable growl. "Do it now, before I break this vial and throw mercury on you."

Amanda had pulled the vial from inside the medallion and lifted it over her head.

Mayor laughed. "You are a fool to think you can win against me. Your human body is too clumsy." She released him. "I could snap your neck before you even manage to break the glass."

Coughing, he sagged to his knees at her feet.

"It is always *not the time*." She looked at Gabriel, her lips curled into a snarl. "Enjoy your friend while you can, big brother. I will destroy you in time, yes? Your cruelty is far worse than mine. I have never let a person rot in some dark cave, unable to do anything but lay there alone. If not for that man who chanced upon me.... When the fool removed the medallion and was stupid enough to loiter, I found the strength to snap his neck. Unlike with him, I am not going to be so merciful to you."

Suddenly, a gray-white fog formed, swirled, and then thickened around Mayor until it engulfed her from all sides, obscuring her body from view. Then the mist exploded in all directions. Raising a hand against her face, Amanda flinched and stumbled back.

Mayor had disappeared. The bloodstained snow remained as before, the only sign that she'd been there.

Amanda blinked. Had she missed something? She pivoted, tension cutting a swath across her back and shoulders. To her left, Gabriel rubbed his throat as he used a hand on his knee and rose to his feet. "I don't understand. Where did she go?"

"My sister evidently decided to leave."

She shivered as Mayor's laughter lingered in the air. That was the laughter she'd heard when she was at the Jeffersons' property and stumbled upon Clark Swanson's body. The insane woman had been there watching her. She could have easily killed Amanda if she'd wanted to. "What do you mean? How can she just vanish? Are you able to do the same?"

He met her gaze. She undoubtedly looked frazzled, but it wasn't every day someone vanished like in some horror movie. Maybe she should have used the vial on Mayor when she had a chance, but she'd been too afraid of injuring Gabriel in the process.

"No. I can't do what Mayor does. She's stronger, capable of doing things that are beyond me."

"Why?"

The question hung in the air between them. "I think you know," Gabriel whispered. "Mayor gets her strength from feeding on others."

"That's sick." But he was right. Some part of her had already suspected. "How can she... How…"

"She's lost what she once was. Her humanity has been gone for a long time now. I thought at one point she might change, but she's beyond my or anyone's reach."

"If it wasn't my threat that made her vanish…"

"No. I wish it were. I wish we were both able to stop her tonight." He nodded toward the flashing lights through the trees. "She's smart enough to know having the police involved is only going to get her into trouble. There comes a point she can only run so far if a mob is after her."

A patrol car raced into the parking lot and skidded to a halt. "Right now, she knows police aren't going to help her agenda."

"This is just great," Amanda muttered, shoving her gun into its holster at her waist. "How are we going to explain this?"

"We're not." He walked toward her, brow dipped into a frown, jaw rigid with tension. "At least not what really happened. Also, we both know they're not going to connect a woman to the killings, so I wouldn't even bother going there. Talking about smoke, mercury, and someone disappearing into thin air is going to get both of us locked up, and it might not be in prison."

Amanda made a face. "I've never been good at lying, but I seem to be doing that a lot lately."

The grim expression on his face didn't soften. "You do things you normally never do when it comes to survival."

She palmed the vial and eased it into her front pocket, not having enough time to get it back into the medallion without someone seeing. Glancing over at the snow peppered with Mayor's blood, Amanda swore under her breath. One time she'd like things to go right for her. Just once.

When Warner stepped out of the department car, Amanda didn't relax. Yeah, he was new and green, but that didn't mean he was naive or stupid. New could be dangerous. Inexperienced cops were more likely to be quick to prove themselves, quick to act, quick to use brute force.

"Hey, what's going on?" Warner asked, glancing at them briefly before scanning the parking lot.

Amanda lied. Gabriel was right. She didn't see any other choice. "A guy was hitting on me, and Gabriel here told him to knock it off. I guess he didn't take to kindly to being told what to do and started a fight." Amanda stuffed her balled fists into her jacket pockets and forced herself to keep her gaze away from the stained snow. "Why? Someone call it in?"

"Yeah, they heard yelling outside and possible gunshots." He shrugged. "No one wanted to go outside to investigate. Not that I blame them with all these crazy killings happening in the area."

Amanda looked over at the bar. None of the windows faced the parking lot. Maybe things might be turning in her favor.

Warner pulled a flashlight from his belt and scanned the area to the right and beyond the parking lot.

With his attention in the other direction, Amanda casually moved to where Mayor had stood and just as casually scuffed her heel into the snow and covered the bloodstains.

Warner pivoted and walked toward her, but frowned and glanced over at Gabriel, then gave him a funny look. "I didn't think you were into the bar scene. And especially places like Wild Willy."

Gabriel shrugged, both hands stuffed into his pockets. "I didn't feel like socializing. I am not known here."

"Where'd the guy go?"

Gabriel nodded in the opposite direction of where he'd been fighting with Mayor. "Down the main road. On foot."

Warner frowned again. "You're sure? He just shows up, hits on your girlfriend, and takes off? Did you see him actually harassing her?"

Amanda stiffened at the nasty way he said girl-friend. She wouldn't be surprised if Freer was trash-talking behind her back, especially with the way Warner was behaving.

Gabriel's gaze narrowed. "What is with you? I'm on your side, remember?"

Warner rubbed the back of his neck. "Yeah, I know. Hell, it's just all these killings are getting to me."

"To all of us," Amanda murmured.

He pressed the communication button on the radio at his shoulder and called dispatch for backup. He grimaced at the both of them. "I don't feel like doing a search. It's colder than shit out right now."

Amanda nodded but knew no one was going to find anyone. Not unless Mayor wanted to be found.

Then her heartbeat stuttered. She'd been so focused on trying to explain, she hadn't thought beyond the moment and her own self-preservation. Mayor could be God-only-knew where. Furious at how the evening had played out, the woman might be going after Nicole that second. Her daughter probably wasn't safe, even with two able police officers in the same house. "I've got to go." Amanda glanced over at Gabriel and met his gaze. "Nicole."

"Hey, I'm going to need to question you for my report," Warner argued, folding his arms over his chest.

"It can wait." Amanda dug in her pocket for her car keys and raced to her vehicle.

"But—"

"It's not like we're going to skip town, Warner," Gabriel called over his shoulder as he rushed to his SUV.

A few minutes later, Amanda ran into the house with Gabriel only a few feet behind her. She'd never forgive herself if Mayor touched or came within one foot of Nicole. In the living room, she stumbled to an abrupt stop. The only light illuminating the room was from the television. The antics of some comic-book character played across its large screen.

Katie jumped to her feet. "What's wrong?"

Amanda must have looked a sight, hair mussed, face wild with worry, and Gabriel rushing in behind her. "Where's Nicole? And Josh and his friend? They were supposed to stick around until I got home."

"She's in bed asleep. And the guys took off to grab some fast food. Why?"

"I-I just need to know." Amanda hurried down the hall, unable to relax until she double-checked.

Her daughter was curled on one side of the bed with the covers up to her ears and sleeping. The soft sigh of her breathing filled the room and only when Amanda realized Nicole was safe did she relax. With Gabriel waiting in the doorway, she adjusted the bedding around Nicole, who shifted deeper under the covers and cupped a hand under her chin.

She backed out of the room and warned Gabriel in a whisper, "I swear if she touches Nicole…"

"She won't. She's never touched children, not with

what happened to her daughter." He moved down the hall with her.

Katie stood at the end of the hall leading into the living room. She folded her arms against her middle, her brow dipping in worry. "She's okay, right?"

"Yes, sorry. She's fine. I'm just a little paranoid right now."

"Well, I haven't seen anything or anyone acting suspiciously in the neighborhood that I know of. I would have called otherwise."

Amanda nodded sharply. "Yes, of course. Sorry for alarming you."

Katie shrugged. "Just glad everything's fine." She glanced down at the cell phone in her hand. "I just texted Josh to let him know you're here now and he doesn't have to come back. Did you want me to hang around a bit longer tonight?"

"No. No." She turned to Gabriel and asked, "Can you make sure Katie gets home?"

"Yes, of course. I'll tail her until she gets inside."

"Oh, there's no need! Josh is dropping by my place in just a bit."

"Yes, there is," Gabriel insisted. When Katie disappeared into the kitchen to get her things, he murmured to Amanda, "Just make sure you have got that medallion around your neck. I can feel you have the mercury on you right now by the way my strength has been ebbing."

Amanda bit her lip. Until that moment, she hadn't noticed the ashen color to his face and the faint sheen of sweat on his brow. His injured hand was inside his jacket pocket. "How bad is the damage?"

"Some antiseptic will take care of it. Also, once I get away from the medallion, my strength will fully return. I'll head on over to the bar and see if things have quieted down. I'll also check out another bar in the same town, but I'll be back later to see how you're doing." He paused, then kissed her hard and fast before following Katie outside.

She locked and dead bolted the door behind him, which probably wouldn't be much use for protection. If Mayor really wanted in, she'd find a way. Scared, nervous, and alone—she hated feeling so damn weak—with Gabriel gone, she rolled her shoulders and straightened her back. Courage. *Come on, get a grip.*

After shrugging out of her jacket and toeing off her boots, she hung up her coat, but then pulled the vial from its pocket and gently set it in the hidden compartment of the medallion and slipped the cross around her neck.

Even with the necklace's protection, she felt anything but safe. Okay, no thinking of herself as some sacrificial lamb waiting to be slaughtered. She needed to do something, anything to protect herself and Nicole. The last thing she wanted was for Nicole to somehow get in the middle of Mayor's trajectory. But how could she stop Mayor if bullets didn't work and she only had the mercury as a weapon? There had to be something else. But what?

Ugh. And how? Gabriel hadn't exactly been forthcoming with his past.

She needed answers. If she dug into the past, decades, centuries ago, she might find some clue or leverage against Mayor. Taking a detour to the kitchen for a glass of wine, she then booted up her computer in her office. Staring at the screen with narrowed eyes, she took a sip of wine. Maybe if she researched the myths of that era, she might uncover something.

After 30 minutes of searching, she'd finished the wine and had grown decidedly sick to her stomach. Alcohol had nothing to do with the feeling, but rather the subject matter. Now she could understand why Gabriel didn't talk much of his captivity. The brutality was mind-numbing. She'd thought her world was filled with crazy, inhumane acts…. The scope of capturing, torturing and sacrificing neighboring tribesmen and women was both horrifying and incomprehensible. The Spanish were brutal in their genocide of the Aztecs and other local tribes in their thirst to conquer. Women, children, frail, or innocent—it didn't matter who they subjugated.

As for the human zoo Gabriel had mentioned… She skimmed through several articles on the subject. The zoo was considered a blessing for the captive's family members, who were given compensation for their relative residing within the zoo's walls. But as for slaves, Amanda could only imagine what they'd been subjected to or what degradation they'd had to perform. Beatings, scorn, ridicule. Probably worse than the freak shows back in the 1920s and 1930s. All because they'd been considered odd and different from their own race. No doubt they hated the Spanish. All that hatred must have been impossible to survive unscathed. And she could understand how the natives had found Mayor peculiar with her coloring. She suspected they thought Gabriel and his brother equally strange being related to her. Or maybe they'd hoped to have them mate and create a child with similar coloring.

Amanda cringed at the idea of an incestuous relationship between any one of them and quickly clicked out of the article. She then scrolled through several other web pages, some reputable and others just plain nuts. But then she was also looking for crazy or some type of myth or legend that might have been based in fact at one point in history. The word obsidian jumped out of a paragraph. Her fingers stilled on the mouse. During sacrificial ceremonies, priests were known to use obsidian blades to cut open their victims.

Brent had used such a weapon. She'd known the knife had been unusual, even an antique, but she hadn't been aware of its history. Her sole focus had been on getting Nicole out of her environment and into a safe home. She'd killed Nicole's stepfather, and she'd thought at the time she'd eliminated the problem, but Brent continued to have tremendous sway in Nicole's life. She wondered if the nightmares would ever go away

Amanda did a quick search on obsidian. Hard volcanic glass.

And what about the murder victims now? Blunt and the others? Had an obsidian blade been used on them? Had Mayor used it? But what about the tattoos? Why would Mayor tattoo that symbol on their bodies?

Starting another search, she couldn't come up with the exact symbol she'd seen on the victims. The tattoos now had a completely different meaning. She should have thought of it earlier, but she'd been still reeling from everything around her.

Jennifer.

The medical examiner had told her the knife had a residue she hadn't been able to identify. But did her friend say obsidian? Ugh. She couldn't remember.

She hurried out of the office and grabbed her phone and paused to quickly text Jennifer to see if she'd gotten the lab reports on the weapon yet. Yes, it was late, but knowing Jennifer, with her chronic case of insomnia, she was awake.

Could Brent have been something other than human? Was it possible? She paced from one end of the living room floor to the other and back again.

NO. Impossible. Amanda had killed him herself. A bullet, not mercury, had killed him. She'd seen the body, the coroner's report. But there was a tie. There had to be. It was too much of a coincidence. But the question was…what?

Or maybe she was grasping at straws….

Lights from a car arced against the living room window. A car engine died.

She quickly peered outside.

Gabriel. Tension she didn't know she'd been holding released from her shoulders. She opened the door, unable to keep the smile of pleasure from her eyes or lips. Then her heart collided against her chest when she caught the heat in his gaze as he quickly shrugged out of his jacket and hooked it on the coat rack by the door. "I'm glad you're here. I wanted to—"

Gabriel caught her mouth in a hungry kiss, cutting off her words and any logical form of thought. Desire— hot, wild, and oh-so-delicious—flared and roiled through her body. Heart pounding, she latched onto his shoulders to keep her balance and arched against his body. How could one man send her in complete disarray to the point where she couldn't think of anything but him and only him?

But she needed to stop. She really should. This passion wasn't going to go anywhere. It couldn't.

CHAPTER 22

A groan rumbled from Gabriel's chest as he brought Amanda closer to him. She tasted amazing. The feel of her plump breasts against his chest and the swell of her hips in his hands threatened to crack his already limited self-control. He slipped one hand beneath her sweater to glide a thumb along the curve of her spine. He wanted to taste the salt on her skin. He wanted to lose himself in her body and forget everything but the two of them. He wanted a normal life. A life with her in it... Holy Mother....

He wanted what he could not have.

When she stiffened, he drew back to find her gaze dark and turbulent. "What's wrong?"

"Nicole's asleep in the other room..." She bit her bottom lip, uncertainty darkening the light of desire in her eyes.

"How is she?" He had been blinded by the moment to the point where he had forgotten everything but the two of them.

"Yes, yes. She's fine." She frowned and shifted, looking suddenly awkward, which was unlike her.

"What is it?"

"I don't want Nicole walking in on us... That's not something I'm willing yet to..."

"I understand," he murmured. He swept back

several strands of hair that had escaped her ponytail, before cupping her jaw and neck. The pulse below her ear throbbed against his fingers. In a voice too thick and needy to his liking, he muttered, "Does she usually knock before coming into your room? You have your own private bathroom. Showers can hide a multitude of sounds or sins. She'll never know. I'll make sure and leave long before she gets up in the morning."

Her lips parted, while her eyes flared with unmistakable desire.

Gabriel's groin tightened in response. He waited tensely for her answer. She could easily refuse, but his need and he hoped hers overshadowed any propriety. He was not in the mood to be proper, tame, civil, or anything resembling it. Holy Mother, he wanted to be selfish. She wouldn't leave the house without Nicole, and he never would expect her to. But the idea of leaving her alone was out of the question. While still holding her hip with one hand, he pressed against her until her breasts flattened against his chest once again. Her agitated breathing filled the foyer as he stared down at her parted lips.

"I shouldn't…"

"Maybe not," he whispered back, caressing her jaw with a thumb. "Life is filled with shouldn'ts. Many come with regrets, but I can promise you'll not regret tonight or the next couple of hours."

When she licked her bottom lip, he didn't wait but took her mouth in another slow, deep kiss.

She gasped against his lips and clutched his shoulders, digging her fingers into his skin and pressing harder against his body. Then she slipped from his arms, grabbed his hand, and urged him from the foyer, down the hall and into her bedroom.

Heart pounding, he followed. He would have followed her anywhere—over a cliff and into a roaring sea, through the searing heat of the Gobi desert, or into another physical dimension or alternate universe. One kiss from Amanda would be enough before he died.

In the bedroom, after locking the door with a soft click, she turned on a bedside lamp as he shrugged out of his shirt and draped it over the back of a bedroom chair. An archway led to a shadowed bathroom. He sat down to take off his boots as Amanda disappeared inside it. He stilled for a moment. Last time he really hadn't paid attention to her room. His entire focus had been on Amanda and getting into her bed.

A book sat beneath the bedside lamp. Gabriel read the title, surprised at the deep spiritual theme. He'd been wrong thinking Amanda was all about facts and logic. Knowing that, though, made him appreciate her that much more. The sound of a shower filtered into the bedroom as her shadow appeared briefly before muted light bloomed from the other room, shifted, and flickered.

Candles…

Then suddenly Amanda reappeared minus her shirt and pants. The black lacy bra and panties accented her pale skin and curves. Every centimeter was raw woman. He had lost much of his humanity over the years, but watching her walk toward him made him want to be better, be the man Amanda could admire, but most importantly, he wanted her to look at him with not only love, but trust and respect. The last two didn't come free. He needed to earn those, too.

She knelt by his feet and grabbed his boot.

"You don't have to—"

"I want to," she murmured, looking up briefly to meet his gaze.

His chest tightened at the expression in her eyes. Their depths held something beyond desire, something deeper, even transcendental. He sucked in a breath. Moments like now, he found it near impossible to believe she wanted him. Only him. No one else. Even with his deep flaws and otherworldly characteristics. He couldn't remember a time where he felt needed, wanted. The possibility of love after so many decades caught at his chest with such force that he grappled for breath.

Forcing himself to breathe normally, he stared down at her bent head as she pulled one of his boots off. Hating the idea of her kneeling at his feet, he bent in one fluid motion and swept her up to stand in front of him. He toed the other boot off impatiently and shucked his pants and underwear. When she reached behind herself to unhook her bra, he caught her wrist and tugged her close. "No. I want to do that, and I want to watch."

The confusion in her eyes shifted quickly when he nudged her up against the bathroom counter between the two sinks. The mist of the shower crept into the bathroom as pillar candles flickered and added a creamy texture to her already beautiful skin.

They both faced the counter. He caught her gaze in the mirror as he placed both palms over her shoulders and slid them down to cup her elbows. The act sent her breasts thrusting forward, the dark, erect tips visible beneath the black lace. With their eyes still locked, he pressed his cock against the crack of her ass and unhooked her bra with slow, measured movements. With a quick flick of both thumbs, he slipped the straps from her shoulders, and the wispy material fluttered to the counter.

As her nipples pebbled, Gabriel groaned, the chill of sweat along his back sending a shiver across his flesh. Her quickened breathing matched his own as he cupped her breasts, lifted their weight with unsteady hands, and brushed their tips with his thumbs.

Her head fell back against his chest, and she pressed her ass harder against his erection as she stared at his hands on her body. He kissed the long sweep of her neck until he reached her ear and nibbled the lobe, while his hand left one breast to glide across the smooth expanse of her ribs and belly. Her skin quivered beneath his fingers as he slid his index finger along the elastic of her panties. Then he skimmed his hand lower until his fingers dipped into the dew of her sex and he slowly penetrated her with his index finger.

For the briefest moment, she stiffened.

Then Gabriel withdrew his finger and slid it back in again, higher this time. Then he did it all over again.

She cried out, slapping one palm on the counter and grinding her drenched sex against his hand.

Lust. It pounded into his body, left his mind blind except for the animal need to take. He wanted to mount her right now, press her over the counter and...

"My God, Gabriel," Amanda breathed. "I—"

Before he had her coming and he lost the last of his control, he withdrew his hand from between her legs and flipped her around and set her down on the counter. Sweeping his fingers in her hair and anchoring her head, he caught her mouth in a kiss.

She groaned into his mouth before sucking his tongue into her own, wrapping both legs around his waist and bucking up against cock.

He met each thrust with a jerk of his own, rubbing her mound and soaked panties again and again.

Her entire body jackknifed against him.

His lips muffled her cry of release. He eased back long enough to look into her dazed eyes. She was beautiful. The candlelight gleamed off the sheen of sweat on her face, breasts, and stomach. He was losing himself, and he didn't care. All he wanted was to be inside her and to drown in her scent. He roughly tugged at her panties and couldn't stop the tremble of his hand as he guided her into the shower.

The warm water sluiced down their bodies while mist swirled around them. Sheltering her from much of the water's spray, he nudged her chin upward to take her mouth in another hot kiss.

She sank into him, rubbing her stomach against his cock as her slick breasts slid up against him. Her hair snaked around her neck and shoulders.

Gabriel swept the wet strands to one side and tongued her neck and the lobe of her ear as he cupped her breasts once again and kneaded them, brushing their peaks with his thumbs until her breathing quickened once again. When she started to kneel, he caught her by the elbow. "Not this time. If you go down on me now, it's all over."

He turned her around until water sprayed over her back and ass, accenting every feminine, nerve-wracking curve and dimple. He shifted, shielding her further from the onslaught of warm water. It sprayed against the back of his head as he widened his legs and kneaded and shaped her ass cheeks beneath his fingers. Her hand slapped the shower wall as he nudged her legs wider and fingered her folds and opening. He squeezed his eyes shut, his breath sawing into his lungs as he forced himself to go slow when all he wanted to do was slam into her heat. Inch by slow inch, he eased inside her opening. Holy Mother. She was tight, hot and wet around his cock. While anchoring her against him with one hand on her hip, he stroked his other hand over her neck, shoulders, back, ribs, ass—touching, kneading as he slowly withdrew and slid back inside her body. Then he found the perfect rhythm. Until...

She reached around and caressed his balls. Her touch sent him over the edge, and he slammed into her, covering her hand against the tile with his own palm to keep himself from collapsing against her. His hips pistoned, nailing her again and again until she cried out, stiffening, shuddering against him, her fingers clawing at the tile. Then he, in turn, grew rigid as spilled his seed into her.

They both stilled for a moment. Then she slumped.

Before she pitched forward, he caught her around the waist and held her for a long moment, savoring everything about her.

Once out of the shower, he grabbed a plush towel and helped wrap her hair and then used another to dry her gently. After quickly rubbing himself down, he carried her to bed and made love to her again. This time, he went slow. He showed her with his body how much he loved... yes, *loved* her...

He loved this beautiful, fierce woman, this mother,

this amazing and incomparable lady he had been blessed to have in his life, no matter how briefly. To find love after all this time when he had shied away, even hidden from the emotion, was a miracle in itself.

When it looked like she might melt into the mattress a good fifteen minutes later, he smiled down at her as he rested on his side, propped on one elbow. He'd managed to get her to forget for at least a couple of minutes. He brushed a damp tendril of hair from her temple, pleased at the rose tint to her cheeks and the sated look in her eyes.

Her gaze slid down his chest and paused on the scar. It was almost 12 inches across from nipple to nipple. Another incision cut downward, making a T pattern. She touched both lines with the whisper of a finger and met his gaze. "They've faded a lot."

"Everything fades, given time." His voice was gruff and unsteady from this deep, unfamiliar emotion he could not kill off even if he wanted to. He spoke the truth; time had dulled the horrors of years before, but even if faded, he would never forget. They had made him the man he was this moment, this day in time.

He caught her hand and kissed the tender, inner side of her wrist, then over the fleshy pads of her hand before he moved along a finger to suck on its tip. At the look of unmistakable desire again flaring in her eyes, his entire body tightened with hunger

He never thought he would surrender to a woman with a badge and a fierce independent streak, never mind surrender to love.

CHAPTER 23

Amanda woke to screams. She jerked up from the bed and shoved her hair from her face, momentarily disoriented as to where she was or what time it was. Darkness filled the room, but the warmth of Gabriel's body had long disappeared. She blinked at the clock's red numbers. 4:44.

She kicked to break free of the sheets twisted around her legs and ankles. As another scream crashed into the night, Amanda tumbled from her bed and grabbed a housecoat. Heart pounding, she shoved her arms into the sleeves and rushed from her bedroom, almost falling to her knees and slamming her elbow against the doorjamb in her hurry.

Nicole! Heartbeat clamoring, she snapped on the hall light and rushed into Nicole's bedroom.

Alone in bed, Nicole thrashed at her covers and swung out at some imaginable thing above her with both hands.

"Nicole!" Amanda scrambled onto the bed. "Wake up! You're having a bad dream." She shook her daughter's shoulder roughly while ducking her flaying hands. She finally managed to catch both wrists and pressed them against her chest. Biceps and wrists straining, she held tight as her daughter twisted and bucked beside her. "Nicole!"

Finally, the young girl stilled and stared up at her. The beam from the hall's light illuminated the blind look in her eyes. She was in some other world.

"It's okay, baby. I'm here. You're not alone. You're safe. No one's going to hurt you." She shifted closer and gathered her close.

Nicole lay limp in her arms and continued to stare back with a distant look in her eyes. She didn't seem aware of her surroundings or didn't seem to care.

"Nicole," Amanda whispered, rubbing her daughter's hands between her warmer ones. "Come back to me, sweetie. Come back."

A breath shuddered through her frail body. Then Nicole blinked and shifted, her gaze focusing finally. It had taken minutes to reach her, and even now she seemed like she'd shut herself down from her surroundings.

Amanda had been an idiot, fooling herself. She'd thought things had gotten better moving to Spirit Lake. Yes, the nightmares had lessened in frequency, but what was worse, in truth, was that they'd increased in intensity. This one seemed more brutal than the others. The recent murders had to be fanning Nicole's fears. It was getting to the point where Amanda didn't know what to do. Flee with her child? She didn't care if running made her look like a coward. At the same time, Nicole had just started adjusting to their new home. What if Amanda uprooted her again, and this time her daughter wasn't able to adapt?

Worse still…

What if the next time Nicole had a nightmare, she couldn't pull herself back into the real world?

Just the idea sent a tremor of dread through Amanda's body.

She tenderly swept back Nicole's hair from her brow. "It's only a dream. Nothing more. Your stepfather is never going to hurt you."

Suddenly Nicole violently shook her head back and forth. She opened her mouth, tried to say something, and shook her head again.

"What is it?"

"The knife. They're going to cut me open. They're going to kill me."

Amanda sucked in a breath of shock. "No, you've got it wrong. That's all a dream. Your stepfather is dead. You saw yourself, I killed him. He can't come back. It's impossible. There's no way he can hurt you again."

Right now, if she could, Amanda would kill the bastard all over again. But this time, she'd kill him slowly. HE deserved nothing less than a slow, brutal torture.

"It's not the same dream. This one's different."

Amanda sank back on her heels. "How so?"

"That woman was in it."

Amanda stiffened. She already knew the answer, but she asked anyway. "What woman?"

"Mayor."

"And? Can you talk about it?"

"She let me die."

Fear crawled across Amanda's skin. The idea that Gabriel's sister was getting into Nicole's subconscious was horrifying. Some part of her wondered if the woman could do something so supernatural. She said, more to convince herself than anyone else, "It's a dream. Only a dream."

"No, it isn't. It's not a dream." Nicole pushed away from her.

Amanda tried not to show how the action hurt. Nicole wasn't thinking. It would take a good 24 hours at least for her to get back to normal. Thinking back to the other day and the missing newspaper clippings and how looking at them might be triggering Nicole's nightmares, she had to ask, "Did you go in my desk the other day and take anything?"

"No. Why?" Nicole looked genuinely puzzled.

"No reason. I just can't find some papers since the move, and I thought you might have accidentally moved them." She shrugged. "No worries. I'll stay with you the rest of the night in case you have any other dreams."

"No. I want to be alone."

Amanda thought to argue, but something about Nicole's expression stilled her tongue. She hadn't seen that look in her eyes before. Dead. Nothing. She'd seen an array of others—terror, horror, sadness—but never something that lacked any emotion. "Sure," she murmured. "I'll at least leave the hall light on. And if you need anything…"

She turned her back to Amanda and faced the opposite wall.

Amanda slipped from the room, an incredible sadness banding around her chest and throat. She'd been snubbed many times throughout her life, but Nicole's cut the deepest. Her rejection was only part of Amanda's sorrow. It was also having this child she'd brought into her home dealing with insurmountable pain. Amanda had lost her own parents, but she'd managed to create her own life before their deaths. She had other people, other interests, and a separate and adult identity. She'd been devastated, almost like a part of her had lost a limb when her mother died. But she'd known what was coming when her mother had been diagnosed with cancer. She'd had months to deal with a loss. Nicole's life was still so focused on her immediate surroundings and the people in her circle. At that age, she didn't have any concepts of a larger view of the world around her.

The next morning when she dropped Nicole off at school, her daughter appeared solemn, barely talked, and when she did, her responses were all monosyllables, free of any emotional inflection.

"Are you going to be all right?" Amanda asked as Nicole unbuckled her seatbelt. "You can take the day off." She pulled to a stop behind the next car in line. The car's cabin buffered the noise from other car engines, doors slamming, and the chatter from the students outside. It also magnified the lengthening and uncomfortable silence between them.

"It doesn't matter. I don't care anymore."

"What do you mean?"

Nicole quickly opened the vehicle's door, slipped out, and shut it without answering.

As she watched her troubled child join the other students in the yard and then disappear into the school, Amanda strangled the wheel with both hands. It sounded like Nicole was giving up. Impossible. She'd come this far. She couldn't now. Not with what she'd already been through. She'd healed so much since her mother's murder.

Amanda frowned. She wasn't going to let her

daughter give up and fail now... Amanda somehow needed to show her to have faith, to believe everything would work out. Nicole was too young. Life still held the possibility of something wonderful happening.

Yes, with those wonders there was also pain. But life was a blessing. Amanda refused to think otherwise. Maybe it was time to find another psychologist, but who? Options in a small town were few. But she needed to do something to help Nicole. Moving away from a large city wasn't enough. It went deeper than that.

When Amanda went home, she didn't sleep, too agitated about her daughter's mental state. Granted, working the night shift kept her from getting a good rest many a night. After a couple of hours of battling the sheets, she gave up and instead cleaned the place, even resorting to scrubbing the floor beneath the fridge and stove. When it was time to pick Nicole up from school, she left the house with a mixture of hope and dread. She walked across the snow-dusted walkway toward the car, which was exposed to the elements. Like many in the neighborhood, her place, several decades old, had been built without a garage.

She pulled up her collar and glanced across the yard and both sides of the street, unable to kill the tension in her body as she looked for any sign of Mayor.

Nothing. But that didn't mean Amanda was safe.

She hit the unlock button on her key as a gust of wind flung her hair to one side. Shoving the strands aside, she got in and quickly closed the car door behind her. It wasn't like she'd be safe inside, considering what she'd seen Mayor capable of. The temperature had dropped during the day and the wind had picked up.

The forecasts warned of a storm coming in with several inches of snow. She was tired of the winter and there were still a couple of months to go.

Maybe they'd take up skiing. Get Nicole out into the fresh air after this thing with Mayor ended...

Amanda swore. There had to be a way to get the woman away from them. Away from town. Away from Gabriel. What was it that motivated a person? Sex? Money? What else? Power?

She swore again. She didn't think any of those things would work on Mayor. After all, the woman, creature, monster—whatever you wanted to call her—didn't have normal human motives except maybe revenge. So how to get someone thinking they don't want vengeance? Exchange it for something that they wanted even more? But what exactly?

Behind the wheel, she turned the key in the ignition. The engine didn't turn over. She tried again. Nothing but a clicking sound each time.

Shit. Not good. Not good at all. Not when Nicole was in the state she was in...

She rummaged in her purse for her phone and quickly glanced at the time. She had ten minutes before the school's bell. She could walk, but she'd get there too late. The idea of Nicole standing in the yard and finding no one waiting for her made Amanda feel awful. Really, more than awful.

Katie. Of course. The older girl wasn't far from the school.

She called but didn't get an answer. Grunting in frustration, she hung up. Who else?

Gabriel, of course, but she hated calling him. But

hadn't she just been spouting about Nicole needing to have faith? Didn't she need to learn that herself? Didn't she need to have belief in not only herself but in others? Like Gabriel? Slowly, she'd grown isolated, lost touch with many of her friends, using work as an excuse, but the death of her mother had left her reeling. She'd lost her sense of purpose, having spent almost a year ensuring her mother had the best care, the best of everything as her health declined and she succumbed to cancer. Amanda had been left with a hole and no purpose, so she'd focused on work. But then her life had intersected with Nicole's during one violent, senseless, and evil act, and she'd found a new meaning, but in the process, she'd lost sight of herself and what she needed.

She really did need to take that leap herself, trust Gabriel and have faith that counting on him was a good idea. Being vulnerable was just fine. How else could she grow as a human being?

His phone barely rang once before he picked up. The tension in his voice was unmistakable. "Are you okay? Nicole?"

"We're fine. It's just that my car won't start, and I can't get to Nicole before school ends. I'm trying not to panic, but your sister is still out there…"

It was Gabriel's turn to swear. "I'm over twenty minutes away. I'm in Estherville right now. It looks like a woman with Mayor's description was registered at one of the hotels there. Did you want me to swing by the school?"

"Um…" She'd have to walk. There wasn't any other option. Nicole didn't have a cell, and her best friend didn't either. Amanda was calling herself all kinds of stupid for not giving her daughter a phone. But she couldn't do anything about it now. She just hoped... "Sure, if you could. I'm heading that way by foot. Hopefully, I'll get there before you, but if you do, just let her know I'll be right there."

"Of course."

She didn't want to think about Mayor and what she was capable of for any length of time. If she went down that route, she'd have a full-blown panic attack.

She left everything in the car except her phone, locked the doors, and headed toward the school. Five minutes in, snow started falling from a darkening sky. When she reached the school's property, only a few students lingered near the building. One or two cars were parked along the perimeter, while a few other vehicles dotted the parking lot.

No need to worry yet, even though she didn't immediately see any signs of Nicole. She hurried up the sidewalk and stepped into the office. All the chairs lining the wall were empty.

"Hey," she called to the receptionist behind the desk. "I'm late picking up Nicole Douglas. She's not out front. Did she leave already?" Amanda gripped the edge of the counter that separated the public from the staff. It was a clear but feeble barrier to keep the crazies at a distance.

"I'm sorry. There's no way I can tell you that." The woman with a bun the size of a grapefruit on top of her head rose and walked from behind her desk. "Do you have your ID?"

"No." Of course, she'd been stupid to leave it in the car with her purse. She'd gotten lax living in a small town.

The woman didn't know her. Amanda hadn't bothered making friends with the faculty or other parents. Keeping to herself and being relatively new to the town wasn't in her favor for bypassing the school's protocol.

"Then I can't give you any information." The woman adjusted her thick black-framed glasses, which reminded Amanda of Harry Potter's, but these ones seemed far larger.

Or maybe they just seemed to magnify her suspicious brown eyes unusually so. Or maybe it was just Amanda feeling like she was in a panic and imagining every little thing. "I usually pick her up, but my car wouldn't start and…"

The woman shook her head, the bun on her head swinging dangerously to one side. "Sorry, I can't help you without an ID."

A mask of resolve and coolness settled over the woman's face, so no amount of cajoling was going to get Amanda anywhere with her. She swore under her breath and shoved away from the desk. Adding several other choice words, she pivoted and rushed back outside. She hurried across the yard and peered down the open walkways between the buildings. She couldn't get in because of a wrought iron fence. It was sad that walls and fences in schools were turning out to be a standard protection for the young.

She reached the end of the building with no sign of Nicole.

Nothing. The rest of the students had left and no one was around. Panic was starting to set in. There was no way Amanda could have missed her if she'd walked home.

She grabbed her phone and dialed Katie's number. This time the girl answered. "Hey, Katie? Has Nicole showed up at your place?"

"No. Why?"

She isn't at school, and I haven't been able to find her."

"I'm sorry, no. I'm sure there's nothing to worry about."

"I'm sure," Amanda lied. Nicole never wandered off. At times, she acted older than Amanda.

But maybe this time she'd been so upset with dealing with her nightmares and past that she'd decided to run off? Amanda chewed on her bottom lip. She hated to think that way, but the alternative sent chills racing through her.

Mayor was dangerous. But was she dangerous enough to harm an innocent child?

She pushed the thought from her mind. She didn't dare focus on that now. Instead, she called every friend of Nicole's she could think of, but no one had seen her since school had been let out.

At the sound of a car engine drawing near, she turned.

Gabriel pulled up to the side of the curb.

She rushed to the driver's side, relieved at his appearance. She didn't feel so helpless, so alone.

His window hummed open. "Any sign of Nicole?"

She grabbed the open window where he rested his elbow. "Nothing." She glanced down at her phone. "It's twenty minutes since the kids were let out from school. It's not like her to take off like this. She'd be the first to wait in the office or have someone from the school call me."

He engulfed her hand in the warmth of his own and squeezed gently. "Get in."

She hurried around and jumped into the passenger seat while brushing impatiently at the snow clinging to her hair. "Take me home. I'll point out the exact way we always go, but drive slow just in case I missed her for some reason."

Gabriel traveled the route, each road and house as familiar as the clothing on her back. The knot in her stomach tightened until they reached her street and she thought she might vomit. "I'm going to notify the department. If I don't find her soon… Maybe they can issue an Amber alert."

"Try to be positive. I'm sure there's an explanation."

She glanced over at Gabriel and saw the shadow of doubt in his eyes that belied his words.

When Gabriel pulled into the driveway, a layer of snow covered the yard and sidewalk. Even though she didn't see any signs of footsteps, she still rushed inside and called out, "Nicole? Are you there?"

Nothing. Only silence. Then the sound of Gabriel stepping into the house and the door closing behind him.

She pivoted and faced him, hating to ask the question but unable to stop herself. "What would Mayor do if she took Nicole? Would she kill her?"

CHAPTER 24

The question hit him in the face, which was stupid on his part. He should know Nicole's safety would be the utmost in Amanda's mind.

"No," he replied as she shrugged out of her jacket. He hung up his next to hers on the coat rack and followed her into the kitchen. "She's never hurt a child, no matter how emotionally distraught she was."

She pressed a thumb and finger to each side of her temples and closed her eyes briefly. Sighing, she dropped her hand to her side. "She has a fixation with Nicole. It's more than revenge, I think. There's some type of bond between the two. I don't know what it is. Maybe because she lost her daughter before and she thinks Nicole can somehow replace her? But whatever it is, I don't like it.

"I'm calling this in now. I have to." She swiped her phone and frowned down at it. "I just don't know how to do that without sounding crazy. They're going to think I'm ranting. Who's going to believe such an insane story?"

"They're not. And even if they did, it would take not just hours, but days. We don't have time. I've got this." Gabriel pulled his own phone from his back pocket. "What we'll do is separate them. They're two different situations. No one would believe a woman the size of Mayor was capable of physically taking down those men. But taking a child. That's different. They'll jump on that."

Gabriel called into the department, he reached Warner, talked to him and told him the details of Nicole missing and that his sister, a woman who had a vendetta against him, might have kidnapped Amanda's daughter. It was close to the truth, as close as he could get without sounding off an alarm.

He hung up and said, "They are going to get someone down here to question both of us. From there, hopefully they will get an alert on the broadcast system."

"I guess that's something." She pulled a cup from a cabinet. "Did you want some tea? I can get you something stronger, but for myself, I don't dare. If I start drinking alcohol, I don't think I'll be able to stop, and right now, I need a clear head and to do something mundane to keep my sanity." When he shook his head, she started the electric kettle. "What did you find out at Estherville? Anything?"

"The manager at the hotel where she was staying didn't have anything helpful."

Lips pressed into a grim line, she grabbed the cleaner from under the sink and a towel and wiped down the island. "I figured. You would have said otherwise. No-no sign of Nicole or a struggle?"

"No, not at all. Mayor didn't leave any belongings behind, but I learned she does have a car. The manager didn't know what type, other than a white sedan. It could possibly be a Toyota Corolla or a Ford Fusion or Focus. It's hard to say. I was not able to get a license number."

She dug her fingers into the towel, then squeezed it into a tight ball, before she pivoted sharply and put it and the cleaner back in the cabinet.

Then she turned again to the electric kettle to pour her tea, but he caught the flash of fear in her eyes. He walked up behind her and placed his hands gently over her shoulders, but he could not offer much comfort other than saying, "Mayor has always loved children. She would never hurt Nicole."

She pivoted and rested her head against his shoulder and sniffled into his shirt.

He slid a hand over the cap of her hair and the thick, silken wand of her ponytail before pressing her deeper into his arms. When she clung to him, Gabriel's chest tightened with a pain he had not felt in decades. The sudden, unexpected and intense surge of empathy caught him off guard. He drew in a ragged breath and closed his eyes. He opened his mouth to insist that he would protect Nicole, but he realized it was a useless promise and an outright lie. He couldn't protect Amanda's daughter if he couldn't find either the child or Mayor.

After several moments of silence, Amanda shifted, easing backward until he released her. Frowning, she met his gaze. "I was thinking of the ritual or spell that was done on you and your family. What they did to you must be branded into your mind. I'd never forget such a horror." She paused, bit her bottom lip for a moment, then asked, "Have you ever tried doing it on someone else?"

"No. I had thought of it a long time ago, but it's too dangerous, and there is little guarantee of it working.

Plus, I would never inflict that type of pain on another living being."

"What about Mayor?"

"She'd never do something like that now," he quickly said, but he couldn't keep the doubt from his voice or his thoughts.

"What do you mean by 'now'?" Amanda's voice rose. "Are you saying she's tried it before?"

"Once," he admitted, but quickly added to lower Amanda's escalating alarm, "She would never do it now. Not when it ended so badly."

She rubbed the heel of her palm against her brow. "This is sounding like I've traveled to hell and can't find a way out. How bad is bad?" With narrowed eyes, she stared back at him, and then shook her head. "Forget I asked. I don't think I want to know the details."

"You don't," Gabriel agreed. "And knowing does nothing to stop Mayor today." He thought back to what Mayor had done. He still remembered the man's name: Hector. He had fallen for his sister's laugh, luminous eyes, and charm. When she was lucid, she could turn a man into an idiot with a word or look. Hector had trusted Mayor. The poor fool had not seen the other side to her. Maybe because he had somehow curbed the hatred inside her. Who knew, but he had paid for his love. He had paid with his life. Gabriel had walked into the scene, frozen in horror, but he had not been in time to save Hector.

"Still, if she's done it once, she's more than capable of trying it again. She might have gotten it into her head to somehow replace her daughter with Nicole."

"I hope Mayor wouldn't be so stupid as to try

something like that." Holy Mother. Amanda's fears had real substance. "If she's thinking of Nicole as a daughter, the last thing she would do would be to harm her."

"I'd like to believe it, but your sister's a serial murderer. You can't tell me she values human life."

"She did once." But that was long ago and a lifetime away. She had changed so much. Yes, she had a mental condition, but it was more than that. It was the hatred that fed her irrational behavior.

"But this is now." Jaw inflexible, Amanda lifted her chin. "Why did she try to turn this other person?"

"Love."

"Oh." She tugged on her ponytail. "Somehow that seems worse."

"Hector adored her and she felt the same, or at least as much as she's capable of. I thought for a time that she might change for the better. I guess they were willing to hold onto that feeling…"

"And then he ended up dead."

"Yes." He rubbed at the back of his neck, pivoted, and looked out the front living room window. He didn't like talking about the couple's doomed relationship. And he hated talking about the past even more.

"I've changed my mind. Tell me. What did Mayor do?" Hands fisted, Amanda asked. "I'd like to know the details. Maybe it will help me in terms of what she's capable of." The unrelenting look on her face said she wasn't going to let it go, and she would push, push until he told her the truth in every bloody detail. He wouldn't be able to skirt around it.

So be it.

He cleared his throat before saying, "I walked in after Mayor had performed much of the ceremony she had replicated from memory. The priest ties the victim down to ensure they don't move for fear of injuring the body. When we were chosen, their objective was to create a better, stronger person who is reborn from the womb of *Temazcal*. This particular ritual was never recorded or documented by any historians, although there are other in-depth studies of Mayan and Aztec rebirth ceremonies. Few of the natives talked about it while we were held captive. Probably fear kept them silent because of the priest's great magic. He was fascinated with Mayor and her coloring, and knowing we were related, grouped us into that same fascination.

"I have blocked the actual words used during the ceremony from my memory. Somehow Mayor had memorized each inflection, storing the syllables in her brain. While the incantation is performed, the sacrifice is bathed in a purifying hot vapor and has their face, arms, and legs painted with various symbols in red ochre. They use the same paint to draw a cross over the chest and stomach. Then a knife is blessed and heated beneath a flame in the center of the room." When Amanda's expression changed, he paused and asked, "Do you want me to go on?"

She cut the air with a hand. "Why not? I'm already having nightmares."

He hesitated. He wasn't fooled by Amanda's snappy response. Even though she tried, she hadn't been able to mask the dread in her eyes.

Amanda sighed. "Please. I need to know."

He rubbed at the bridge of his nose and dropped

his hand to his side. "I'm sure you've heard stories that Aztecs were a bloody lot, but the conquistadors were no better, slaughtering the native children and women, respected leaders, war veterans, and codex interpreters in their greed for gold and riches." Gabriel rubbed at his neck as memories sifted from his subconscious. "We were herded from the main sacrificial temple during the festival of *Tlacaxipehualiztli* where they worship Xipe Totec, the god of rebirth. The whole energy is filled with a mix of terror and celebration. It's a dizzying combination. The three of us could not escape; we had learned those who tried died far more painful, lengthy deaths." Memories of the others captured threatened to take hold of his thoughts. They had gotten to know a few others, their history, and the families they left behind. So their deaths hit harder than the others.

He hooked both thumbs around his leather belt, and the chill of sweat formed along the seam of his spine. He braced his legs to stop himself from pacing or turning away from Amanda's all-too-knowing eyes. He wished he could just as easily turn away from the past. "The usual method of sacrificing their slaves or captives was a slice from the abdomen up through the diaphragm. With us, their incision was smaller, more inclined to help us heal in the event we were reborn. From a small earthen pot, they poured mercury into our chest cavity."

Amanda gasped. "No one can live through something like that."

Gabriel forced a laugh. "Exactly, and we didn't. We died and somehow came back. I'm not sure how. Luys, fascinated for years with what the priest had accomplished without a state-of-the-art medical center, has been doing research for decades to try to decipher how."

"So it's magic?"

"I don't know. Luys seems to think otherwise. He's a big believer in science and a rational explanation, but he hasn't found one yet.

"As of today, all the science in the world can't explain how we are living. And yes, I have lived for centuries, but I would never subject myself to such inhumane methods to do it again. They tied us all down over a ceremonial rock slab. I think they believed the more pain they inflicted, the greater chance there would be able to launch us into the womb of *Temazcal*. They wanted us to scream—the louder, the better. After all, childbirth is a painful business, and they didn't want us to escape this world without experiencing the worse they could inflict upon us. The blade was surprisingly sharp and made of onyx instead of flint…"

A visual of that same knife flashed inside his head. The wicked point and how it had sliced through his flesh as they carved a line from nipple to nipple while he had been still breathing and fully aware. They had deliberately cut him slowly and retraced the knife's path, again and again, to push him over the edge. He could still remember Mayor's and Luy's screams and then his own. Even hear and smell the scent of burning flesh, the chanting, the screams from others sacrificed around them. And the pain…Holy Mother, he had never felt such pain …

He stepped backward until he hit the edge of the sofa. Grabbing the arm to steady himself, he grappled for breath. The priest's face, painted into a monstrous mask, appeared over his head…

"Gabriel."

He blinked.

"Gabriel! You're fine. Everything's fine. You're not there anymore."

He blinked again. Then Amanda's face swam before him and eventually came into focus, and he realized she was gripping his arms. She must have been shaking him.

With one hand, he wiped at his face, and with the other, he cupped her hand against his arm. With one hand, he wiped at his face, and with the other, he cupped her hand against his arm. "I'm sorry. I shouldn't have gotten carried away like that—"

"Don't. I should be the one apologizing. I'm making you remember something painful and beyond anything I can imagine, but I also need to know about what is driving your sister. Mayor's past is somehow tied to her future. Everyone's is. We're always trying to grow past our childhood or early adulthood issues. And Mayor's issues have become Nicole's and mine and they're the reason why she's taken my daughter."

At the sound of a car's engine, Amanda's hand stiffened beneath his own. Quickly, he wrapped his arms around her and held her for a moment, wishing that somehow by holding her she could draw more strength.

She shuddered and pulled away before taking a steadying breath.

For a moment, he thought she might crack; raw fear flashed in her eyes before she turned away. He followed Amanda to the front door. From the living room window, he could only identify Warner as two men stepped from a squad car.

~☙~

Amanda opened the door. Warner stepped inside, followed by Freer. At seeing Freer, Amanda sucked in her breath and forced herself to calm down. She hated the idea of him seeing her being anything but contained, and she'd be damned if today was going to be any different.

"You want to tell us what's going on?" Freer quickly asked. "She's been missing since the kids were released from school today, correct?"

"Yeah. It's not like her." She stepped farther into the house to make room for both officers. She explained how she'd been late picking her up, but never found her on the school grounds and went into a little more detail than Gabriel had when talking to Warner earlier.

Freer patted her on the back. "Don't worry, if your girl is alive, we'll find her. We'll see if we can get an Amber Alert broadcast going in a bit." He shrugged and made a face. "We'll find her, either way."

Gabriel glared at Freer. "There's no either way. She'll be found alive."

Amanda stepped in front of Gabriel, afraid he might do something physical to the other man. She'd never seen Gabriel act so protective of her. It was soothing and surprising at the same time. She couldn't remember, other than when her mother was alive, anyone championing for her.

Freer flushed, looking uncharacteristically contrite with everyone frowning at him. "Martinez, I understand you're getting worked up, but I'm on Amanda's side." He nodded at Amanda. "Take the next couple of days off work."

"But—"

"No arguments. Just focus on finding your daughter. Make some calls around town. That type of stuff."

"I don't want—" Amanda's words stumbled to a halt at the sudden static.

Then dispatch announced from the radio on Freer's shoulder, "We have a 187. The address is 1607 Oak Ave."

Gabriel sucked in his breath behind her.

At his reaction, Amanda turned sharply toward him. "What?" She widened her eyes. "Oh, shit. That's your address."

CHAPTER 25

On the porch of Gabriel's house, Amanda glanced over at Gabriel standing in the middle of the yard, but he wasn't paying attention to her or pretty much anyone. Gaze blank, he was staring off at something across the street. Neither one of them wanted to go back inside; the stench of death was too overwhelming.

All four of them had rushed to the scene. The front door had been locked, but the killer had broken in through the back door. Freer was the first to find the mutilated body lying on Gabriel's bed and identify the man as Ken Nelson. The victim's heart had been cut out, while a symbol, like the other victims, had been carved into his flesh. Mayor had decided to get artistic on the man's stomach.

Amanda had never been so terrified from the time the dispatcher's voice came over the radio to when she reached Gabriel's home and found an adult male victim instead of her daughter. For a wild moment, she thought she was going to crack right then and fall to the ground and would never be able to get back up.

Nicole was still missing, though. There might be a slim chance Mayor didn't take her, but Amanda didn't believe it. Nicole wouldn't leave willingly without first letting her know. She just wasn't that type of girl.

Amanda stepped down from the porch and walked across the yard to Gabriel as someone from the Medical Examiner's Office wheeled the body down the driveway to the government vehicle.

Waves of despair radiated from him. He looked broken.

She'd been there before with the death of her mother and knew how god-awful that felt. Amanda whispered beside him, "She really hates you."

He didn't turn to acknowledge her but said in an equally low voice with a distinct bite to it. "There was a time when she looked up to me, thought I could do no wrong."

"Being flippant doesn't suit you."

He turned then and met her gaze with dull, tired eyes. "I don't know what suits me anymore. I've never felt this powerless. Nothing I've done so far has made a difference."

"Don't think that way. I need you, Gabriel," she whispered in a voice crackling with emotion before rubbing at her face with a shaking hand. She didn't care if Gabriel saw her near cracking. She'd lost any desire to hide behind a façade of control. "I need your strength. I've never asked much of people, but I'm asking you to help me get through this."

He ate up the distance between them in two steps and dragged her into his arms in a crushing grip. Then he let go and caught her face in both hands and forced her to look up into his eyes. "Don't ever worry I'll turn my back on you or Nicole. I'm here to the end. Even if it means my death."

Amanda caught his hands and pulled them up against her chest and clung to them. "Don't say that. Don't ever say that."

He pressed his brow against hers. "I love you."

She squeezed her eyes shut and let his words wrap themselves around her. "I love you, too."

She hated how ironic life could get. Those three words should make her happy, but they just made her even sadder. It would be obscene if she relished the possibility of happiness with her daughter out there somewhere with Mayor, in danger, afraid, alone.

"We'll get through this," he whispered against her brow. "I have to regroup and find a way to locate Mayor. I tried calling my brother for his input. So far no answer. Luys lives in Phoenix, so it would take some time for him to get here." He kissed her temple. "I will find her— she can only hide so long—and end it between us for good. Her hatred and rage have to stop."

Amanda pressed deeper into his embrace. Life was too painful, too raw. Only the strong survived it, and she was feeling far from strong right now. She could just imagine how Gabriel was feeling.

She didn't know how she'd react to having a sibling like Mayor. She'd been an only child. After her parents' divorce, her relationship with her dad had been non-existent. For years she'd blamed him. Her mom never remarried after the divorce, while her father had soon moved out of state to be with his new wife's family. At first, she'd suspected her mother had stayed single because she hadn't been able to get over her dad and didn't want to get hurt again from another man. It wasn't until she'd found her mother's love letters that she

realized her mother had been in love with another man.
Their affair had lasted over five years and then nothing.
Amanda didn't know why the letters stopped, whether
her mother's lover had been married or died years later,
but she'd never tried to trace the letter's origins, feeling it
best to leave the past alone.

All those years she'd considered her mother perfect
as she focused on Amanda, her close circle of female
friends, and spent her remaining time supporting one
of the local shelters for women and children affected by
domestic violence and human trafficking. All those years,
Amanda had tried to live up to her mother's standards, all
the while subconsciously competing with and emulating
her. All those years, she'd mistakenly thought of her
father as the one who'd walked out on his family. Sadly,
all that time she'd thought wrong.

Far too late, she'd come to the realization she never
could be her mother, but only the person she was meant
to be. The only power she had was to focus on being the
best person she could be with what she could do and
what she knew.

But what was her best now? She'd failed so much
already.

"I need to get to work. My shift starts soon. I'll be out
there with everyone else looking for Mayor." He caught
several strands of hair that had escaped her ponytail and
slipped them behind her ear, before stepping away and
breaking off their embrace. "How about you get a bit of
sleep. The medallion you have on will keep you safe. It
doesn't take long for me to feel its power."

"I can't. I need to do something," she said in a
choked voice. She pulled the medallion from beneath

her shirt. "I should have given this to Nicole. I should have—"

"Don't." He stepped farther away from the medallion and her. "At the time, we thought she was only after you. How were either of us to know otherwise?"

A cold breeze cut into her jacket and cut across her exposed face and hands, and she shivered. Until then she'd been unaware or uncaring of her whereabouts.

Gabriel must have noticed. He rubbed her arm and urged her toward his car. "Let me get you home before you freeze out here. Let Freer do his job. He might be an ass, but he does know what he's doing."

Lips thinning, Amanda followed him, but not before she glanced back at Gabriel's house. She wondered who was going to be next. It couldn't be Nicole. Just the idea…

No. She wouldn't think it, because she knew she'd never be able to live with herself if that ever happened.

The house was heart-wrenchingly quiet when she stepped inside and pulled off her jacket and boots. She spent the next couple of hours cleaning, scrubbing every corner of the kitchen, dusting picture frames and light fixtures, and vacuuming places that didn't need vacuuming. When she'd completely exhausted herself, she moved down the hall to her bedroom. She avoided looking into Nicole's room and rubbed at her gritty eyes. A headache pounded inside her skull. After stuffing her clothes into the hamper and setting the medallion on the bedside table, she turned on the water in the shower's stall, then stood under the hot water until it nearly scalded her skin and steam rose and filled the room.

As she rubbed herself dry, she bit back tears and

grabbed a pair of jeans and a shirt. The simple task of dressing herself seemed difficult. She tried to ignore the ache inside her chest as she slipped the necklace back on, but it was impossible. Food was impossible too, yet she needed her body and mind functioning, so she forced herself to shovel down a yogurt.

Sudden shouting from outside drove her from the kitchen, but not before she grabbed her Glock from above the refrigerator. Someone started banging on the door. A quick scan out the front window didn't reveal anyone. Hand tight around the Glock's handle, she looked through the peephole. Her heart stuttered then launched into a full gallop.

With shaking hands, she unlocked the door and yanked it open. "Nicole!"

Nicole launched herself into her arms. The paper bag her daughter was holding dropped to the floor in the foyer.

She barely noticed, too caught up in seeing Nicole standing there, seemingly unharmed. Amanda hugged her daughter with her free arm and glanced over the girl's shoulder to check if her daughter was alone.

No sign of Mayor in the yard, street or driveway. Or anyone else, for that matter.

"Are you hurt? What happened? How did you get home?" Amanda couldn't stop the questions flying from her mouth, even knowing she needed to back off and let her daughter get her bearings. "I looked everywhere for you. I called your friends and anyone else who I thought might have seen you. I was sick with worry!" She stepped back far enough to get a good look at her.

Tear tracks stained Nicole's cheeks, her hair was

mussed and uncombed from her flushed face, but she didn't appear bruised or physically hurt in any way.

Nicole wiped at her eyes and shuddered. "She's crazy."

"Who? Mayor?" Amanda closed and locked the door and pulled Nicole deeper into the house.

"She said she was worried about you and I needed to go with her."

At Nicole's nod, Amanda couldn't help but say, "But I warned you about her."

"I thought you had to be wrong or were just being super protective. She was so nice to me the times she talked to me." Her daughter walked into the kitchen and slumped into one of the kitchen chairs.

Amanda wanted to yell with frustration, hit something, but reacting and giving in to her baser feelings would only upset Nicole and not solve a thing. Instead, she nodded once, turned and walked across the kitchen to put her Glock on top of the fridge, taking the time to get her expression under control. But she couldn't calm her insides. No one warned her that by adopting a child, she'd grow vulnerable like she'd never been before, that she'd get so attached to someone else to the point where it hurt like the devil when that child suffered in any way. The love she held for Nicole was bone-deep, profound, and far stronger than she'd ever imagined possible.

"She didn't hurt you, did she?" She failed at keeping the anger from her voice. Everything would be easier if she were dealing with someone normal, not some unbalanced woman with crazy strength.

"No, but she broke a couple of things when she thought I wasn't listening. She got really scary at the beginning. She picked me up when I tried to get away, and she's *strong*. Stronger than Matt."

Amanda had dated Matt for a time, mistakenly thinking he might be the one. A dedicated athlete, he'd participated in the Ironman triathlon for several years. Other than Gabriel, she hadn't met another man with such physical superiority.

Nicole rested an arm on the table and propped her chin on a hand. "She didn't like me crying. But I couldn't stop."

"I'm *so* sorry!" She pulled a chair closer to Nicole, sat, and took the girl's cold and clammy hands and rubbed her fingers gently to get warmth back into them. Thank goodness Nicole had escaped with her jacket. Being out in the elements could have been equally dangerous.

"Crying made her angrier. But I started pretending I really liked her and I agreed with everything she said." Nicole rested her head against Amanda's shoulder.

"That was very smart of you." She let go of Nicole's hand. "How did you escape?"

Her daughter sniffed and rubbed at her nose. "I thought she locked the bedroom door, but I guess she thought I wasn't going to try to leave. When it was really quiet, I left the room and couldn't find her anywhere. So I ran out the front door."

Mayor was probably off killing Ken Nelson. At the idea of Nicole being in such danger, Amanda struggled against an onslaught of nausea. She inhaled a couple of times to get it under control. It had been a miracle Nicole had escaped with her life. "Do you know where she took you? Was it a house, cabin or something else?"

"A house by a bunch of trees somewhere." Nicole

shrugged out of her jacket. "When I managed to get out from the trees and off the back road, I recognized the highway where we've gotten gas before. I didn't want to go inside the store or get help, because I was afraid I'd run into her and she'd get me."

An incredible sadness engulfed Amanda, but she wasn't about to argue with Nicole's reasoning. Fear made you think of doing strange things that had nothing to do with logic. Her daughter had traveled 3 miles to get back home. That was a long way, especially when you were a child of eleven and alone and frightened. "I have to call the police. They've been looking for you and need to hear you're safe. They're going to have questions about what happened, too."

Nicole frowned but nodded as she tossed her jacket on an empty kitchen chair.

As it slid from the seat, Amanda got up to retrieve it from the floor and put it up on the coat rack, and then she called the police department. Gabriel was unavailable—probably being questioned about the killing of Ken Nelson. She hadn't a clue how he was going to be able to skirt around Mayor. While waiting for someone to show up from the department, she texted Gabriel that Nicole was safe and at home. He'd get there as soon as he could.

Warner showed up for questions. She was glad it wasn't Freer, who was too gruff and taciturn for a sensitive girl. She tensely watched Warner question Nicole, ready for any sign that he might step over the line of interrogating a child, but he was professional, asking the right questions, using a gentle, respectful tone that Nicole didn't find intimidating.

When he finally left, Amanda locked the door

quickly after him and stepped back in the kitchen to find Nicole standing with the refrigerator door open and looking inside.

"Is there any leftover pizza from the other day?".

"Yeah, sure." Amanda grabbed a plate from the cabinet. "Sit down, and I'll get you something to drink with it." She put a piece in the microwave and filled a large glass of milk. The scent of cheese hung in the air after she set the plate of pizza on the table. She glanced at the clock on the microwave.

Blue neon glowed 1:13. There were still a couple of hours of night. Maybe they might be able to get some sleep.

She forced herself to sit down beside Nicole. All she wanted to do was hover, unable to stop herself from imagining what Nicole must have gone through. A quick look above the refrigerator door reassured Amanda that her Glock was still there. Certainly, she wasn't going to unload the bullets and lock both up like she usually did. She felt a little better knowing it was close at hand, even though it wouldn't keep Mayor at bay for long.

"Something's really off with her," Nicole muttered around a mouthful of pizza. "She kept calling me Maria."

Amanda tensed. That was the name of the woman's dead daughter. "Do you know why?"

"No. A couple times she talked about her daughter. Every time she did, she got super upset." The girl gulped down some milk. "It was strange. I think sometimes she thought I was her."

She took in a shuddering breath. So it was true. Mayor had decided to substitute Nicole for her long-dead daughter. How could she combat such a crazy idea?

None of it had any logic. She absently touched the chain around her neck, and her fingers stilled on the metal. She should have given the necklace to Nicole from the very beginning. None of this would have happened if she'd been wearing it.

They could run from town, find another place and hide, but running wasn't going to keep Mayor from finding Nicole or Amanda. She'd found Gabriel easily enough. There was only one option that would keep Nicole safe. Standing up from the table, she pulled the medallion from around her neck. "I have something for you."

"What is it?"

"It's a medallion. Gabriel gave it to me. It has mercury hidden inside a compartment. It's something that will protect you from Mayor. She's actually Gabriel's sister. They go back a long time and have been fighting against each other for probably most of their lives. He's been trying to stop her from hurting people." She ran a thumb over the compartment that held the mercury. "It's something I hope will protect you from Mayor. It has some power that will keep Mayor away from the person who wears it."

After she slipped the necklace over her daughter's head, Nicole fingered the cross that hung almost to her waist. "It looks dirty."

"It's just old."

"Is it magical?" Nicole frowned as she slid a finger over the design.

She thought of lying. "I think so."

A tentative smile touched the girl's lips. "I like that."

"How about you keep it on until we stop Mayor

from hurting anyone else. Promise you won't take it off?"

"Sure." Nicole dropped the cross back down against her stomach. "Who has she hurt?"

"Innocent people who haven't done anything to her."

"So what did she do?"

Amanda didn't lie but she also didn't elaborate. She'd always been an awful liar. "She broke the law."

Nicole's jacket had fallen from the coat rack, so she walked over, picked it up and put it back on its hook, but then saw the paper bag Nicole must have dropped when she'd first gotten inside. Bending back down to also pick that up, she wrinkled her nose. The paper was crumpled, smelled a bit, and had dirt smudges all over it.

"No!" Nicole cried out.

CHAPTER 26

W hat?" Amanda jerked her hand from the bag, swiveled, and stared at Nicole, who stood rigid, hands opening and closing in rapid succession at her sides.

"Don't touch it!" Tears flooded Nicole's eyes and tumbled from her lashes and onto her cheeks. "I had to take it. I had to!"

"But—"

"Please. Please!" Nicole raced over and clawed at Amanda's hand and forearm.

She backed off from the bag and eased her daughter's fingers from her wrist, but Nicole clung tighter. "Where did you get it?"

"It was in her bedroom."

"It'll all be okay. But how about I pick it up and put it on the kitchen counter? Having it by the front door isn't a good place. Someone's going to trip over it."

When Nicole finally nodded and eased her grip on her arm, Amanda rubbed at her wrist.

"I want you to hide it." Her daughter folded her arms across her middle as she backed away.

Slowly so as not to alarm her, Amanda picked up the bag and moved it toward the kitchen's island. "You do know I'm going to have to open it and see what it is.

From your reaction, what's inside is clearly important. I can't let it just sit there without at least knowing why you're upset."

Nicole's lips thinned, but she didn't argue.

Gritting her teeth, Amanda unfolded the top with trembling fingers, the paper bag crackling in protest. She angled the bag toward the light and looked inside.

Shit. A knife. She didn't dare pull it out and leave damaging fingerprints. It was bad enough she'd put her hands on the bag. She was equally shocked Nicole had smuggled the weapon from Mayor's place. Her daughter's phobia had dictated every action she'd made when it came to any type of knife.

What was inside wasn't just any knife, though. She suspected the blade was made of onyx. It gleamed beneath the kitchen's bright light as if honed again and again to get the edge as sharp as any modern blade. She couldn't tell if there was any blood residue on the knife.

Nicole wiped at her eyes and nose. "They used that knife."

"What do you mean?"

"They killed lots of people with it."

"Is that what Mayor told you?" Amanda tried not to show her shock and horror as she gingerly set the bag on the kitchen island. Just what the hell was that woman trying to do? Intentionally terrify Nicole to control her? It was yet another low from Mayor.

"No, but it was in my dreams."

In my dreams. Amanda didn't like the sound of that. "What do you mean by 'they'?"

"The people in my dreams."

Nicole had never mentioned any other people in

her dreams. Her nightmares had always been about her mother and stepfather. She then noticed the dark circles beneath Nicole's eyes and the almost translucent quality to her skin. No doubt lack of sleep and acting on adrenaline alone were clouding her thoughts. Having the police and Amanda bombarding her with a ton of questions probably hadn't helped either. "How about you take a shower? I'm sure it'll make you feel better. And then you can try to get some sleep. We can talk more about it tomorrow." With a fresh mind, maybe she could also unearth more about Nicole's dreams.

After she had Nicole settled for the night, she'd call the department regarding the knife. It was probably one of the murder weapons from Mayor's arsenal. It could be the knife that had carved out—nope, she wasn't going there. Not when she was beyond exhausted. Getting the department involved was the only option. Things were beyond her scope. Mayor was just too big an adversary.

"You have to hide it," Nicole insisted.

"I don't know—"

Panic flared in Nicole's eyes. "You have to. Please. It's a knife." With each word her voice rose. "It can hurt someone. Hurt them bad! Even kill them—"

"Sure." Amanda quickly conceded. "I'll put it in a good hiding place." She inwardly sighed. Maybe one day they could work through Nicole's phobia of knives.

Nicole twisted her fingers faster in front of her. "No. No. Don't hide it. I NEED to know where it's at at all times."

Amanda frowned, rubbed at her face, and tried to get a handle on her own emotions. Tears pricked the back of her eyes. She was supposed to be this strong woman, a mother a child looked up to, who could be relied on. A woman who knew how to be a mother. She wasn't any of that, and feelings of inadequacy and failure swarmed through her. She tried to bat them away, but they still crowded in and stung like hell.

Blinking to clear her vision, she nodded sharply, grabbed an oven mitt, picked the bag up with it and walked over to the pantry on the other side of the fridge. She snapped on the inside light and made sure Nicole saw her clearly. "It'll be on the top shelf, closest to the door. See?"

Nicole's fingers stilled. "Okay."

Amanda sucked in a slow, relieved breath. "Everything is good now. How about that shower, and then get in your pajamas? I'll be right there."

When her daughter disappeared into the hall toward the bedrooms, she latched onto the kitchen counter and struggled not to fall apart. *Keep it together. Just keep it together. Nicole needs you to be strong. To be able to protect her.*

At the slam of a car door in front of the house, she stiffened, then snagged the Glock from the top of the fridge, and strode to the front door. Legs spread, the safety off and her hand steady on the handle, she eyed the closed door, wondering if Mayor could slam through the metal door. The woman was strong, but she didn't think she was that strong. At least she hoped to heaven that wasn't the case.

"Hey, it's me!" Gabriel called out.

A wave of relief washed away some of her dark thoughts. She wasn't alone. She had to remember that. There was Gabriel. She snapped on the gun's safety, then unlocked and opened the door.

Mayor slips from the forest while moonlight glows against the snow around her. She licks her fingers. The kill, even the taste of blood, doesn't soothe her. Nor did the look of horror on the human's face as she took its life. Rage bubbles through her as her thoughts turn to Gabriel and Luys. Gabriel is the worse of the two, the perfect one, the moral one, always regarding her with a superiority she despises. He makes her feel crazy, inadequate, lacking in everything. He doesn't deserve happiness, or to feel love, not when love is forever out of her grasp.

But she has not always been alone. Sudden sorrow hits her from all sides.

Memories like savage shards cut into her mind.

"Maria…" Mayor murmurs as night air caresses her face and flicks at the tendrils of her hair. She had a husband, a child, a family… once.

The years tumble away… *Blood everywhere. Screams. Terror. Her husband is cut to the ground with an ax by one of the villagers, ordered by Alonso Rodrigo de Avila. Then Alonso rapes her. Furious at her rejection, the don accuses her of witchcraft and inflames the villager's superstitions. Days later, fearing for her life as an angry mob advances toward her modest home, she flees with her daughter to the forest but they hunt them down just as Gabriel and Luys arrive from their travels. She fears her brothers are too late. The villagers surround her, grab at her hair, tearing the strands from their roots. Luys miraculously appears as she is thrown to the ground. He rips her from their grasping hands. Then they all flee, running, grabbing Maria, Gabriel yelling to hurry, the whinny of horses, the pounding of hooves in the distance, and Luys riding alongside.*

Gabriel slaps the reins across the horse's hindquarters, urging them even faster as the sound of their pursuers draws closer. The wagon careens around the corner of the road too quickly. The wheels lift from the ground. The wagon lists to one side. Clutching Maria to her chest, she realizes Gabriel has lost control of the horses and the cart. Wood creaks, then howls as the wagon careens to the side. The horse's screams mingle with her own as she flies from the wooden seat.

Gasping for air, she finds herself in a gulley adjacent to the road. Bushes scrape her exposed arms and legs as she struggles to her knees. Maria. Fear of being discovered keeps her from saying the name aloud. She will not be able to help her daughter if she is slain. Gabriel lies motionless on the ground while Luys, fists raised, circles Stegan, one of the village leaders who wants her dead.

Maria lurches into view from the side of the wagon. Her brow is cut while what looks like blood stains the side of her waist. Josef, the monster who testified that Mayor was a heretic and a witch, advances toward her daughter.

New terror snatches Mayor to her feet. "Leave her be!"

She limps from her hiding place, while fury compels her across the road even though bone protrudes through the skin at her ankle.

Josef rounds on her, then screams, "Witch!"

He bears down on Mayor. Moonlight flashes against the sheen of an ax as he raises it above his head.

She stumbles backward. Pain explodes from her ankle as she twists around to save her fall with a hand. As she turns, she glances over a shoulder and across the brush to meet the horror in her daughter's eyes.

Her head hits something hard as she crumples to the ground. Her peripheral vision clouds. New screams carry over the night as her sight fades.

She comes to in the back of the wagon with Gabriel behind the horses, urging them onward and farther from their home. Maria is sitting in the corner as they bounce and jerk over the dirt *road. Mayor runs her hand up and down her arms and over her legs. When she touches her ankle, she gasps and tears up at the pain. But she is whole.*

She later learned Luys had managed to kill Josef before the villager used the ax on her.

When she fled from her country with Maria, Luys, and Gabriel, she didn't realize she would sail to a new nightmare, one far worse than the last. This new horror would break her like nothing else had. And the sorrow would turn to rage. A rage she relished, thrived on, welcomed.

Because it deadened the pain.

Holy Mother. He didn't give Amanda a chance to say anything when she opened the front door but swept her up in his arms and held her. The heat of her body emphasized the chill from outside and his own body, and he quickly closed and locked the door behind him. He caught her head in both hands and gave her a deep, long and thorough kiss. When her tongue slid into his mouth, he pressed harder against her body and shuddered with a mix of hot desire and wild relief. Before he lost control, he dragged his mouth from hers and took a step away.

He finally noticed the gun and nodded toward her hand. "What happened?"

"Nerves. I didn't want to take any chances just in case Mayor was at the door." Amanda caught his hand and backed up, pulling him along with her. Excitement flashed in her eyes. "I know where Mayor is. Maybe not her exact location. She's close to the gas station on 71. There's a house nearby on the edge of a crop of trees.

I'd go myself, but there's Nicole. Plus, I'm not capable of taking on Mayor on my own."

He followed her into the kitchen as she set her gun on top of the fridge. "I'll take a look, but before I leave, I want to make sure you're fine."

She shrugged and sent him a twisted smile. "I've had better times."

"Those better times will be here for you very soon. This is going to end now. I will find this house and will not stop looking for this place until I do. Surprise is the only way I can overpower her. I have some mercury I have saved from years before. If I am careful—"

"Gabriel, the last time mercury got on your skin, you almost died."

"That was a freak accident. I couldn't have foreseen coming across that particular medallion with its mercury at Wombats. And to have it break—"

"That was my fault." Amanda bit her bottom lip.

"No. It was an accident. Yes, mercury's dangerous for the average person, but how could you know I would have such a reaction?" He met and held her gaze. "I'll be prepared this time. The silver is secured in a lead container until I am ready to use it." No more would he think of his sister and their shared history. No more would he allow her to harm another.

"Hey, Gabriel." Nicole appeared in the doorway that led from the bedrooms. The smile on her face flashed briefly before her mouth dipped and she started twisting her fingers in front of her. The child looked exhausted; the usual sparkle in her eyes had dulled.

He noted the medallion around her neck with relief. As long as she kept it on her, it was better than any weapon against Mayor. That he had brought Amanda and her into Mayor's crosshairs would always fill him with guilt and horror. "I'm sorry. You should never have been treated so terribly by my sister."

Nicole flushed. "Yes, well, she didn't hurt me."

"But I'm sure she frightened you." Gabriel tamped down his outrage. "I'm going to find this house she took you to. Do you remember how far away it was from the gas station?"

"Twenty minutes, I think. I walked along the highway. There's a big ditch beside it. I kept close to it and any trees along the way. I was afraid she might find me out in the open. I got on the highway from another road. I'm not sure the name…" She squeezed her eyes shut for a second. "It was a person's name. But it was also the name of a bird, I think. There was a sign on the corner of that and the dirt road I started out on. From that road, I'm pretty sure the house was near the end of it. It was by itself. I think so, anyway. I didn't see any lights from anywhere else."

"I'll find out soon enough." Gabriel walked over to Amanda, who stood by the sink with dark, sad eyes, her hand on the counter. He covered her hand and squeezed gently. Uncaring of Nicole watching, he bent and brushed his lips across her mouth and lingered for the briefest of moments, taking in the plump curve of her lips, her distinct, feminine scent, and the warmth of her body. He took a shuddering breath. Would this be his last kiss before dying?

He took an abrupt step backward. He could not think that way. He needed to believe he could protect the two of them.

"I'll be back as soon as I can." He was unable to mask the uncertainty in his voice.

Amanda met his gaze. She looked like she had the same doubt about him returning.

Ten minutes later, behind the wheel of his SUV, Gabriel slowed about a mile after passing the convenience store. A street sign came into view behind several large trees. He slowed even more as the words came into focus. Robin. This had to be what Nicole was talking about. He didn't have much farther to go, and he turned down the road for a bit before noticing a dirt road a quarter of a mile in. He turned onto it, parked after several yards, and rolled down the window.

Silence filled the night. No wind. No call of a bird. The feeling was eerie and unnatural.

He jogged down the side of the road, conscious of the snow beneath his feet. After a good five minutes, a house appeared, darker than the sky, but blending into the trees beside it. Breath sawing into his lungs, he slowed to a walk and paused at the driveway. The house was silent, its windows absent of light. A blanket of snow covered the yard. He didn't see any footprints or tire tracks anywhere. That didn't mean Mayor wasn't there waiting inside.

The snow crackled a protest beneath his feet as he walked across the yard. He winced, even knowing the sound was barely above a whisper. Beneath his touch, the screen and interior doors opened easily on surprisingly silent hinges. He slipped a hand into his jacket's pocket and palmed the lead container. Even with it being completely covered in thick, resistant metal, he could feel the mercury already corrupting his senses. He hadn't told Amanda that the metal, given enough hours, would start having adverse effects, slowing his movements, his thoughts, until he could do nothing but be a broken vessel of a body.

Light from a half-moon streamed through the screen door and into the foyer, but only went so far before it bumped up against the rest of the house's deeper shadows. Even so, as he stepped farther from the door, he noticed a figure sitting in a rocking chair, the sole piece of furniture in the room. No amount of shadows could disguise the person's platinum hair.

For a moment, they stared at each other as the chair creaked back and forth, making him feel just about as old and worn as the wood.

"She left," Mayor whispered. "She ran away from me."

"What did you expect?" Gabriel scoffed. "No one likes to be kidnapped."

With one hand still cupping the lead case, he stepped into the living room and snapped on the light switch by the entryway with his other hand. He blinked to adjust to the sudden light that flooded the room.

Fury flared in her eyes. "I didn't kidnap her! She came willingly!"

"Maybe in the beginning. But not later when she realized how twisted you are."

Her rage disappeared as quickly as it had started. "We were enjoying each other's company, even laughing like we used to do before she left me all those years ago."

Gabriel frowned. "She never left you."

"Of course she did. Unlike this time, back then, she didn't have a choice. They killed her."

"What are you saying?"

"Do you not understand?"

He shook his head, wondering why he was even talking to her. His chest tightened with incredible, unexpected, and unwanted sadness, because family bonds were impossible to break and clouded a person's best intentions. They twined around a person, cut and seeped into the mind and body to the point they smothered, even suffocated the will to break free.

"She is Maria. She has come back to me."

His hand tightened on the lead. "No one has come back to you, and especially not Maria. She died long ago. I saw her. You saw her. All of us saw her being—"

"Butchered? Yes, they cut her down, treated her, you, and me, worse than any animal. Nevertheless, she is reborn. She is my daughter come back to me!" Mayor shook her head, her lip curling in disgust as she continued to rock in the chair, the wood sighing against the floor. "You look at me like I am stupid. Like you always do! But you are the one being stupid! You are too blinded by today's modern beliefs."

"Your daughter?" Gabriel sliced the air with one hand. He shook his head. Even for Mayor, she had gone over the edge. "You need to stop. Now. Nicole is not your daughter. Your daughter is dead." He sounded cold, but he didn't care. She needed to see reason. Somehow. Which made it all seem stupid on his part. Mayor didn't see reason. Never had from the moment she lost her daughter and even before.

"You are completely clueless. You have no idea what the truth is!" She curled her fingers around the wood arms of her chair and stopped her rocking.

"You're not going near Nicole! I forbid it."

"Forbid?" She laughed. "You are a bigger fool than me. I will do what I want. I am stronger than you. I can easily break you. You can't stop me from making sure Maria is with me forever. She will never die again."

He sucked in a breath. "You are not going to hurt the child. Why would you even think of putting her through that ceremony? Your lover died at your own hands."

"What do you think I have been doing? I have not been just killing for the sake of killing." Her eyes narrowed. "You thought that, yes? Why am I not surprised? I have been testing large, strong men while performing the ceremony to see how long they survive. I'm perfecting it. Soon, I'll be able to kill someone and bring them back. Once I do that, I will be able to ensure Maria's life for centuries."

She jumped to her feet.

Gabriel tensed, locking his legs, pulling the mercury out from his pocket. With a quick flick of his thumb, he unhooked the clasp. He expected her to charge at him, scream her profanities, but instead, she flung her arms wide, and in a whirl of smoke, disappeared.

He stood frozen, stunned at how easily she had played him. He had been a complete idiot. She had wanted him to follow her here, to lure him away from Amanda and Nicole.

Pivoting, he fled the house. Holy Mother. He wouldn't make it to Amanda's house in time.

CHAPTER 27

Amanda sat in a chair by Nicole's bed as the girl slept. Every now and then her daughter would shift or whimper. She hated watching her when she knew Nicole was in some awful dream scene of her own making. For a time with a pillow cradled to her head, she'd rested beside her daughter and inhaled her scent, a mix of lavender and lemon from Nicole's favorite shampoo, all the while concern for Gabriel's safety and fear of Mayor kept her eyes open and her mind racing. Too restless and afraid of disturbing Nicole from her sleep by moving around on the bed, she sat in a nearby chair, but even then after several minutes of trying to stay glued to the cushion, she got up to go stand out in the hall, listening for any sign of Gabriel…or God forbid…Mayor.

The faint hum of the refrigerator was the only noise that filtered toward her. She rubbed at the bridge of her nose and took a deep breath. Thirsty and needing to clear her head, she walked down the hall on bare feet. She'd changed into a pair of flannel bottoms and a sleeveless T-shirt. The chill in the air brushed against her exposed arms as she stepped into the kitchen and turned on the light above the stove. She filled a glass from the sink's filtration system, added a couple of ice cubes, and drank the entire contents. Rolling the chilled glass against her brow didn't do a thing to combat her exhaustion as she eyed the closed pantry. Knowing she shouldn't, but unable to stop herself, she grabbed an oven mitt—which would leave fibers and a path back to her own front door—opened the pantry door, and pulled the bag off the top shelf.

A scream sliced through the house.

Nicole!

Oh, God. Not again. Not this soon. Tossing the oven mitt, plus the bag and its contents on the counter, she rushed from the kitchen, scraping her arm against the pantry door in her hurry. She rubbed at the stinging skin as she ran into Nicole's bedroom.

Light from the hall illuminated her daughter sitting up, blankets around her ankles, hair wild, her hands wrapped around her raised knees, and her head buried against them.

Amanda slid up on the bed, cupped her shoulder and gently rubbed. When Nicole didn't respond, she whispered, "You're back in your house. In your room. Safe."

Nicole pulled her hands from her face and glared. "I hate these dreams! They're so REAL!"

Amanda edged backward. "I think it's time we saw someone for them. We'll go to the city."

"No."

She wasn't going to let it slide anymore. "You need help, Nicole. You can't continue having nightmares like these. They're getting worse, and they'll start affecting your schoolwork again, keep you from making friends—"

"No one is going to be able to help."

"How can you say that, when you haven't even talked

to a professional? I don't have the tools or knowledge to fix this." She sank back on her heels. "You didn't see any horror movies I'm not aware of, have you?"

"NO!"

Amanda stiffened.

"This dream isn't the same. I've had it a bunch of times now. I'm somewhere different. Nothing looks familiar. The houses are different. They don't look like anything I've seen here or around our old house. They talk differently too. They look like Indians, but they're not."

"Maybe you heard Gabriel and me talking…" But for the life of her, she couldn't think of one minute where she'd talked to Gabriel about his past with Nicole nearby, unless Nicole hadn't been sleeping but eavesdropping. Still, she'd been very careful—

"THE KNIFE IS THE SAME."

"What do you mean?" Dread crawled across her flesh. Something was off.

"The knife that I stole from Mayor is the same one in the dream. The same knife that killed my mother."

"That's impossible."

Her daughter scrambled onto her knees, lurched forward to grab Amanda by the arms, and said in a hard, urgent voice, "It is! You have to believe! It's the one that killed me."

"But it's just a dream," Amanda insisted.

"NO. YOU DON'T UNDERSTAND." Her daughter's face tightened in frustration. "Mayor is in the dream with me. And some other people. It looks like *Raiders of the Lost Ark* you had me watch with you, but different. Older. Scarier. And they don't talk English. There's this guy with a scary face and darker skin than me. But it's his eyes. That's what so SCARY. His eyes…"

"What about his eyes?"

"They're the same. His and my stepdad's. They have the same look."

"That doesn't mean they're the same person."

"But they said the same thing to me…"

Amanda was being drawn into Nicole's fantastical story, almost believing. Almost… "And that is…?"

"*The blood—the blood—*" Nicole scowled. "*The blood of an innocent will purify the abo—abom—*" she struggled with the pronunciation "*—the abomination of others.*"

"How could you know that if they're from a different time, from a different culture?"

"I don't know. I just understood them. It was like I could speak the language too." She sank back down on the bed. "But like right now, when I try, the words don't come."

"Do you know you're sounding—" Amanda stopped herself from saying crazy. "I don't know what to say."

"Mom, you've got to do something. Someone is going to kill me with that knife again." Her hands tightened on Amanda's arms, gripping the flesh until she winced with pain.

"I'm not going to let that happen!" Oh, God. She'd left the knife on the counter. A chill seeped through her skin and went deeper until her whole body shivered with unease.

"Or I'll kill someone with it." Nicole released her grip as if she'd burned herself on Amanda's arms. "THAT'S IT. I WAS WRONG ALL THIS TIME. I'M GOING TO KILL SOMEONE."

"Nicole, calm down." The second the words were out, she wished she could take them back.

"I can't be CALM!" Tears welled in her daughter's eyes. "Please hide it. Please hide the knife!"

This was all coming too fast. Too hard.

BOOM.

They both jumped.

"What's that!" Nicole cried out.

"I don't know."

BOOM.

Jesus. That didn't sound like anyone at the front door, but more like a crash. From somewhere INSIDE the house. Her gun. She needed to get to her gun. It might not do much, but it was better than being completely defenseless. She hurried from the bed, trying not to panic, trying to keep her thoughts from fraying into a shredded mess as she locked her gaze on the medallion around Nicole's neck. Knowing her daughter wore the protective necklace eased her fear somewhat, but she still couldn't control the rush of adrenaline. "Stay here. Don't leave this room!"

In her hurry to leave, she collided with the wall in the hall. Slapping a hand against it, she pushed off and raced into the kitchen. Locking her hand around the Glock's grip, she paused in the middle of the room.

CRASH.

Glass breaking—it had to be—sounded like it was from the living room. Sudden light from that same room flooded from the hall to filter into the kitchen.

Amanda tightened her hand on the gun as she edged toward the doorway. Weapon steady, both hands locked around its grip, she pivoted into the hall and edged toward the living room. As the room came into full view, she saw Mayor standing in the middle.

At her entrance, Gabriel's sister clasped her hands in front of her. Her blonde hair framed her beautifully cold face and fluttered from the winter breeze rushing through the broken front window.

Amanda's heart free fell into her stomach as she aimed the gun at Mayor and stepped into the living room. "Get out or I'll shoot."

"I have come for my daughter." Her lips flattened. "You know that is not going to make me go away."

"Like hell." Amanda's finger tightened on the trigger. "She's not your daughter."

"Have you asked her?"

"I'm not about to subject her to stupid questions."

"You don't want to ask, because you know it's the truth. She knows. She will tell you she is."

Amanda wasn't going believe such craziness. Nicole couldn't possibly be Mayor's daughter, and forget Nicole's latest nightmare. It was too insane. But then, wasn't the woman in front of her, wasn't Gabriel's life inexplicable?

"Now get out of my way!" Mayor advanced.

Amanda pulled the trigger.

The gun exploded, and the bullet hit Mayor in the head. A circle of blood bloomed on her forehead, but the shot didn't stop the woman as she moved toward Amanda.

Another blast of the gun. This time, the bullet hit Mayor in the chest, dead center, where her heart would be.

Mayor still approached.

Damn it! The bitch wouldn't die. Amanda scrambled backward, tripping over her feet in her hurry to evade Mayor's hands. She pulled the trigger again. Her aim went wild. The bullet smashed into the wall, sending chips of plaster and paint flying.

Mayor backhanded her in the face.

Amanda tumbled sideways, smacking her skull against the wall. Lights flashed along her peripheral vision. She struggled to focus, to get back her equilibrium, but Mayor didn't give her time. She seized Amanda's upper arm and flung her across the room. She landed on the sofa, her head snapping against the furniture's arm with a loud whack. Lying half on and off the sofa, she blinked as Mayor's face swam into focus.

The front door vibrated. It took Amanda a moment to realize someone was hammering on the door.

Gabriel's shout echoed into the house.

Mayor's lip curled at the corner. "Oh, my very predictable older brother is here to save the damsel in distress."

But it was too late. It had always been too late. Too late for Amanda to save Nicole. Too late for Gabriel to save either of them.

"Stop it! Stop it!"

Oh, God. Nicole. What was she doing? Amanda had told her to stay in her room!

Mayor jerked above her.

Amanda blinked again, struggled to focus, as she fought to stay conscious. Gasping for breath, she climbed up on the sofa.

Blood stained Mayor's shirt by her stomach and hip. But the wound wasn't from a gunshot.

Nicole backed away from Mayor, gripping the onyx knife with Mayor's blood dripping from its blade.

Just then, Gabriel hurled himself through the cracked and broken window and landed on his hands and knees, yards from Amanda and the sofa. He lurched to his feet.

"Nicole," he yelled. "Use the necklace. The mercury."

The girl grasped the necklace in a trembling hand as she waved the knife in Mayor's direction.

"Why?" Mayor cried out, staring at Nicole with hurt and disbelief.

"She's innocent. She's not an ab—abomination!"

Mayor's eyes widened. "You DO know." She lifted a beseeching hand. "Come with me. We can live forever. I know a way where you will be stronger than you can ever imagine. You can be invincible. No one will ever hurt you again."

"I can't." Nicole glanced over at Amanda. "She saved me. I'd be dead without her. You can't hurt her. If you hurt her, you hurt me!"

Amanda recognized the sadness and despair in Nicole's eyes and realized a part of her wanted to follow Mayor. That thought hurt like hell. There was a history she could never comprehend.

The relationship between her daughter and Mayor went far deeper than this life.

As Amanda struggled to her feet, Gabriel caught her up against him. She sank against his side, drawing on his strength.

"I will save you," Mayor insisted.

"You've never saved me." Tears rolled down

Nicole's face. "I died that day." She stared at the knife in her hands and lifted the blade in her bloody hand. "This is the knife that killed me. Brent tried to use it on me."

Mayor flinched. "I just found you. I didn't know Cuetzpalli would try to kill you again in another life with the mask of a different man. How could I know he would be reborn as a man of a lower caste? But you lived. I found the articles about the killing in this woman's desk. I know everything now…"

"And that I've died, but I've had other lives," Nicole whispered. "Other mothers. Ones I can't ever hurt. Amanda is one of them. She saved me from Cuetzpalli. He called himself Brent, but I knew. His eyes were the same. The evil there was the same."

"Mayor, stop," Gabriel ordered. "Leave Nicole alone. Let her live her life. She is just a child! What if your attempt to make her like you, Luys, and myself, and it does not work? Do you want to be the one who kills her? Stop now before anyone else gets hurt."

"You ask too much!"

"Remember Maria?" he asked. "She was such an inquisitive child, always asking questions, wanting answers."

"Maria?" Mayor breathed the name on a sigh.

Amanda waited tensely, hoping Nicole had the sense to stay silent.

"Yes," Gabriel replied almost as softly. "Everyone loved her smile, the way she made everyone laugh. Remember that one time when you were sick? She cared for you, wiping your brow, feeding you broth?"

"I loved her so much," Mayor whispered.

"I know you did. I know you did. Remember how

that love felt? It was selfless. You always put Maria before your own welfare, no matter the cause. You need to do that for Nicole. If you turn her, make her into what you are, she will never grow into an adult. She will always be a child. Do you want that? Can you live with that?"

"I do not know how anymore. All I know is I can't continue living like this! If I leave Nicole, I will not survive! I barely did when you put me in that cave. I despise you for that!"

Amanda hated feeling a strange sense of compassion for Mayor's anguish.

Mayor's gaze narrowed on Gabriel. "Do you think I do not know that I am different? That there is this dark, sick side of me? But I can't get rid of the hatred. I will not. It is what keeps me going. And even if I wanted to become normal, there is no cure for any of us."

"Luys is working on trying to find a way to fix what was done to us."

"And how long has he been trying? Decades, yes? He has had no success. I am not going to be a fool like you and wait for something that will never happen." She spat out the last word.

"Then we will always be enemies," Gabriel stepped in front of Amanda.

"Come with me!" Mayor demanded, holding out a hand toward Nicole

The young girl rushed across the room and barreled into Amanda's side. "No!"

Amanda cuddled her daughter.

"Please, Maria! I am begging you."

"I can't! You're not the mother from my dreams anymore." Nicole dropped the knife, which thudded at her feet, and pulled the clasp of the medallion open to reveal the mercury inside. "You scare me. You're evil. You've become like Cuetzpalli."

"Do not say that!" Mayor stepped toward the three of them but stopped as Nicole raised a threatening hand with the small container of mercury.

"NO!" Mayor clasped her hands into fists against her breast as tears slid down her cheeks. "I love you."

"Then leave me alone."

Tears continued to stream down the anguished woman's face. "I will be back when you are a young woman. When you realize what power you have. Right now, you do not understand. You are still a child."

"You're the one who doesn't understand, Mayor. Leave her," Gabriel ordered. "You're playing with something none of us understands. If you put her through that ceremony and she survives, she will never grow up or know an adult passionate love. How could you do that if you think Nicole is your daughter? It's beyond cruel. You say you love her, then show her! Holy Mother! You can't think of keeping her a child forever!"

Mayor dropped her hands to her side and stared at the three of them standing beside each other, a unified force. She wiped at her eyes, then slashed a hand in the air. "It has come to this, yes? I am alone again? It seems you have won, brother." Her gaze darkened, unmistakable sorrow in their depths. "So this seems the end."

Amanda braced for the attack. Gabriel tensed beside her.

Screaming, Mayor fisted her hands to the ceiling and exploded into a cloud of gray mist that swirled through the room, wrapped around all three of them, then vanished, leaving the room in stunned silence.

Amanda buried herself in Gabriel's arms as she held Nicole against her other side. "Do you think she'll kill herself?" she asked against his shoulder.

"I don't know."

"But she's gone, right? For good?"

"I'm not sure. But I've never seen her like that before. At least not since we were children. So solemn. Beaten, even. As if the rage she'd been holding onto vanished."

Amanda closed her eyes, relieved yet saddened. She could only imagine walking through decades, even centuries alone, filled with hatred and unable or unwilling to find a path from such a crippling emotion.

"Mom?"

She turned to Nicole. Her daughter had picked up the knife. With a steady and calm gaze, she handed the onyx blade over. Amanda took it with tentative fingers. She sucked in a breath as the realization hit.

Nicole wasn't afraid. She'd picked up the knife without showing one ounce of fear. She'd lost her terror of the weapon.

In silence, they stood together in the middle of the room. There was a feeling of finality to it. Maybe it was her wishful thinking, but Amanda didn't think so.

Then Gabriel whispered, "We are going to be okay. We are all going to be okay."

EPILOGUE

Hey, sweetie." Gabriel followed the direction of Amanda's pensive gaze. A stand of trees marked the end of the street. "She's gone."

A cool fall breeze flicked at her hair as she stood on the porch of their house. It had been over six months since Mayor disappeared from her living room. Gabriel had since moved in, and they were getting used to being a family, not just a couple.

Nicole seemed to enjoy having him around. The knives were no longer hidden away. Strangely, her daughter had lost the phobia that had gripped her from the night her mother was murdered.

As for Nicole being Maria? Amanda still didn't know what to make of it. She'd never thought much of reincarnation, but there were too many loose ends, too many unanswered questions.

Nicole didn't talk much about her dreams anymore, and thank goodness, she didn't have a reason to. Her nightmares had vanished along with her phobia. She was thriving at school, had discovered new friendships, and had spent several nights at her friends' houses. It seemed like her anxiety at separating from Amanda had also dissipated.

At times, Amanda was selfishly saddened by that.

"Are you sure she's gone for good?"

"No, but there's never a guarantee on anything or anyone. Something in her broke, though, this last time. I'm not sure if it was to the point where she will heal or not. That's not up to either one of us. I can't save Mayor. For too many decades I tried to, even going too far, to the point of hurting the people I love."

"I think she'll be back." Amanda nodded, hating the thought. "She's going to come back for Nicole when she's an adult."

"We can't worry about that now. If we do, we'll waste the years we have now."

"I don't know if I can handle you staying the same as I grow older with each year."

Gabriel kissed her brow. "You don't know that. We don't know the future. No one does. Miracles happen every day. You don't hear those in the news." He closed his eyes and brushed his lips tenderly against her brow. "Luys is smart. He's the smartest of the three of us. If anyone can fix us, he'll be the one."

"But you don't need to be fixed."

He eased back to look down and search her face. "Says who?"

She broke into a smile. "I say."

"Well, then, who am I to argue?" He laughed and pulled her close, thanking God for his own miracle.

THANK YOU!

Thank you for reading *A Kiss Before Dying*. I hope you enjoyed it, and if you did, don't forget to leave a review.

For latest releases, contests and other news, you can signup for my newsletter at hdthomson.com. Also, if you feel like contacting me, you can always catch me on Facebook (https://www.facebook.com/authorhdthomson).

BIBLIOGRAPHY

https://www.smithsonianmag.com/history/discovery-secret-tunnel-mexico-solve-mysteries-teotihuacan-180959070/

https://en.wikipedia.org/wiki/Tlaxcala

http://www.houstonculture.org/mexico/tlaxcala.html

http://www.aztec-history.com/aztec-empire.html

http://www.latinamericanstudies.org/aztecs/aztec_human_sacrifice.pdf

http://rubens.anu.edu.au/raid1/student_projects97/aztec/ACosWorldView.html/World1a.html

https://en.wikipedia.org/wiki/Spanish_conquest_of_the_Aztec_Empire

http://aztecsandtenochtitlan.com/aztec-names/aztec-boys-names/

http://mexicounexplained.com/three-martyred-children-tlaxcala/

https://www.thoughtco.com/hernan-cortes-and-his-tlaxcalan-allies-2136523

http://www.cs.cmu.edu/~kvs/heraldry/spanish16/male-given-alpha.html

http://www.cs.cmu.edu/~kvs/heraldry/spanish16/

http://www.bcmj.org/premise/history-bloodletting#4

History of Mercury

http://www.dartmouth.edu/~toxmetal/mercury/history.html

https://www.rt.com/news/252985-mexican-tomb-king-mercury/

http://www.dailymail.co.uk/news/article-3054296/Hunt-ancient-royal-tomb-Mexico-takes-mercurial-twist.html

https://www.history.com/news/7-unusual-ancient-medical-techniques

COMPLETE LIST OF TITLES

ROMANTIC SUSPENSE

SMOKE & MIRRORS SERIES

ANXIETY
DUPLICITY
IDENTITY

PARANORMAL ROMANCE

ONYX & MERCURY SERIES

A KISS BEFORE DYING
A LONG KISS GOODBYE

SHADES SERIES

DEADLY SHADES #1
SHADES OF HOLLY #2
KILLER SHADES #3
SHADE SERIES BOX SET #1-3

CONTEMPORARY ROMANCE

THE LONG ROAD HOME
PROTECTING KATIE

ABOUT THE AUTHOR

H. D. Thomson moved from Ontario, Canada as a teenager to the heat of Arizona where she graduated from the University of Arizona with a B.S. in Business Administration with a major in accounting. After working in the corporate world as an accountant, H. D. changed her focus to one of her passions–books. She owned and operated an online bookstore for several years and then started the company, Bella Media Management. The company specializes in web sites, video trailers, ebook conversion and promotional resources for authors and small businesses. Now, when she's not heading her company or enjoying small-town life in Spirit Lake, Iowa, she is following her first love–writing. You can read more about her and her books at HDThomson.com.

What they're saying about H. D. Thomson's books:

"My applause to the author on an entertaining read."
– *Romance Novel Junkies*
"Author H.D. Thomson does a great job of keeping the reader guessing."
– *Paranormal Romance Party*
"Bravo H. D. Thomson!"
– *Writer's and Reader's of Distinct Fiction's Top Read.*
"Thomson's writing is spot on…"
– *Confessions of a Bibliophile*

Made in the USA
Middletown, DE
18 May 2022

65883979R00198